HOWARD FAST
The Confession of Joe Cullen

The Outsider

"A novel to be savored . . . bristles with ideas . . . Fast's flair for sure-handed storytelling weds ideology securely to a driving narrative . . . a wise and generous novel, enlarging our sense of what it means to be fully human."

—*Philadelphia Inquirer*

The Confession of Joe Cullen

HOWARD FAST

A Dell Book

Published by
Dell Publishing
a division of
Bantam Doubleday Dell Publishing Group, Inc.
666 Fifth Avenue
New York, New York 10103

ISBN: 0-440-20669-3
Reprinted by arrangement with Houghton Mifflin
Printed in the United States of America
Published simultaneously in Canada
June 1990

10 9 8 7 6 5 4 3 2 1

OPM

For Austin Olney

The First
Confession

JOE CULLEN came in out of the rain, his hat soaked, his trench coat sodden across the shoulders, and leaned his weight against the bar and waited for Billy Sullivan to look at him and recognize him. It was early in the afternoon and there were only three other customers in the place, two men at the bar and a woman who sat drinking alone in one of the booths. One of the men, at Joe Cullen's left and far down the bar, nursed a shot glass of whiskey. He was a fat man in jeans and an old dirty shirt, and he seemed to be half asleep over his drink. The other male customer was lean, middle-aged, with hard hands. He looked as if he might be one of the construction workers on the high-rise that was being built on the other side of Ninth Avenue.

Billy Sullivan made no effort to keep his voice down. He was telling the drinker how he had come to buy the place. It was a good story, and though Joe Cullen had heard it at least five times before, he didn't mind listening to it again. In a way, it was reassuring. It made him feel secure; it enforced the reality of his being back here in New York City in November of 1987 and not in a place that he thought of as the black pit of creation. Billy Sullivan was at that part of the story where he had rolled eleven passes in the great legendary crap game in Saigon, which had happened just a week before the last American troops pulled out. The winning pot held fourteen thousand, one hundred and sixty-two dollars, ten thousand of which Billy used as a down payment for the Shamrock Bar at Ninth Avenue and Nineteenth Street. And at that point in his story, he shifted his glance and noticed Joe Cullen.

He dropped his story in the middle and went over to Joe Cullen and leaned across the bar, gripping Joe's arms in a sort of half embrace.

"I sure as hell thought you were dead."

"I'm not dead," Joe Cullen answered. "Maybe I'm not a hundred percent alive, but not dead."

"You walk out of here," said Sullivan, "and

three months go by—hell, that can wait. What are you drinking?"

"Beer."

Sullivan drew him a beer. "You walk out of here," Sullivan began again. "Jesus, we're all crazy, more or less, all of us. You remember that big black guy, Moses Something-or-other, he was in Charlie Company, and last week he took a big bite on a forty-five automatic pistol and pulled the trigger and blew the back of his head away. I had to go ID him because they know this is a hangout for some of the guys who were in Nam, and all I could think of is that you were somewhere—"

"With the back of my head blown away."

"Yeah."

"Not likely. I was always scared of guns. I'd never put a pistol in my mouth."

"You want another beer? For Christ's sake, where were you? I remember you walking out of here with Oscar Kovach. He never came back. That didn't break my heart. I never liked that shithead."

"Around."

"Yeah. That says it."

"What the hell! I was never any good at family history. I did a couple of things and I made some money."

"Yeah."

Joe Cullen was a tall man and well built, an

inch over six feet, wide shoulders and a mop of brown hair. Billy Sullivan was smaller, skinny, more demonstrative. He kept reaching across the bar to touch Joe Cullen, and though Cullen did not like to be touched by another man, his feeling for Sullivan was too deep for him to reject him. They had seen too much together.

"Because I seen you walk out of here with Kovach, and I had a feeling he was bracing you for something, and I felt like saying to you, Culley, for Christ's sake, dump him."

"Maybe you should have."

"You want to talk about it?"

Cullen shook his head and then nodded at the woman who sat alone in the booth. He had glimpsed her out of the corner of his eye when he first walked into the bar. Now he looked at her. She had a handsome bony face, dark eyes and black hair, and a good figure. She wore a black suit, and her hair was combed back and cut in a long bob.

"Who's she?"

"She's a hundred-dollar hooker, name of Sylvia. Some kind of Spanish, but she was born here."

"What's a hundred-dollar hooker doing here?"

"She don't work out of here," Sullivan said. "She lives around the corner. She'll have a drink here because I don't let anyone crap around with her."

"That includes me?"

Sullivan shook his head. "You got a hundred bucks, talk to her, Culley. I didn't want to ask about Frannie?"

"There's nothing to ask. I haven't seen her for almost two years. I never wanted anything from Frannie. I never took anything from her. I don't blame her for taking off. I had no job. I was flying with a little commuter line up in the Mohawk Valley, and making decent pay, and wham, they go out of business, and Frannie never took any shit. That's the third airline goes out of business. It's just a lousy time for the small carriers, and no jobs. Even the hot-shot old men on the 747s and the L10–11s are getting dumped, and they're still suspicious as hell about the guys from Nam."

Sullivan turned to his cash register, punched it, and took out a few bills.

"Come on," Cullen said. "I ain't poor."

Sullivan shrugged. "The beers are on me." He refilled Cullen's glass, and Cullen took it and walked over to where the dark lady sat, and squeezed into the booth opposite her. "The name is Joe Cullen," he said.

"The booth is occupied." The voice was low and rich.

"You're Sylvia. I'm an old friend of Billy's.

I'm civilized. I'm not violent. Tell me to blow and I blow. I don't push ladies around. I'm cold and I'm tired." He took a roll of bills out of his pocket, riffled them, and found two fifty-dollar bills. He slid them across the table.

"For Christ's sake," she said, "it's half-past three in the afternoon. I'm not working. I don't work this place."

"You work the Plaza."

"You're goddamn right I do. And the Saint Regis and the Pierre."

"I didn't say you don't have class. You're a beautiful woman. You don't see many women as good-looking as you."

"Thanks for nothing."

"I'm sorry." He pushed the bills toward her and started to slide out of the booth. "Keep it."

"Hey, wait a minute. Are you crazy? Or do you give a yard to every bimbo that spits in your face?"

"You're no bimbo and you didn't spit in my face."

"Sit down."

Cullen sat down and stared at her, smiling wanly.

"I just don't work here," she said. "I work the hotels, the johnny rooms. I work alone because I pay off the bell captains, and I can live without any lousy pimp sucking my blood."

"Billy says you live around the corner."

8

"Billy should keep his big mouth shut."

"He didn't mean any harm. We go back a long time."

She nodded. "I got a little apartment, but I don't take johns there." She regarded him thoughtfully. "Who are you? What do you do?"

"I'm a pilot. I fly."

"Are you working?"

"Not right now. I walked out of a job, but it was good money. I got enough to stuff a pig."

"You one of the guys from Nam who hang out here?"

"Does it matter?"

"No. What the hell, you're no crazier than anybody else, and crazy ain't in short supply these days. We'll go up to my place."

Billy Sullivan made a circle of thumb and forefinger as they left.

Her apartment was on the seventeenth floor of a new yellow brick high-rise, and from the windows you could see the Hudson River, a piece of the harbor, and north to the George Washington Bridge in the misty distance. The living room measured twelve by eighteen feet, as did most living rooms in the new high-rises, and standing in the tiny foyer, Cullen could see the open door to the bedroom, as well as the cubicle of a kitchen. In the living room were three overstuffed pieces, two armchairs and a couch, violet carpeting on the floor, and three flower pictures on the walls. He had his own taste in matters of furnishing or decoration, and the place was all right in his mind, neat and nowhere disheveled, and it was clean. Sylvia started toward the bedroom, paused to tell him that he could sit down, and then went into the bedroom and closed the door behind her. Cullen went to the window and stared at the Hudson River and the Jersey shore. The rain had stopped, and the sky over the Hudson was streaked with gashes of silver, gray, and white, the blue sky as a backdrop to the latticework of cold, ripped clouds.

She opened the door slightly to tell him to take off his coat, for God's sake, and put his hat and coat in the closet. In the coat closet, opening off the little foyer, he saw a mink coat, a silk coat with a fur lining, and three cloth coats. Well, it didn't take much to have a mink coat these days. He had bought Frannie one for three thousand dollars, and a hundred-dollar girl who worked without a pimp could pretty damn well afford what she wanted. He couldn't think of her as a hooker. As a matter of fact, he hated the word, even though it had been explained to him by a post librarian in Nam as having nothing to do with the prostitute as a hook, hooking in the poor johns. He was told, then, that during the American Civil War, a certain General Hooker had seen to it that his men did not lack for female companionship, whereby camp followers were dubbed hookers. Whether or not that was the case, he disliked the word.

He had finished hanging up his coat, and turned around to see Sylvia come out of the bedroom in a lacy negligee that left little to his imagination. She was a tall woman, at least five feet and nine inches, with strong rounded limbs and good breasts. "I should have my head examined for this," she said. "I never had a man up here before. So I'm stupid. Would I be a whore if I wasn't stupid?"

"I'm sorry. Do you want me to go?"

"I got your money—Joe—Joe Cullen?"

"My friends call me Culley."

"I don't know if we're friends, Culley, but you paid your money and you got your choice. You want to go inside and take your clothes off —or what?"

"Suppose we sit down and smoke a cigarette."

"Whatever you say. I don't go uptown until six o'clock or so. I'm in no hurry. Tell me what's with you? You're a good-looking guy, and you got a nice face and you're not crazy—I know crazy, and I run like hell—and you could walk into any singles bar and take your pick for a couple of drinks and whatever, so

11

what is it? You got more pain than anyone needs."

"How do you know that?"

"It shows. Come on, get out of your clothes and we'll fool around."

He lit her cigarette and then his own, but made no move toward the bedroom. Instead, he dropped into one of the armchairs. "No damn use," he said.

"What does that mean?"

"It means I can't get it up and I'd crap out—"

She went into the kitchen then, and Cullen listened to the sound of water and ice. She came back with two oversized old fashioned glasses, loaded with ice and whiskey.

"You drink bourbon?" she asked him.

He nodded.

"I grew up in New Orleans with sweet whiskey. Drink up. You'll feel better. You always had this trouble?"

"I don't want to talk about it," Cullen muttered.

"Oh, shit. Grow up. They sell condoms on the TV now."

"If I always had it, I wouldna come on to you. I got more sense than that. If you came out of that bedroom, looking the way you look, six months ago I would have popped my pants."

"What happened?"

He took a drink of the bourbon. "Good. I like bourbon. Nobody drinks it anymore."

"I drink it. Come on, Culley. What happened?"

The bourbon was warm inside him, and on top of the two beers, it warmed him and eased him. This was a beautiful woman. He could see the deep red discs around her nipples, the hard thimbles of her nipples erect and ready. Some damn fool had once argued with him that prostitutes could not be aroused. This woman was aroused. He could taste the hot scent of her, and as he drank the whiskey, raw over the ice, he felt the change and the hardening in his loins.

"I can't tell you."

"You can tell me anything. You know how it goes—a whore's a slob who'll listen to anything."

"Why do you have to call yourself a whore?"

She smiled, rose, and walked behind Cullen and kissed him on the top of his head. Then she dropped down in front of his chair with her arm over his knee. "Because that's what I am, lover."

"Can I have another drink?"

"Makes you nervous, me sitting here."

"Like hell it does. I just need another drink."

"OK, OK, don't bite my head off." She rose

and took his glass. "It's not water. You say you're a pilot. What do you fly?"

"Anything. If it has wings, I can fly it. I'm a damn good helicopter pilot, as good as anyone in the business. That's how I was trained, Jesus God forgive me. What in hell difference does it make to you?"

"Just asking." She handed him the drink. "You really blow hot and cold, don't you?"

"You got another name besides Sylvia?"

"Why?"

"Why? Why? I don't know." He felt the second whiskey. He was not the kind of a drinker who could put down a fifth of whiskey and then walk away. The two beers had put a fuzz on his head, and now he was getting truly drunk. It was a warm, comfortable feeling that was nevertheless threaded through with fear, and he fought against the feeling of being enshrouded with fear, like a fly laced into silk by a spider. "You're a lady. Oh, shit, do you know what I mean?"

"Maybe."

"Trouble was, Frannie never knew what the hell I was talking about."

"Sylvia Mendoza. No secret. Who's Frannie?"

"My wife. Once."

"So tell me what you want, Culley. Right now, you're sitting here and getting stinking drunk. If you couldn't do it before, you're sure as hell not going to do it now. You want to take the money back and get out of here before you get sick and vomit on my rug. That rug cost me twelve hundred dollars."

"I don't vomit, and I don't want the goddamn money back. I want to talk to someone. I got to talk. Can't you understand that—I got to talk."

She dropped onto the couch, indifferent now to her nakedness as a fact of sex. She had let go of seduction. Seduction was business, and she had dismissed Cullen as a client. "I'll tell you what," she said. "I got a john who's a shrink. I'll make a date for you, and for a hundred dollars an hour, he'll let you talk your head off."

"The hell with that! I don't need no hooker to put me down." He was bristling now. "Who the hell are you to put me down? I paid."

"Come on, come on," she said, getting up and going to him and taking his hand. "I didn't want to make you mad. I'm not putting you down, Culley. Come on to bed. I don't need to be satisfied, I'm not your wife."

"I want to talk."

"Then talk," pulling back from him. "Talk. What's eating you?"

"I'll tell you what's eating me," Cullen said, spacing the words so that each word stood by itself, the way some drunks speak. "I murdered a priest. That's what's eating me."

At first, Sylvia Mendoza did not react. She stood facing Cullen, her mouth slightly open, and that tableau, the two, the man and the woman, facing each other, staring at each other, silent, maintained itself for at least ten or fifteen seconds, and then she whispered, "Say that again, what you just said."

"I murdered a priest."

Now she reacted, her voice shrill, almost a scream. "Get out of here! Get out of here, goddamn you, you crazy motherfucker, you crazy bastard, get out of here or I call the cops!" She ran into the kitchen and returned with a ten-inch butcher knife in her hand. "Don't come near me, motherfucker, or I'll cut your heart out."

Cullen staggered to his feet, his hands spread, palms down. "Hey, take it easy. Be cool. I'm not going to hurt you." He shuffled to the outside door, opened it, and she followed him, the knife outthrust, for all the world like a bullfighter going in for the kill.

"Jesus God," Cullen begged, "get that damn knife away. I ain't going to hurt you."

The door slammed. A moment later it opened, and his hat and coat were flung out into the hall. Other doors were opening now in response to the shouting. Heads peered out, but no one came out of a door and into the hallway. Shocked back into a sort of sobriety, Cullen kept his finger on the elevator button until the car appeared. When at last he left the building to stumble out into the rain, he breathed a sigh of relief.

The Second
Confession

THE CATHOLIC CHURCH of Saint Peter the Rock, in the West Twenties, had long since fallen on hard times. The docks that had once been a base for the loading and unloading of the goods of America, and the world too, had moved across to the Jersey shore, and the stevedores, the Irish and Poles and Italians who had made their living as longshoremen on the downtown docks, had drifted away to other places. Saint Peter the Rock had never placed among the great Catholic churches of New York, but it had been built with love and care out of the same brownstone that had built thousands of New York houses, and its stained glass windows were the gift of an Italian immigrant who had made a small fortune in the ice business, and who went to Verona himself to order the windows and supervise their construction. But that was a long time ago, and now Saint Peter the Rock served only a handful of old people who clung to the neighborhood.

None of this was known to Joe Cullen, who had spent most of his childhood in Broad Channel on the edge of Jamaica Bay, where you see the towering skyscrapers of New York in the misty distance; but he had some recollection of seeing a church not too far from his apartment on Eighteenth Street. On this day, some three days after his encounter with Sylvia Mendoza, he found himself in front of the old church, standing there and staring at it for at least five minutes, after which he sat down on the steps, lit a cigarette, and smoked it until the heat of the butt touched his fingers. He then snapped it away, shook his head, closed his eyes for a long moment, and entered the church. Once inside the doors, he stood still, blinded by the dark shadows, waiting for his sight to clear.

His eyes focused now. The only light in the church came from a few candles and the glow from the stained glass windows, and in this dim light an old woman was straightening out the hymnals on the backs of the pews. Cullen took a few steps and then stood in the aisle, watching the old woman approach him. All unconscious of his presence, intent on her work, she glanced up suddenly and let out a shrill gasp.

"Please," Cullen said.

"Oh, you did startle me, sir."

"I didn't mean to. Is there a priest here now who could hear confession?"

"Oh, yes. Father Immelman is here, but he's having his afternoon nap. He's getting on, you know, and he needs his nap. He's seventy-three. When you get to that age, you want a nap in the afternoon. Not myself, of course; there's so much work to be done. Do you come here often?"

"No."

"I should have known. I know all the churchgoers, but my memory's so poorly these days. What time is it, sir, if I may ask?"

Cullen looked at his watch. "Ten minutes to three."

"Well, there you are. In another ten minutes, he'll be down. You can sit in the booth—the one over there," she said, pointing. The moment he comes down, I'll tell him you're there."

He nodded, mumbled a thank-you, and then went to the confession booth and sat there, breathing the musty air and remembering his childhood without joy. The smell had not changed, and he had a notion that anywhere, in any booth, the smell would be the same.

The smell was his childhood. He remembered hearing, somewhere, that the deepest memory was odor, the deepest impression, the link of man to an ancient time when he was not man at all, only becoming, and this odor was filled with the fears and frustrations of an adolescent boy. Cullen did not want to remember the adolescent boy. There was a great deal that Cullen didn't want to remember. There was the odor that came from the body bags, and there was the odor of mud when your face is in the mud, and there was the odor of sheer terror the time he was shot down with VC all around him. He was beginning to sweat, and in another moment he would have leaped out of the confession booth and fled the church.

Then, on top of that thought, pinning him to his seat, there was the sound of the old priest's slow steps, and the opening of his door to the booth.

"My son?"

Cullen opened his mouth but no sound came from it.

"My son, you wish to confess? To receive absolution?"

"Yes."

"How long is it since your last confession?"

Long moments passed before Cullen could count the years.

"My son?"

"I'm trying to think about it, Father." It was before Vietnam. Was it 1970? That would make it seventeen years. Or was it 1968? Nineteen years.

"I think—nineteen years."

From the priest, a long silence—to the point where Cullen had the feeling that he had left the box, and then when he spoke, he asked whether Cullen was still a believer. "You said you were, my son—or that you had been in the past. You have not put the church out of your life, have you?"

"Things happened, Father. I was in Vietnam."

"And that kept you from confession?"

Cullen was not used to self-examination. It was only recently that he had begun to look into himself, trying desperately to find motives and see himself as another might see him.

"I don't know," he answered. "I'm not sure. In some way, it made it too hard to confess."

"Yes." The old priest's voice was without rancor. He had lived a long time and heard too many confessions ever to be surprised. When he asked Cullen what he had done that brought him here today, after so many years,

25

he could almost have anticipated a tragedy of some sort.

"I murdered a priest," Cullen replied, each word torn out of his gut.

"You murdered a priest? Is that what you said? My hearing is not of the best." There was not surprise nor anger nor horror in the old man's voice.

"Yes, Father," Cullen whispered.

"A little louder, please, my son."

"Yes, Father. I said that I had murdered a priest."

"I see." Then silence, silence. Cullen heard the old man's breathing, his own breathing. Then the old man asked, his voice unshaken, "Were you conscious of what you were doing?"

"Yes, Father."

"And tell me, how do you feel about what you have done?"

"Terrible."

"And sorry? Contrite?"

"Yes, Father."

"Tell me, my son, do you believe in God?"

Cullen's hesitation was so long that the priest asked his question again. "My son, I asked you whether you believed in God. Can you answer that question?"

"I don't know," Cullen said finally.

"That is not an answer, and you know that,

my son. Look into your heart, and then tell me what you believe or disbelieve."

"I was in Vietnam," Cullen said forlornly. "How can I tell you that I believe in God?"

"You saw what man does and not what God does. Can you accept that?"

"No," Cullen whispered.

"Please, louder, my son."

"No. No, I can't accept that what man does isn't what God does—I mean, I guess I want to. I can't."

"Then I must ask you again—do you believe in God?"

"Father, I want to."

"But do you?"

Cullen felt every muscle in his body tighten. He knew what the priest's question meant, and as much as he wanted to lie, he couldn't.

"No," Cullen said.

He heard the priest sigh; there was such sorrow in that sigh that Cullen's eyes were wet with tears.

"Then why are you here in God's house?" the old priest asked gently.

"I don't know. I had nowhere else to go."

"Don't you know, my son, that murder is an offense against God, a terrible offense against God?"

"I have guilt," Cullen managed to say. "I'm filled with guilt, Father. I can't sleep, I can't rest. It's not like Nam. It never happened to me that way in Nam. This is something else. I'm sick with what I have done. I thought—if you could forgive me, if you could give me some kind of absolution?"

"How can I, my son? When you say you are filled with revulsion at what you have done, I believe you. But what can I do? A pagan can come to me with guilt, with conscience, with revulsion, but I cannot give him absolution. He must understand that his offense, his sin, is against God, not against man. It is the same in your case. You don't believe in God, so there is no absolution, no forgiveness."

"Why? Why are you turning me away?" He was a little boy again, pleading.

"I am not turning you away, and even if I spoke words of absolution, they would be meaningless. Pray, pray, and seek inside yourself, and when you have found God, come back here and I will give you absolution."

"Junk in every size," Cullen muttered miserably, and then, louder, said, "Thank you, Father."

From the church, Cullen walked west, remembering that once an elevated highway had nestled alongside the river and the piers until it bore witness to the municipal crooks who had built it so poorly that in time it came tumbling down. Well, if a murderer like himself could walk around in the city, with nobody giving two damns about it or what he had done, then why bother with common crooks? Nothing was as it had been once, and nobody really gave a damn about anything, and the old priest would have been happy to give him absolution if only he had stood up and said forthrightly that he believed in God. He should have lied, and he was not sure but that everyone lied.

He walked on alongside the river, and then out onto an ancient pier. He sat down on a pile of wooden planks and lit a cigarette and thought about things. In time, he came to two conclusions: one, that he would never sleep again or be able to face himself unless he confessed to what he had done; two, that the only confession that mattered was one with chapter and verse underlined.

The Third
Confession

THE PRECINCT HOUSE was an old building on an old street. It had been built at the turn of the century, and the street had not changed very much since then. The precinct house had a front of gray stone, and on the arch over the doorway the word POLICE was engraved, and on either side of this simple word two iron sconces held blue light globes. Most of the streets in the West Twenties had not been subjected to the city's penchant for tearing down old buildings with character and replacing them with new buildings that had no character at all; the nod to modest antiquity was most evident west of Eighth Avenue. The buildings along the street were each of them close to a hundred years old, loft buildings now turned into warehouses, garages, film-processing labs, computer companies, software houses, and at least fifty other kinds of modern production that happens in New York. But the face of these grimy buildings had not changed, and as Joe Cullen walked down the street, east to west, he experienced at least a trace of the comfort that familiarity brings. The dirty gray front of the old precinct house reminded him of the Carnegie libraries he had haunted in his childhood.

There were kids in the gang he ran with who never set foot in a library. His dreams had been different. His retreat into the wonderland of books was secret. Drunk once, his father asked him where he had been. When he replied that he had been in the public library, his father belted him across the face and sent him reeling. He never mentioned the library to anyone again.

The police station was something else. The only time he had ever been in this particular police station was when his father, drunk again, got into a fight at a bar, and the man he picked the fight with hit him across the side of his head with a heavy beer mug. Cullen was then living uptown near City College, a place he fought his way through because he had only one dream, to be an airplane pilot; and to have the air force train him for that, he needed a college degree. His mother telephoned him at that time, and he came down to this police station to hear what they could tell him about his father. They told him that his father had been taken to Bellevue, but when Cullen got there, his father was already dead.

Thoughts are quick. On the steps of the precinct house, Cullen paused, the image of his dead father, almost twenty-five years in the past, so clear in his mind that it might have been a photograph hanging in front of him. The face, forever angry and hate-filled, was now relaxed and peaceful, the eyes closed, the mouth without bitterness. Death purified him, and Cullen, who had hated and feared him and wanted so desperately to love him, found his eyes moist, even as they had been twenty-five years ago.

Cullen went on into the precinct house. The public room was small, crowded with cops, since it was the moment the shift was changing, among them at least four women, a dozen cops in the room and no one paying any attention to Cullen. A heavyset sergeant behind the long high desk, wearing a gold badge, tried to talk on the telephone, vent his anger at one of the cops, and pay attention to the desk at the same time. The cops were horsing around and laughing, the female cops quite pretty as they laughed and tossed their heads—all of them so very young to Cullen, like the kids in the infantry. But it was a beautiful November afternoon, the kind of cool fine weather that would make most people feel good, and even Cullen was able to shake off some of his depression and despair.

A fat old woman in front of the desk was weeping. The sergeant slammed down the telephone and snapped at her, "He's not dead. No way. You understand me?"

Her weeping was not interrupted. The sergeant turned to Cullen and said, "I'm listening."

"I murdered a man," Cullen said clearly.

The instant quiet in the room was like the sound turned down on a television set. The picture continued, but suddenly the talk and laughter were gone, and Cullen felt himself gripped from behind, hands passed around his body and up and down his legs.

"He's clean, Sarge."

The desk sergeant nodded, his gaze fixed on Cullen. The room was quiet and interested.

"What's your name, mister?" the sergeant asked.

"Joseph Cullen."

"And who did you kill, Mr. Cullen?"

"Father Francis O'Healey."

"You mean a priest? Father O'Healey, a priest?"

"That's right."

The sergeant rubbed his chin and stared at Cullen thoughtfully. Then he said to a cop who was standing behind Cullen, "Take him upstairs to the squad room, Harry."

Harry was tall, skinny, and young. He looked at the sergeant, who shrugged. Cullen held out his hands, an indifferent gesture. "We ain't going to cuff you, Mr. Cullen," Harry said.

"You're not going to arrest me?"

"I don't know. I don't know what you done yet. Talk to the detectives."

Harry led him through to the back and up a staircase to the squad room—the squad room small, about twelve by twelve, two desks and four chairs, all very old, and a door that led out of it to the lieutenant's tiny office. The windows were almost opaque with dirt, the wall paint so ancient that the original color could only be surmised. "A shithole," Cullen said to himself, wondering why the cops put up with it. If it had been the army, everything would be spanking clean, the furniture new, the desks polished and clean instead of being piled up with filing forms. But in the army, without a war, there wasn't much to do except to keep things clean and fancy and order something new the moment the old thing showed a scratch.

Evidently the desk sergeant had phoned up, because the very tall man who came out of the tiny office explained that he was in charge, Detective Sergeant Hosea Ramos. "This is Detective Leary," Ramos said, nodding at a heavyset detective with a bulging waistline, "and this is Detective Jones."

Jones, a good-looking black man of about thirty, pushed a chair toward Cullen and told him to sit down. He had just confessed downstairs to murdering someone, but nobody here appeared annoyed or troubled. Leary sat down behind his desk. Jones leaned against another desk, and Ramos, slender and handsome, black hair, mustache, started to say something and then heard the phone in the office and went in there to answer it, closing the door behind him. While he was there, the two detectives said nothing, simply studying Cullen amiably.

"You want a butt?" Leary asked, lighting his own cigarette. Cullen nodded, and Leary rose, handed him a cigarette, and then leaned forward to light it. Ramos came out of his office.

"Joe Cullen?" Ramos said.

Jones sat down behind his desk and picked up a pencil and a pad. "C-U-L-L-E-N?" he asked.

"Right."

"Joseph—got a middle name?"

"Patrick. I don't use it, even on my Social Security card."

Ramos said, "We got no reason to search you, Mr. Cullen, but we'd like to see identification—if you don't mind?"

Cullen opened his wallet and began to lay out his cards. "I don't mind," he said as he put down driver's license, pilot's license, air force reserve ID, Social Security card, MasterCard, and American Express. The three men crowded around to look at the identification, and then Ramos told him to put it all back in his wallet and his pocket.

"You say you killed a priest," Ramos said, "and you want to tell us about it. Is that right?"

"Yes, sir," Cullen agreed.

"Have you any objections to having your confession put on videotape?"

"No, sir."

At that moment, a uniformed policeman came into the room, his arms loaded with a portable video camera, spotlights, wires, aluminum light stands, and spare tapes. He began setting up his equipment immediately.

The telephone in Ramos's office rang again, and the sergeant went to answer it. Jones said, "We might as well get a few facts about you, Mr. Cullen. To begin, how old are you?"

"Forty-four."

"Born in 1943?"

"July tenth."

"Place?"

"Broad Channel."

"Where the hell's that? South Bronx?"

"Queens," Leary said, "although why anyone lives there, God only knows."

"You can say that," Cullen agreed. "We moved to New York when I was a kid."

Ramos came out of his office and asked about the video.

"Whenever you're ready."

"OK." He turned to Jones and asked him to run through it again. "And try to grab the pertinent points so we don't have to run the whole tape. I want it typed out tonight," he said to the cop who was handling the video.

"Sergeant, I'm off duty at five."

"Now you'll do overtime." And to Jones, "Go ahead. Start taping. Give it to him again."

Jones repeated the questions he had already asked Cullen, and while he did so, Leary whispered to Ramos, "What do you think? Is he for real?"

"He's a lieutenant in the air force reserve." He turned to Cullen. "Mr. Cullen, when did this killing take place?"

Jones let him take over the questioning.

"Where? In Honduras."

"I asked you when?"

"On September twenty-third," Cullen said.

Ramos waved to the cop with the video. "Cut it! And cut those damn lights for a minute." He pulled up a chair and sat down, facing Cullen. His telephone was ringing again. "Leary," he said, "will you tell Conway to hold those damn calls? If they're serious, switch them to Manhattan South. Call Manhattan South and tell them we need an hour of peace."

While he was speaking, another detective entered, a tall, tightly built man, glasses and curly red hair. He draped his trench coat on the coat tree and studied Cullen curiously. After a long moment, he said to Cullen, "I'm Lieutenant Freedman." He turned to Ramos after studying the TV equipment.

"You think it's worth that?"

"They got an army up there at Manhattan South. We got a corporal's guard without a pot to pee in."

"I know what we got. You don't want to send him up there?"

Ramos grinned slightly, walked over to the lieutenant, and whispered, "Very big, Lieutenant, very big. Give it to Manhattan South? Fuck Manhattan South."

"All right. Fill me in."

Cullen watched the cops and listened as Jones and Ramos repeated what they had learned from him. It was only here and now that Cullen began to think about punishment.

His only purpose up to this point had been to remove a scab that, he felt, had attached itself to his soul. He had never felt that before, and he had killed other men in Vietnam—and women and children as well. He had told the old priest that he did not believe in God, and now, suddenly, fear clutched at his heart, not the fear of death in terms of the retribution that would be taken of him but a deeper, older fear of judgment. If the old priest was right, then it mattered not a little whether he believed in God.

Lieutenant Freedman said to the cop with the camera, "Hold on, Lefty, until I give you the nod. I want a few words with him before we start recording."

Lefty nodded, and Freedman said to Cullen, "You come in here and confess to the murder of a Catholic priest, name of O'Healey. There was a piece in the *New York Times*, maybe two, three weeks ago, about the disappearance of Father O'Healey." He turned to Jones. "George, get the *Times* and find out what O'Healey's first name was and what they can tell us about him. I'm pretty sure it was O'Healey, but if it wasn't, find out what they got about a Catholic priest disappearing in Honduras." Jones went into the little office, and Freedman said to Cullen, "When did it happen?"

"On September twenty-third," Cullen said.

"Do you also remember what day of the week it was?"

"Wednesday. I'm not some nut coming in here to plead for attention. I know what I did."

"You're a Catholic?"

"I was born one and I was raised that way. What I am now, God only knows."

"If it wasn't a priest, would you be here confessing?"

"I don't know," Cullen answered slowly. "Maybe not."

Freedman said, "All right, Lefty, start recording." And then to Cullen, "Take it from the top. We'll begin with your name."

Cullen repeated the information he had already given them, and then Freedman said, "You say you were in the air force—what rank?"

"Lieutenant."

"And you were in Vietnam?"

"Three tours," Cullen said. "I was trained as a regular pilot. Then they sent me back for helicopter training. I spent nine months in Nam flying helicopters. I was damn good." He didn't know why he said that, but he felt that the five policemen were putting him down, degrading him as just another killer. He wasn't just another killer. "Goddamnit," he said to himself, "I'm Joe Cullen, I'm not dirt. You don't take that away from me."

"Honorable discharge?"

"I'm in the reserve. That's honorable enough."

Freedman was watching him, measuring him, trying to crawl into his mind. Freedman was in no hurry to get the confession over with. He sensed that he was touching something explosive and dangerous, and he wanted to move into it slowly and thoroughly.

"After Vietnam?"

"There were a couple of years just getting my head together, which wasn't so uncommon with the guys from Nam. I had enough back pay to drink too much and be stupid. I got a job in Utah, flying with a tiny commuter line, and they washed out bankrupt, and then I got another job with West Texas Carriers, but they were picked up by Unity, and the big carrier fired all the pilots. I came east, and I got a pretty good job with Cayuga Mohawk, and I got married, but Cayuga Mohawk couldn't make it in Reagan's big push for deregulation, and they folded. My wife left me, and for the next year I didn't do much of anything until I met Oscar Kovach and got into this Honduras thing."

"OK," Freedman said. "You're doing fine."

The telephone in the office was ringing.

Leary went in to answer it, and returned and said, "That was the *Times*. They ran the story on November ninth, and what they had came over the wire from Reuters in London, which is kind of strange, and the priest's name was Father Francis Luke O'Healey, a missionary priest out of San Francisco. The only thing they got to add to this is that according to their inquiry at the time this Father O'Healey was 'solemnly professed,' and I got a vague notion of what that means. I think vows of poverty or something like that."

"Total poverty, total renunciation of ambition," Ramos said.

"Should I stop the camera?" Lefty wanted to know.

"No," Freedman replied. "Keep it rolling." And to Cullen, "You say this man Oscar Kovach got you into the Honduras thing?"

"Yes, sir."

"Tell us about it and how it happened."

Not as easy as the question sounded. Cullen recalled how he had felt that day, a hot, miserable day. He was washed out, tired, his head bursting with pain, still hung over from the day before, and thinking how good it would be to sit right now in the cockpit of a plane and put on the oxygen mask and let the cool flow of oxygen wash away his pain. How to spell out his condition, how to make them understand his mood of defeat and hopelessness that day, the mood of a man who all his life truly desired only one thing, to fly, to experience the sheer ecstasy of flying, to have it day after day—and then to find every door closed to him.

"You see," he explained, "there were enough younger pilots who had not been in Nam. They never felt easy about us. Sure, we could get a job in the 'seventies, but then a whole new generation of pilots was on line, pushing for jobs."

They were listening, waiting. He expected them to come up with a question, but Freedman simply nodded, waiting for him to continue.

"I had eighteen dollars in my pocket. The way it is now, with the inflation, eighteen dollars is worth about twenty cents."

"Was that when you made your Honduras connection?"

"Yes, sir."

"You don't have to apologize for what you did. Just tell it plain and directly. We know what it is to be broke."

There was no anger in Freedman's voice. He spoke gently, encouragingly. The others, too, regarded him without malice. No one walking in on the scene would have suspected that they were talking to a self-confessed murderer.

"I went into Billy Sullivan's saloon over on Ninth Avenue. You know the place?"

They knew the place. It was right around the corner. How could they not know the place?

"Billy's a vet, so the vets feel comfortable there. You want to meet someone who was in Nam, you'll find him if he's in New York. Just wait long enough. That's how I ran into Oscar Kovach. He was standing at the bar, and when he saw me, he waved me over and bought me a beer. I hadn't seen him for years. We flew together with West Texas, I mean we both had jobs there, and he was no great friend of mine, but you know, you see a guy you haven't seen for a long time—well—and he looked good, good clothes, a big grin and a big handshake. He tells me how glad he is to see me."

When Cullen paused, Freedman asked, "Does he figure importantly in this—Oscar Kovach?"

"Yes."

"Tell us about him."

"I guess you want the spelling. Oscar K-O-V-A-C-H. Lieutenant in the air force, told me he did a tour in Nam, but we never met there. I guess he's maybe a year or two younger than I am, early forties. Also in the reserve. He's a good enough pilot."

"Do you have an address for him?"

"No, not a street. He lives in Ridgefield in

Connecticut. A lot of pilots live there because it puts them just outside emergency jobs at Kennedy and LaGuardia. You could probably find him in the phone book."

"Go on then. You met him at Sullivan's. What happened then?"

Once, in Vietnam, a little drunk, Cullen got into a discussion with another pilot, who put forth the proposition that birds lived in a perpetual high. It didn't matter, this pilot insisted, that they had practically no brains and that their lives were short; the high of flight made up for that, and however brief their time on earth, it was damn wonderful. He asked Cullen whether he understood, and Cullen had said, Sort of. It's something only a pilot can understand, I guess. Well, how do you tell a bunch of cops what you felt like when Kovach offered you a chance to fly? How do you tell anything the way it happened.

"He asked me whether I was working," Cullen said. "Well, I wasn't working. I had eighteen bucks between me and hard diet, and I guess at that moment I would have given damn near anything to sit in a cockpit again. So I told him how it was with me, and he said, 'Great. I got a job for you.' Well, you can imagine how I felt, and then when he tells me it's five grand for a flight, I'm ready to kiss his ass."

"Five thousand dollars a flight?"

"That's right."

"And it never occurred to you," Freedman said, "that only dope gets flown at that kind of price?"

"Sure it occurred to me. But you're wrong, Lieutenant. It ain't only dope that gets transportation at that price."

"What else?"

"Guns. You see, that's what he told me. He told me he was working for an outfit that flew guns and ammo into Honduras for the contras. I didn't see anything wrong with that. The president was dumping on the commies and the secretary of state was dumping on them, and I figured that anything to help the contras couldn't get me into too much trouble."

"Where did this operation take place?"

"In Texas, at a place called Salsaville."

Freedman looked at the others. They shrugged. "Where the hell is Salsaville?"

"Western Texas, in the White Mountains, which is just about as far from anyone and anything as you can get. It's an old mining town, with a population of maybe two hundred people—if that. It's no place. It's like one of those godawful places you see in the movies, with sheds to keep off the sun and a few rotting buildings."

Freedman said, "Leary, go downstairs and

see if you can hustle a map of Texas. We had a stack of maps in a shelf behind the booking desk." Then to Cullen, "Go on. Tell us about these people. Who are they and what have they got there at Salsaville? Salsaville? How do you spell that?"

Cullen spelled it.

"Go on. The people?"

"They come and go. Two of them are there every time we hit the place. One's a retired general, name of Swedenham—mostly they just call him General."

"Does he have a first name? Give me both names when you mention someone. What kind of a general? Does he wear a uniform?"

"No. No uniform. The colonel's retired too. His name is Yancy. I don't know his first name. They call him Colonel or Yancy. They're both West Pointers, I think."

"Why? Why do you think?"

"Because when I told them I wasn't, they dropped the nice-guy treatment, and I became a hired hand, like the rest of the pilots. Not that I gave a damn. I was flying and I was being paid. There was a guy there. Everyone brown-nosed him."

Leary came back into the room with an open map, a big folded sheet that he was studying as he walked. Freedman told Lefty to

50

cut the lights and the camera, and then they all crowded around the map.

"I think I got it. Right here."

"Looks like fly shit," Ramos said. "If they were flying into Honduras, why weren't they close to the border?"

"OK, Lefty," Freedman said, and Lefty started the camera.

"Because the landing strip at Salsaville was three thousand feet above sea level," Cullen said. "We were flying 727s, and we crossed the border at twenty-five thousand feet."

"Come on," Jones said. "We could pick a plane out of the sky at that altitude."

"Only if you want to."

"Tell us some more about Salsaville. You say they had an airstrip big enough for 727s. Was it tarmac?"

"No, dirt. But hard and even. It doesn't rain much there, and they have a pair of bulldozers keeps the ground smooth."

"What else do they have there?"

"They got a three-thousand-gallon gas storage tank, a couple of Quonset huts where they store the guns and ammo, and a couple of tents if you have to spend the night. They have a food truck with a stove and a water tower that they rigged. The guns were trucked there by big Mercedes truck rigs. Everything was top dollar."

"And where did all of these top dollars come from?"

"Mostly they came from a millionaire type, name of Fred Lester. Should I spell it?"

Freedman shook his head.

"Maybe he was just a funnel. Oscar figured he was the source, but he took orders and sometimes crap from another man, name of Monty—M-O-N-T-Y. No other name."

"Oscar? That's Oscar Kovach, the guy who steered you to the job?"

"That's right."

"OK," Freedman said. "Let's go back a piece and see what we have. This guy, Oscar Kovach, picks you up in Sullivan's saloon. He's a vet, you're a vet. He needs a pilot—wait a minute. He doesn't do the hiring for the outfit?"

"No, but his copilot had a heart attack and was hospitalized. They told him to find a pilot he could trust and someone who could navigate decently. He needs a pilot, I need a job."

"Go on. You meet him. What then?"

"He pitches the job. I tell him yes, and he gives me a couple of hundred for some tropical clothes and a flying jacket, and I meet him the next day and we take a plane to El Paso. Out of El Paso, we take an eight-seater commuter job to Salsaville, and the day after that, Oscar and me, we're flying an overloaded 727 down to Honduras, where we unload carbines, hand grenades, mortars, heavy antitank stuff, and missiles and ammo, and I'm five thousand dollars richer."

Cullen felt better than he had for weeks; his head was clearer, the tension that lived at the base of his neck and around his shoulders had eased off. He had just begun to think of what the consequences would be—ten, fifteen, twenty years in prison, or a lifetime in prison —and they didn't matter. Something inside him had changed, snapped, released him from himself. If he could have thought it through and put it into words, he might have said that he was free for the first time in his life, not only free from a father who beat him unmercifully, a mother who was an alcoholic and another subject for his father's beatings, a father who hated his education, who drove him out of the house when he began his freshman year at City College, but free from savage, semidemented drill instructors, free from hardly-more-sane senior officers, free from the lunatic horror dreams that were with him in Vietnam, free from the contempt and the lack of interest of a country in the men who fought in Vietnam—a freedom that he had tasted only in the air, high, high in the air. But this was more than a taste. He was released. The cops stood and sat around him not like inquisitors, but in his mind at the moment like priests hearing his confession.

"You had no trouble—walking into a 727?" Freedman wondered.

"I can fly anything. So can Oscar—well, he's not as good in a helicopter as I am, but there's a kind of pilot—I don't know exactly how to put it. I read a book of Faulkner's called *Pylon*. Faulkner understood it."

Freedman, who had been studying Cullen thoughtfully, was taken aback by the reference to Faulkner. He had not known that Faulkner wrote a book called *Pylon*. Cullen had not struck him as either very literate or introverted, but simply as a heavyset roughneck with enough of the Catholic locked into him to recoil from the murder of a priest. Nor did Freedman know, at this point, how it had come about. All that in good time. No need to hurry it.

"Just like that"—Freedman nodded—"you waft into Honduras and unload your guns. How do you get there? You and this Oscar guy —who was your navigator? And where? From what I hear about Honduras, it's a stinking pesthole with a couple of million people who are mostly engaged in killing each other."

"No," Cullen said. "No, Lieutenant, it don't work two ways. The army does the killing, the poor people die."

"What about the airfield? Where is it? How did you get there?"

"The airfield's down by the Patuca River— Rio Patuca, not too far from Nicaragua. Oscar and me, we can both navigate. The airfield's pretty good, better than what they have in Texas, because this field was put down by army engineers."

"What army?" Leary demanded.

"What other army? You don't think those clowns down there can build a first-rate modern field."

"And that's what it is?" Freedman asked. "A first-rate modern field?"

"You bet your sweet ass."

"And tell us, was there army personnel there?"

"Not in uniform, except once or twice when a Jeep would pull up for some kind of conference, and then there'd be some uniforms, and they'd stay for maybe an hour or two and then take off. But there were three or four men in civilian clothes, and sure as hell, they were army."

"How do you know?" Ramos asked. "Did they speak English or Spanish? Do you speak Spanish?"

"Four years of high school Spanish, which is not much. I can make out with it. These guys spoke English. Maybe a little Spanish. There was Honduran army personnel all over the place. Also, you don't have to be a genius to spot army, the way their hair is cut, the way they stand, the way they talk."

Freedman began to speak. Lefty, running the camera, cut the lights, interrupting Freedman's train of thought. Ramos stood up and pointed to the office. Once he and Freedman were in the tiny office, the door closed behind them, Ramos said, "You know what we're getting into, Lieutenant?"

Freedman was calling the desk and asking them to pass any waiting calls up to the squad room, not the office. When he put down the telephone, he regarded Ramos bleakly and said, "There's the kind of thing that happens and then you lose your common sense and remember that when you were a kid they still sang 'America the Beautiful.' Did he kill the priest? Or is he some kind of nut?"

"Maybe he's some kind of nut, but he's telling the truth. You're Jewish, Lieutenant. You can't crawl into the soul of someone put together by the church. I can. I look at that man and I can go inside his head. Ask him what he takes back with him into Texas."

"You know, Sarge, you and me, we're—honest cops. That's right. At least we got only a minimum of glue on our hands, but God Almighty, that's all we are, a couple of cops in a tiny third-rate precinct house that's so old and rotten it would fall down if somebody coughed too loud. Ten months now I been writing letters pleading with them to paint the place."

"I know," Ramos said.

"I wonder what the vintner buys, one half so precious as he sells."

"Poetry?"

"Sort of. Ah, fuck it! Let's go ask him."

They returned to the squad room. The detectives were on their phones, catching up on the calls that were on hold. Lefty said that he was ready to go. Cullen asked to go to a john, and Ramos went with him. When the calls had been handled and Leary had taken off with something that couldn't wait, Lefty turned up the lights and started his camera again. Cullen took his place in the same chair.

"I'm going to ask you about this murder you say you did," Freedman said, "but before I do I want to be very clear about one or two things. First: how many flights did you make, round trips?"

"Twelve."

"Give me some dates."

"I started at the end of June and I made my last flight on September twenty-third."

"All right. You went down with guns—every time?"

For the first time, Cullen hesitated, looking from face to face before he spoke. He knew what was coming. It was, strangely enough, more difficult to talk about than murder.

"No. Twice we went down empty."

"Empty? Why?"

Cullen looking at Cullen was at the edge of despair. The peace and relief that had pervaded him were suddenly tied into knots, and for a long moment he sat with his eyes closed, seeking himself desperately in the darkness. He felt tears in his eyes, but whether they were for the dead priest or the live killer or the answer to the question, he did not know, and perhaps they were for none of those but only for himself, Cullen, whoever Cullen was.

"Let me suggest it," Freedman said gently. "You went down with guns and you came back with cocaine."

Cullen nodded.

"You went down empty to bring back cocaine."

"That's right," Cullen said.

"You brought back cocaine on every trip?"

"Yes."

"How much on each trip?"

"It varied. Sometimes as little as forty pounds. Once, two hundred pounds."

Jones let out his breath in a long whistle. Ramos whispered, "Mother of God." Freedman said, "They didn't need guns. For that kind of money they could buy the Pentagon." Jones said, "You brought it in on every trip?"

Cullen nodded. Murder did not put their backs up like this. Murder was normal in this precinct. Why, Cullen wondered, did he feel defensive about this when he had put aside all his defenses in the matter of Father O'Healey?

"You knew what you were carrying?" Freedman demanded.

"I knew because everyone knew," Cullen said. "I wasn't supposed to know. There was no white powder floating around. The stuff came baled up in heavy sacking. But Oscar knew and he put me onto it, and others knew —but, Jesus God, as far as I knew, I was working for the government. The army was in it and the CIA built the damned airstrip, and maybe two, three times, Oscar would introduce me to some clown, and then tell me he was CIA, and there were two Sikorsky S76s parked there—"

"You're telling me," Freedman interrupted, "that you're so fucken stupid that you figured the government is running in its own cocaine?" It was the first time he had raised his voice.

"What would you think? You just heard it. I lived with it. I come into a situation where the set-up costs millions. Maybe I'm stupid but not so stupid I don't know who's running the contras. Who the fuck knows what a war is or where it's coming from? Did I know it in Nam? Like hell I did."

Freedman nodded. He understood that. He had been in Vietnam. "All right, Cullen. Suppose you tell us about the priest."

It came together for Cullen, simply and directly, another small piece, and his heart hammered less violently. "We had a three-day layover," Cullen said. He paused and drew a long breath. Jones picked up the pack of cigarettes on Leary's desk, selected one, took cigarette and matches to Cullen, and then lit the cigarette for him. If someone had asked Jones why he did this, he might have answered that he wanted to cool the situation, but the truth went deeper. Something in him went out to the big, deflated Irishman, a recognition of mystery like the mystery in himself. Cullen thanked him, nodding his shaggy head.

Ramos, scribbling on a scrap of paper, looked up and said, "Maybe ten million a week, give or take. That's nice money."

"Tell us about the priest," Freedman said again.

"They brought him in by car," Cullen said, speaking very slowly. "There was a lousy little road to the airstrip, and they drove up in one of those big six-wheelers that we build for the army. He came with two Honduran army officers and he was cuffed. He wore a black cassock, and he had red hair and bright blue eyes. I noticed the eyes. They protruded, if you know what I mean. He had a round, chunky face with a pink complexion that was sunburned to high color. They walked him past where I was standing and watching, and he grinned at me. I guess he was about my age . . ."

Cullen's voice dropped away. The words impinged on his memory, and with his eyes half closed, he was back there in that strange tropical place that always reminded him of Vietnam, the air not clean and clear, like northern air, but heavy and scented with all the strange scents of the jungle, his shirt wet with sweat, his tongue dry and thirsty.

"They put him in one of the supply sheds," Cullen said. "They didn't lock him in. There was no door to the shed, just a big opening the size of a pair of doors, and there was always a guard with one of those damn flat poker faces. The guard knew me and let me walk past him into the shed. Maybe if it wasn't a priest he wouldn't have done it, but he let me. Maybe he remembered. Maybe he remembered a priest he knew when he was a kid. So I walked in there and the priest was on his knees praying, and he must have heard my footsteps but he didn't move. So I sat down on one of the crates in there and waited. I must have waited about ten minutes before he moved, and then he got up and turned around because when he was praying his back was to the entrance, and he squinted at me, and then he asked me who I was.

"I told him my name and how I happened to be there and then I asked him what dumb son of a bitch put the gyves on him? He burst out laughing, and he says to me, 'Wherever did you find that name for a pair of handcuffs?' So I tell him that when we were kids on our block, that's what we called them, and then he said something about the persistence of words, and, well—well, that was how I met Father O'Healey."

They waited. Leary returned with a six-pack of soda, fell into the moment of silence, and passed around the soda. Cullen nodded and drank eagerly. He rubbed his forehead. Suddenly, he was confused.

"Take it easy," Freedman said.

"I don't know how to tell it. I could just tell you about the killing, but then it makes no sense."

"Tell it the way you want to tell it. We'll listen," Freedman said.

"All right, I was raised a Catholic. I saw a lot of priests in my time, but I never really talked to one. Like I told you, I had a layover at the strip, and I guess I must have sat and talked but mostly listened to Father O'Healey for maybe fifteen, twenty hours. The day after I met him, we talked until maybe midnight. When I wondered why he'd waste the time on a bum like myself, he said he thought he might save my soul, and when I told him I didn't have any soul to bother about and that I had stopped believing in God, he just shrugged it off and said that nobody has much authority over his own soul. He told me how he had come down to Honduras eight years before and he was supposed to stay for only a few weeks because the priest at the Church of the Blessed Apostles had died and he was to take over temporarily, and that was up in the mountains, just poor Indians and peasants. He told me how they were victimized by the government and the soldiers, robbed, beaten, murdered like they were so many dogs, and how finally they organized a guerrilla movement to fight against the soldiers. We talked a lot about right and wrong. I never gave much thought to things like that. I got through college because I had to for being a pilot, but I took what I was given and I went where they sent me, and it made no damn difference to me whether we had any right to be in Nam or not, and the truth was that I didn't give a fuck as long as I could fly and draw my pay. But O'Healey stood it all on its head, because he turned all my thinking upside down—"

Freedman interrupted him now. It was getting too deep and murky and political, and what Freedman wanted to know was why O'Healey had been there in cuffs.

"Just for what he was doing, being with the guerrillas and being a priest to them and to the Indians. They captured him, and the word was that they were going to send him stateside and that we would carry him in our plane. But a few hours before we were supposed to take off, they got some change of orders and I was told that they were going to fly the priest down to the contra main base. I guess I had shot off my mouth about being a class chopper pilot, so this Honduran officer there—his name is Sanchez—he tells me to pick up one of the helicopters and fly the priest there. So like the asshole I am, I did it, and a soldier brought O'Healey into the helicopter, and Sanchez comes with us and tells me to lift off."

"In Spanish?" Ramos wanted to know.

"In Spanish. My Spanish isn't the worst, but he had a mouthful of marbles and was hard to understand. I ask him where we were going. He says first we take the Christo home, so we go to the mountains."

"Mother of God," Ramos said.

"I should have known, but until O'Healey yells to me, 'Cullen, they're going to kill me,' I don't know, and then Sanchez tries to shut him up, struggling with him, and meanwhile he opens the door of the chopper and I start down. We are up maybe eight, nine hundred feet and Sanchez and the guard throw Father O'Healey out of the copter, and with all the noise I hear his scream as he falls."

"You saw his body?"

"I saw it," Cullen said. "I tried to get down. I guess I was half crazy, calling those bastards everything rotten I could think of and ready to dive and smash the plane and die with those bastards, and then Sanchez points the muzzle of his pistol at me, and maybe I could die in a crash, which was the way I always expected to go, but I couldn't deal with the thought of a bullet smashing my head, so I brought the Sikorsky back and landed it as hard as I could, knocking Sanchez off his feet, and then I began to kick him, landing a few good ones, and then the soldiers pulled me off, and I wrenched myself out of their grip. Oscar was standing, watching, and I yelled to Oscar, 'We are getting to hell out of here, now! Fucken now!'"

Cullen stopped speaking. He was covered with sweat, his shirt wet under his jacket, the sweat beading his face, his hands trembling.

Leary lit a cigarette and handed it to him. He puffed and then drew a deep breath of smoke.

"They let you go?" Freedman said. "Just like that?"

"Sanchez was unconscious," Cullen answered, speaking with visible effort. "I guess the soldiers didn't want to do anything until someone told them what to do, and Oscar didn't know what the hell was going on. Our plane was fueled. I would have taken off without Oscar if he hadn't come with me. He might have stopped me, but I picked up the pistol Sanchez had dropped and told him I'd kill him if he interfered with the takeoff."

"And when you got back to the States?"

"I left my car at the airport in Texas. I got into it and drove. No one tried to stop me."

"So that's it? That's the way it happened?"

"That's it."

"And nobody stopped you there in Texas? Nobody called the cops?"

"Maybe they didn't know what happened."

"Didn't Oscar tell them?"

"I suppose he did. You want them to be crazy enough to call the cops?"

"And the pistol?"

"I emptied it and left it with Oscar."

"Did you tell Oscar what had happened?" Ramos asked.

"I told him."

"And?"

"He said it was none of my fucken business."

"Where is he?"

Cullen shrugged. "I suppose he's where I left him."

Freedman

FREEDMAN told the detectives to get back to their cases and Lefty to give him the tape, and then he and Ramos led Cullen into the small office that adjoined the squad room. There were only two chairs in the office. Ramos pulled in another chair, after which there was not much room remaining if someone wanted to switch from one chair to another. The window in this office had not been cleaned in at least thirty years. The desk was vintage 1920s. When it comes to the place they work, New York City is not generous to its police.

Freedman nodded for Cullen to sit down and pushed a box of Kleenex toward him.

While Cullen wiped his face, Ramos took out his cigarettes.

"Jesus Christ!" Freedman exploded. "You're not going to smoke those damn things in here. We'll choke."

"OK, don't blow your top."

Freedman stared at Cullen for a long moment; then he shook his head and said bleakly, "You're no horse's ass, Cullen. You know which side is up. You're a pilot, you're a college graduate, and you were an officer in the United States Air Force, and if your story is not one crock of shit, you know damn well you didn't commit any crime except running dope. That's a big one, but it's not murder. The way you tell it, you're not even an accessory to a murder. You didn't foresee it, you tried to prevent it, and now you're giving evidence against whoever committed it—if anyone did, if any murder took place. Father Francis Luke O'Healey disappeared. There is no body. As for the dope—we would need evidence and you got no evidence. Do you have any coke on you?"

"I'm not a doper. I hate the stuff."

"So that's where we are," Freedman said. "Leave your name, address, telephone number, and walk out of here. We'll follow up on what you gave us, and if anything comes of it, we'll call you as a witness."

"I'm not a witness," Cullen said stolidly. "Not the way you mean it. I bear witness differently."

"Do you know what the hell he's talking about?" Freedman asked Ramos.

"Maybe. There's another way to bear witness. Tell me something, Mr. Cullen. After you met the father, did you suspect they would kill him?"

"Just before we got into the chopper—yes."

"What could you do?"

The two policemen waited. Through the closed door of the little office, Cullen could hear Jones's voice as he spoke into the telephone. He recalled a story by Edgar Allan Poe that he had read a long, long time ago, where a policeman sat silently waiting for a guilty man to confess. Now the presence of these two silent policemen became intolerable. He had to speak, yet he knew that he was incapable of pulling the thoughts out of his head and turning them into words.

Finally, he said, "It isn't what I could do. I could have done any number of things. I had control of the chopper. If you're as good as I am with a chopper, you can make it teach points to a sparrow. When they opened the door, I could have tossed them out—one of them, anyway. I could have threatened them. I could have spun it—any number of things. The point is, that I knew they were going to kill him, yet I did nothing until they started to throw him out, and then it was too late. I never met anyone like O'Healey before. I never believed there was a good man—I never met a good man. All the hours we talked—it was like I had been blind, and here was Saint Francis. My God," he said to Ramos, pleading, "do you understand what I'm trying to say?"

Freedman watched Ramos, whose black eyes were hooded to slits and who said softly, "I think I do."

"No one paid him. He went to the Indians because they were the poorest people on earth —Oh, shit! You sit up here in New York and you don't know what the fuck goes on, and I don't know how to spell it out."

"You spell it out pretty good," Ramos said. "You did nothing we can arrest you for. We'll look into it."

"Maybe we can get someone to look for that Honduran officer, Sanchez," Freedman said.

"Where do you live?" Ramos asked. Cullen gave them the address on West Eighteenth Street.

"Get some rest," Freedman said. He opened the door of the office and Cullen shambled out.

"Poor bastard," Ramos said.

Cullen closed the door behind him, and for a few moments the two detectives sat in silence.

Then Freedman shook his head. "Fucken strange world. What the hell does he mean with that bearing-witness stuff?"

"I got a notion—sort of, but I can't explain it . . . I mean, I can't make it make sense to you."

"Because I'm not Catholic?"

"I don't know."

Freedman picked up the phone, dialed a number, and then said, "Maybe I can buy you dinner tonight?" He paused, and then, "OK, so it goes. Hell, I understand." He put down the phone and said to Ramos, "What kind of schmuck am I?"

Ramos shook his head.

"We're divorced over a year, and I still try to date her. You ever date your ex-wife?"

"I hate her guts, Lieutenant," Ramos said. "I want to know what you're thinking about Cullen."

Freedman took out a nail clipper and tried to smooth a ragged edge. "You believe him?"

"Maybe."

"Maybe. What the hell does maybe signify?"

"I think he told it the way he sees it. Maybe it's different the way somebody else sees it. Do you believe him?"

"Yes."

"Just like that?"

"This Cullen," Freedman said, "is locked into

himself. I know what that's like. I got a wife locked into herself. Cullen sees a priest killed, a fucken lousy way to die, so goddamn awful that even a priest who believes in God screams in terror as he falls through the air—and that explodes something in Cullen. Cullen really believes he murdered the priest. When we were married, I'd talk to Sheila, I'd plead with her—I couldn't get through. O'Healey got through to Cullen. Look, Ramos, the fact that we both believe him makes a point. I'm going to send the tape downtown to the DA. Let them bust their heads over it. If anything comes of it, we're on page one. That can't hurt the house. We might get a new paint job out of it."

Freedman gave instructions to send the tape downtown to the district attorney, and then, their shift being over, he and Ramos left. Freedman was almost six feet, but Ramos loomed over him, at least four inches taller, stooped, his black mustache drooping. Freedman covered his red hair with a soft Irish hat, and both men wore raincoats. It was about six o'clock, and the bright day had given way to a cold November rain. They turned up their coat collars and hunched over as they walked toward Eighth Avenue.

"Lousy night," Ramos said. "Hungry, boss?"

"When I was a kid, I was hungry. Now I'm never hungry. I eat the goddamn junk food all day, I swear to God it's going to kill me. You know how much cholesterol there is in a ham and cheese or a corned beef on rye? I got high blood pressure and I eat those damn pickles that are soaked with salt. I go to a doctor and I pay him forty bucks to tell me not to eat junk food."

"When I was a kid," Ramos said, "you called a doctor and it was five dollars. And they came."

"Dreams. We could go to a movie now and eat later. Unless you got a date?"

"Tell me something," Ramos asked. "Why do you always try to date your ex-wife?"

"Because she interests me. She's sexy. She's smart. Other women bore me."

"So why'd you divorce her?"

"Because mostly we just ripped each other up. If I'd stayed married, either she'd have killed me or I'd have killed her."

"Yeah—yeah. Let's eat now. I'm hungry."

Freedman nodded. He didn't want to be alone tonight. If Ramos wanted to eat, he'd eat. They went to Tony Polito's place on Eighth Avenue. It was only half-past six, and except for another occupied table, the restaurant was empty. Tony had strong mob connections, such as the mortgage to his place, and therefore was overly polite to cops. "You come early, good. My house is your house. You're not hungry, Lieutenant. I make you a beautiful little salad of arugula, a little olive oil and vinegar, a little spaghetti—"

"How the hell do you know that I'm not hungry?"

"You're never hungry, Lieutenant."

Ramos burst out laughing. Tony brought them a bottle of wine, white Sicilian wine, which, he explained, was the best white wine in the world.

"This is a new line for the mob," Ramos said. "They're building it slow but very serious in the wine business."

"I'll have a beer," Freedman said.

"That's a mistake," Ramos said, tasting the wine.

"I'll risk it."

"You're not a very pleasant person tonight," Ramos observed. "You're ripping up everyone you talk to. All because your ex-wife won't give you a date. You know what I think? I think you ought to marry her again."

"You think she'd be stupid enough to marry me? Forget it, and you're wrong. I gave up on Sheila—for tonight. On the other hand, consider this. Six cops have been shot to death in the last few months by drug dealers, the city is riddled with the stuff, it's fucken ruining the city and the country, and every time we walk through a door, we could be dead on the other side of it, and you and me sit here and stuff our mouths."

"What do you want me to do, Lieutenant? Eat standing up?"

"What the hell is with you, Ramos? Doesn't anything get to you? We just listened to Cullen's story about the biggest drug operation maybe in the world, and cocaine coming in like it owned every seat on its own airline—"

"So what, goddamn it, so what?"

"Like that?"

"Holy Mother of God, Lieutenant," Ramos burst out. "There's army and CIA and the State Department, not to mention the administration itself, mixed up in this business, and we're a couple of cops from a precinct out of *Lost Horizon* . . ." His voice trailed off.

"Yeah?"

"Oh, shit!"

Freedman nodded. "OK, I'm sorry. I'm pissed off. I don't know why the hell I'm dumping on you."

"If you got a date with Sheila, you'd dump on her."

"Maybe you're right." Freedman wasn't hungry, but he ate his spaghetti hungrily. He'd feel sick later, and he realized this and pushed the plate away from him, half eaten. He sat for a little while in silence, observing Ramos, who was devouring all of his food with gusto.

Freedman had an ulcer and he began to feel it now, the initial thread of fire creeping up his gullet.

"It's the lousy food you eat."

"You're eating the same lousy food."

"No, sir, Lieutenant. This is not lousy food. It's the pastrami and corned beef that's putting you under. Myself, I grew up with brown rice and beans. Never had a gut ache—"

"Leave it alone," Freedman growled. "I am sick of that miserable stomach of yours." He called Tony to bring him a glass of milk.

The milk came and Freedman drained the glass and then burst out, "It's a goddamn farce. The whole thing's a joke. A man tells us about a murder and a drug business that could put this whole city on crazy street, and there's not one fucken thing we can do with it, and the whole damn world's coming apart, and you sit there and give me a lecture on Puerto Rican food."

"It still don't hurt as much as your ulcer. Let the DA worry about it."

"I'm going over there," Freedman said.

"Look, Lieutenant," Ramos said, "they got *Casablanca* playing down on Fourteenth Street. We can sit down and relax."

"I saw it six times," Freedman said.

"So what? It's got to be the best picture in the world. So you see it a seventh time."

Freedman shook his head. "I'm going over there, and if she doesn't want to see me, she don't open the door. I'm not going to break it down."

"Suppose she's got a guy there? It's legal. She's not your wife now."

Outside, Ramos watched him walk away, a big, shambling man, stooped, depressed. Ramos never understood why anyone wanted to be a cop. He didn't understand why he was a cop.

It was a dozen blocks to the brownstone where Sheila lived in their old floor-through apartment, three flights up with no elevator. After the divorce Freedman had begged her to move to one of the new high-rises, with a doorman to see who goes in and who goes out, but she preferred her privacy and she wasn't afraid of anything, including Freedman, who had slapped her once and in return received an iron frying pan on his skull.

He opened the street door with his key, walked up the three flights, and then resisted the temptation to turn around and walk out of the place. If he pressed the buzzer and she didn't open the door, he'd be even more miserable than he was right now, and if he did not press it, at least he would avoid rejection.

He pressed the buzzer. Suppose she had a date. Suppose she wasn't home. There was no reason that she should sit at home. Whatever anyone said about Sheila, no one ever denied her beauty. She was a tall, black-haired, dark-eyed woman, half Irish, half Italian, and according to Freedman's mother, not the kind of girl a Jewish boy should marry.

"Who is it?" Sheila asked. "I ordered nothing and nothing's coming and you didn't ring downstairs, so if it's not the Pope, fuck off."

"It's me," Freedman said.

"Oh, God—you."

"Me—just me," Freedman said, feeling that even the three words could be interpreted as a softening of the initial harsh response. "Please, I need to see you, Sheila—please. I'm not drunk—one beer, I'm not looking for trouble —please—"

"Is that Puerto Rican bum you hang out with standing next to you?"

"Ramos? Why would I bring Ramos here?"

"Good question. Why did you bring him around every other day when we were together? Oh, shit—" She opened the door. "Come on in. I'm probably as miserable and lonely as you are."

"Thank you," reminding her of a large, awkward, redheaded dog wagging his tail. She had never been able to explain, even to herself, why she had married Freedman. Maybe it was her Italian grandmother, who told her to

marry a Jewish boy who would never beat up
on her, just because he was a Jewish boy,
which was absolutely not true, as she learned.
Maybe it was his curious gentleness most of
the time, except when wild anger took over,
and his love of poetry. She had never met anyone else who was content to sit facing her and
read poetry. Had she fallen in love with Freedman or the sonnets of Shakespeare and Keats,
or the bemusing wonder of the Rubáiyát, or
the love songs of Carew and Herrick? And this
coming from a policeman, who spoke the language of the streets of New York, had shattered her resistance.

"Why the hell can't you stay away?" she
asked him. "Why can't you give me a break
and not make me crazy? That's all I ever asked
from you. I didn't ask for money. I never
asked for anything."

"I'm sorry."

"You're always sorry. OK, come in. Sit
down."

He dropped into one of the armchairs. The
big, square room was tastefully furnished,
overstuffed pieces with wonderful fabrics, a
colorful hand-woven Portuguese rug, long
white curtains on the high windows—all of it
making him wonder, as it always had, how a
woman almost uneducated could have such
good taste. She was a model at Cornich

Dresses, in-house and photographed as well, and very decently paid—more so than any cop short of the commissioner.

Sheila dropped into a chair facing him and asked, "What can I give you, Mel? A drink, sandwich?"

"Nothing. I just ate."

"Hard day? Don't answer. I don't want to listen to another cop's day."

"This one was different."

"They're all different. Mother of God, you wallow in dung all day—you can't wash it off."

"Beautiful. I need that."

"There we go again," Sheila said. "No. I want to hear about today. Honestly, truly. It did something to you, something deep and a little scary. Forgive me. We won't fight tonight. Tell me about today—please."

"A man walked into the house and told us he had murdered a priest."

"Just like that?"

"Yeah, just like that." And then he went on and told her all of it, and when he had finished, Sheila stared at him without commenting, and he stared back and wondered what was going on in that lovely head of hers. She broke the silence.

"What got to you?" she wondered. "You've seen it all—all the blood and guts and garbage."

"Something shattered," Freedman said.

"What?"

"I don't know. I can't get the image out of my head, the priest flung out of the plane and falling and screaming."

"I wish I understood you," Sheila said. "I don't think we would have made it anyway, because someone like me could never make it with a cop, not in a thousand years, but I'd feel better if I knew how it goes inside of you."

"Any more than I know what goes inside of you?" Freedman asked bleakly. "I'd quit the cops if I could have you back, but then what would I do? Who'd pay me? And for what? All I know is to rut in garbage."

"Oh, shut up," Sheila said. "Nobody goes back. Come on, Mel. Take off your clothes and take a shower and we'll crawl into bed and weep for each other."

**Francis Luke
O'Healey**

CULLEN REMEMBERED, from his very young schooldays, the apple that sat on the teacher's desk. The custom is gone and forgotten, but in that long ago it was still observed. The apple was anonymous, a shining red object that stood there in full view of all the class, and all the class knew that whoever put it there would somehow make himself or herself known to the teacher. But then, in that long ago before a school was a battlefield, the class awaited the teacher's response—although it was always the same and although they knew it as well as the teacher. "Indeed!" the teacher would say, picking up the apple and turning it over, and then continuing, "I see we have an apple polisher in attendance. But they do say that an apple a day keeps the doctor away, and I am sure we shall have no need of a doctor here."

The memory brought a smile to Cullen's face. He had one of those broad, flat Irish faces, and its very flatness and impassiveness made his smile a total transformation. He had a wonderful smile—a good set of teeth and a smile that welcomed the world. Father O'Healey had said to him, "Joseph, you have a unique smile, and when I see it, I think of the moment God smiled. Perhaps you heard the story when you were a kid?"

Embarrassed, Cullen shook his head.

"An old legend. As God smiled, the smile turned into a thousand cherubim."

Perhaps the nicest thing that had ever been said to Cullen, and he thought of it now as he entered the shed where Father O'Healey was kept prisoner. There were two guards now on duty. They knew Cullen and made no effort to stop him, and they were not without a thread of reverence for the priest, even though he had been designated as *el diablo, abogado del diablo,* not to mention *el comunista.* They were very poor and very ordinary *campesinos,* and though O'Healey was of the devil, he was still a priest. Standing in front of the shed in their ill-fitting, American-made uniforms, with their old Springfield rifles—the automatic weapons were reserved for the regular army—they struck Cullen as being more comic than dangerous; and as for guarding, they hardly expected a manacled priest to walk off into the jungle. They passed Cullen through without even asking to see the contents of the brown paper bag he carried.

Father O'Healey watched him spread the contents of the brown bag, and not without a certain amount of awe. Cullen arranged the stuff on a crate: two cans of Norwegian sardines, King Oscar brand—"The very best, for more reasons than one," Cullen said—a package of imported Finn Crisp, a jar of Chivers dark marmalade, made of bitter Seville oranges, a Sara Lee cake with chocolate frosting, and a huge California orange.

"You are a man of miracles," O'Healey whispered.

"If these are miracles, they come cheap, Father. Those local mothers live like kings. The bastards even got a freezer. That's where the cake comes from and by now it's defrosted. The sardines are important, being the whole fish. You got your calcium there and you got your vitamins from the orange and you got your roughage out of the Finn Crisp. You can't live on beans alone."

"I have. But this? Cullen, where did you get all this nutrition stuff?"

"You mean the food? These mothers got a generator and they order anything they want from the States."

"No, I don't mean the food, Cullen. I mean the nutritional talk."

"Oh, that."

"Right. Oh, I'm grateful. Thank you, Cullen, but one thing. If you call them mothers out of respect for me, don't."

"Motherfuckers?"

"I heard the word before. I survived. May I have the orange first? Or does a menu come with it?"

"You're putting me on, Father."

"A little. Tell me about nutrition."

"I dated this army nutritionist in Nam. All she talked about was nutrition."

"Wonderful. You pick up things, Cullen. You see things. You remember things. That's a gift."

Cullen regarded O'Healey suspiciously, but the priest's attention was on the orange, which, although handcuffed, he was slowly and carefully peeling. "Cullen," he said, choosing his words precisely, "doesn't it trouble you, flying the guns down here and taking the dope back?"

"I was afraid you'd ask me that. I was hoping you wouldn't."

"Oh?"

"Damn it, it gets tangled when a priest asks you a question like that."

"No priest. Same question. Oscar is asking."

"That son of a bitch Kovach got me the job. Why would he ask me? Father, does it bug you when I swear? I do it without thinking."

"I know all the words. It doesn't bug me."

"All right. Kovach asks me, but he knows the answer. If I don't, someone else will do it."

"Except that you've never committed a crime. This is criminal—if not the guns then surely the dope."

"I don't know what's a crime," Cullen replied uneasily. "I never said this to anyone else, Father, but the way we did it in Nam, putting a gunship down on a village and raking it, so that every man, woman, and child there was shot to pieces—wasn't that a crime?"

"Yes."

"And a mortal sin?"

"I would say yes, a mortal sin."

"Well, there you are."

"In Nam," the priest said, "you followed orders."

"Does that make it different?"

"I don't think so, but it might make a difference in your own soul, at least the sense that you felt you were doing what's right."

"I don't know what's right. I don't believe I have a soul. I watched our kids being shot to pieces. I watched the VC kids being shot to pieces. Did they have souls? Maybe we were doing good, sending all those souls up to heaven. Father, it's such bullshit. Tell me I'm crazy. Tell me it ain't bullshit."

"I can't tell you that," the priest said gently. "I can't even look at it that way. There's only one way I can deal with it."

"What's that?"

"What I do. If I have a soul, I must find it. Do you want a piece of orange?"

Cullen took the offered orange segment and said, "Father, I met you only twenty-four hours ago, and you already got me more confused than I ever been."

"It's time, isn't it?"

"Time for what?"

"Time to confuse you. Look at it, Joe. You kill, and you work it out. Everyone else is doing it, and if you don't do it, someone else will. You're following orders. You're serving your country. Clean and simple and direct. No confusion. You take a job to bring guns into this place of agony, and what the guns will do doesn't trouble you, because if you don't take the job of flying them down, another will, so what's the difference? And the same goes for the cocaine you take back, and that's all right because up in Texas at the other end are the fat cats who have always run things, and you know that's the way it's always been, and there's a touch of CIA and army, so you figure it's no skin off your back if these wealthy and powerful characters want to run dope into the United States, and that's simple too. So if I confuse you, I have to say it's high time someone did, and if you feel I put you down too much, you can take your ass out of here."

"Jesus, I come to you," Cullen said. "I like you, I respect you, I bring you stuff—you know, I want to help you. Not just because you're a priest and I'm a Catholic, but because —oh, Jesus, I don't know how to say it, but why do you tell me to get out of here? I'm not mad. Only, sometimes I don't know what the hell you're talking about, and I try—believe me."

O'Healey's pink face crinkled. "And sometimes I don't know what the hell I am talking about. When I gave my first sermon, I chose this same question—in Catholic thinking, it has the formal name of 'false conscience.' That means rationalization, the art of working something wrong through your mind until it comes out right. The act of doing a wrong or evil thing and then rationalizing it into its opposite. This was always at the bottom of my thinking—I suppose part of what brought me to the priesthood—and I built it into that first sermon with all the enraged righteousness of an earnest young man who discovers that nothing in the world bears much resemblance to what he had been taught and read. Fortunately, God was good to me and when I delivered the sermon I was in such stark terror that only a whisper emerged from my lips and no one heard it. I am still a righteous type, and I light into a guy like you for no good reason. I like you, Joe, and I pray for you, so forgive me."

Cullen shook his head. For some reason he could not understand, there were tears in his eyes.

"Shall we split a can of sardines?" the priest asked.

"Do you know what I forgot?" Cullen asked excitedly. "I don't have a brain in my head. I forgot the Coke. They got a cooler up there in the executive shack and maybe a hundred bottles of Coca-Cola in it. We're sitting here and both of us sweating, and I forget the Coke."

"Hold on," O'Healey cried as Cullen bolted out of the shack into the blazing sunlight, but Cullen, moving faster than anyone ever moved at that airstrip, was off and running, and a minute or two later he returned with two bottles of Coca-Cola clenched in the fingers of each hand. He was pouring sweat as he put down the bottles.

Wiping his face with a handkerchief, Cullen

then opened a bottle for each of them, took a long drink, and lit a cigarette. "Smoke, Padre?" he asked, offering the pack to the priest.

"Padre. I like that. That's what the *campesinos* call me. It comes easier than 'Father,' trippingly on the tongue, as Shakespeare put it. Ah, Joe, Spanish is a lovely language, music in words. It makes talk a pleasure. No, I don't smoke. It was a pack a day for years, until I came down here. But you don't find tobacco in the hills, so I kicked it. Not easy, not easy at all."

"Someday I'll quit, but not now," Cullen said, taking a long drag. "Right now I feel too good, and if I had my wife, Frannie, here for just an hour, I wouldn't ask for more—but only for an hour, because after an hour we hate each other. Ah, but I shouldn't be talking like that in front of a priest."

"Why not?"

"Well, you know—"

"What do I know, Joseph Cullen? Not a devil of a lot more than you do. Oh, maybe a feeling for God that you have yet to encounter. You don't think you believe in God, do you?"

"No, Padre."

"Then what do you do with the wonder, Joe?"

"What do you mean?"

"The wonder, the mystery? Have you never

97

felt that moment when things come together and it explodes in your mind with the sheer beauty of it?"

Cullen thought about it and then said that he felt pretty good right at this moment.

"Not exactly what I mean."

"No, I guess not," Cullen agreed. "You know, Padre—you don't mind I keep calling you Padre?"

"I told you, Joe. I meant it."

"Yeah—well, what I meant, I mean what I'm trying to say is that I never had this kind of a conversation with a priest before, I mean not in confession but just sitting like this and talking. You know, with a chaplain, well, you don't go to the chaplain, and anyway I hated the bastards, if you'll forgive me, and I'd see them doing their absolution thing when maybe there wasn't even a head in the body bag, and even if there was a head, you couldn't be sure whose body or legs were in there with it—oh, Jesus Christ, I'm really being stupid."

"No. You're being honest."

"I shouldn't say this to you, but I don't mean you, Padre. I mean—"

"I know what you mean."

"Anyway, I think you're the first person in my life I ever talked to about this kind of thing. I mean, God—you know, and then I dump on priests—"

"Go on," O'Healey said. "I'm not putting up any defense of priests. I've seen some cold and heartless bastards who walk around in black nightshirts and I've seen others too brainless to know what was going on in the world, and there are all kinds, so say your piece. I'm curious. I'm interested." He smiled and nodded at Cullen, for all the world a beardless, red-headed Santa Claus, his pink cheeks a bit puffed, his tiny nose peeling and pink, his bright blue eyes in nests of wrinkled flesh.

This was the second time Cullen had talked with Father O'Healey, and he was afraid that he would say something that would cause the priest to tell him to go away and stay away. Certainly, O'Healey had pitted his life and beliefs in a struggle against men like Cullen and Oscar Kovach, who represented, at least in part, the force that was pouring a stream of weapons into Central America, who were supporting the demented military dictators in their slaughter of peasants who struggled against them and of peasants who were suspected of struggling against them and of unnumbered women and children who happened to be in the line of fire or who might be witness to what had happened. Cullen knew this, and his first approach to O'Healey, the day before, had been very tentative. O'Healey, however, had responded with a warmth and charm, and had captured Cullen completely. Yet Cullen, unable to forget what he stood for and what O'Healey stood for, was afraid that the priest might reject him. He didn't want that to happen. He had discovered something in O'Healey that he had never touched before. The priest had turned him inward and with almost magic simplicity had broken through a lifelong resistance to the contemplation of his inner being.

It all burst out now—or imploded, restoring a jumble of memories and happenings that had been squeezed out of his consciousness, a father who beat him until one day Cullen had grabbed him and whispered, "Touch me again and I'll kill you," a mother who was an alcoholic, a childhood of pain and sorrow during which he built a shield of Irish macho and fought with everything and anyone who came his way. It came back now, and the middle-aged man tried to handle it.

He clung to O'Healey. Don't chase me away, Padre, don't put me down as an animal. I need something desperately, and I don't know what I need.

"What you said before . . . ?" He took the last bit of Coca-Cola. "I'll open another bottle for you."

"No. I've had enough for now. Open another bottle for yourself, Joe." Father O'Healey watched Cullen thoughtfully while the pilot drained the Coke in a single long swallow. He was intrigued by the big pilot. He sensed the inner struggles of a man bludgeoned by contradictions, faced with inner antagonisms he could give no expression to. Cullen was a simple man who was complex beyond belief, which was not a new thing for the priest. He also liked Cullen.

"What you said before . . . ?"

"Forget what I said before. Nothing I say is very important."

"No, sir. What you say is important and you said something about the mystery exploding in your mind."

"Something like that—yes."

"Because I want to understand you. I think it happened to me once," Cullen said.

"Tell me about it."

"It was the first time I ever slept with a woman. It was a girl in high school. I really liked her. I guess I liked her as much as I ever liked a girl. But how could I feel that thing if it was a sin?"

"Perhaps it wasn't a sin."

"Anyway, I don't believe in sin," Cullen said. "When I think of the stuff we did in Nam, I'd have to be a fucken idiot to believe in sin—I'm sorry. I talk and I don't think. God's going to put me down because I miss mass for a month, and then he claps his hands when I blow the head off some twelve-year-old VC with a gun in his hands. I'm sorry, God, those are my orders, and can I still go to heaven? Bullshit, bullshit."

O'Healey nodded. "That's a sorry picture you paint. I get uneasy when I talk about God, because I don't know one damn thing about God and I don't think anyone else does either. But the way I tried to explain it before—I sense something inside of me. I know what you mean, sleeping with that girl."

"How do you know if you can't sleep with a girl?"

O'Healey shrugged. "I can sleep with a woman. I have. I'm celibate, not virginal. I'm not the best priest in the world. Like you, I've seen things so terrible, I can find my solace only in the arms of a woman. I'm not like the priests up north in our country, and I don't fault them, because they must do what they must do and I must do what I must do." He lifted a foot. "I wear these sandals, and some-times I'm barefoot, and I've given away my cassock half a dozen times, and I say that with-out pride and I hope with some humility—and where my parish is, sometimes in one part of the hills and sometimes in another, I can go for days without food, but I must not show hunger."

"But you're going home now, and it's over."

"If they send me back to the States, it's only a short interruption. I'll be back here."

But even then, it occurred to Cullen that the priest would never go home and he'd never come back, because they'd kill him. Almost desperately, he asked the priest, "But why do you do it?"

"Ah, why? There's a question, isn't it?"

"Are you sent here? I can't believe the church would assign you here."

"Yes, an assignment. I came for a while, and then I stayed. You really want to know why?"

Cullen nodded.

"Well, two reasons. Number one: happiness. I believe that God created us to be happy. I was never very happy. We were the poorest of poor Irish, and maybe you know as well as I do how that feels. My father died when I was a kid, my mother worked her hands to the bone, and I went to the seminary because it made her happy. It didn't make me happy, and being a priest didn't make me happy, and I never felt that I was a priest. You know when I became a priest?"

Cullen shook his head.

"Down here—out there in the hills, when I gave absolution to a three-year-old child who died because we didn't have a bottle of penicillin tablets that would cost five dollars in San

Francisco, and I gave this little girl absolution and I turned my face up to God and cursed Him, and that day I became a priest; and this is something I never talked about to any other soul—and I'm laying it on you, Cullen, because behind that dumb Irish face of yours, I see something, or maybe only when you smile. I'm here because I found happiness here, and I'm here because I found God here."

In college, Cullen had taken a course in astronomy. It was what was called at the time a crap course, which meant you could slide through it without opening a book. It consisted of a series of lectures, two seminars, and no tests. But if it was a throwaway course, it nevertheless turned out to be one of the most interesting parts of his education, and the slides that accompanied the lectures were fascinating.

It was an hour before midnight here in these Honduran hills, and nighttime had tempered the bitter heat of day. Cullen sat on a bench in front of the tent he slept in, an army issue, and stared at the brilliant canopy of stars and remembered his course in astronomy, and brooded over the immeasurable distances that the heavens revealed from here, the earth, the tiny speck of dust on the outer edge of a minor galaxy. He possessed a deep, subconscious love-hate connection with the Catholic church.

Cullen was neither an intellectual nor an uneducated mental boor; somewhere between
the two, he nevertheless lacked the training
that might have led him around the symbols of
the church to some inner truth. When he
looked at the heavens and considered the presumption of a Pope who declared himself the
vicar of Christ and the spokesman for God, he
could not help snorting in anger, and when he
recalled Vietnam, he reinforced his belief that
a god who put up with this demented slaughter deserved to be put in a straitjacket and
locked up forever. If he had been trained or
educated by the Jesuits, he might have reasoned his way out of this hole.

When he gazed at the star-sprinkled sky like
this, he would feel a cold chill take over his
body, the vastness reducing his own ego to in-
significance. He would feel himself shrink and
vanish, himself and all about him meaningless
and hopeless.

Oscar Kovach came out of the tent, joined
him on the bench, and offered him a cigarette.
Cullen lit up and took a deep drag. Kovach
said, "I swiped a bottle of Jack Daniel's out of
the executive shack. You want to have a few
swallows?"

"Not right this minute."

"You been in that shack?" Kovach asked
him.

"I been there."

"They got everything. They got two cases of champagne, and not just champagne but Dom Perignon, would you believe it, and a case of Jack Daniel's and a case of Haig and Haig, the Pinch Bottle, no less, and just about anything else you want to mention, and these monkeys take what they want, the officer shit I mean. They cut the balls off one of those militia mothers if he even set foot inside."

Cullen nodded. "I brought some sardines and oranges to Father O'Healey. They don't seem to mind what I take."

"We're big shit. We come in and out of here on the big birds. They better damn well mind their ABCs with us. You been spending a lot of time with that priest."

"I like him. He's a good guy. You ought to talk to him."

"No way. I hate priests. They scare me."

"You're a Catholic, Kovach, aren't you?"

"That's why they scare the hell out of me. I haven't been to confession in twenty years, and now I don't have the guts to have someone point out the road to hell. Anyway, do you ever think about getting laid? I mean right here. Some of these Indian chicks are gorgeous, specially the fifteen- and sixteen-year-olds, and they are built. Cullen, they are built, and there's a shower on the other side of the supply shed where you can wash them down, and you lay a dollar on them and they do it. You name it and they do it."

"You're an animal, Kovach," Cullen said sourly. "I got a daughter. I haven't seen her since Frannie and I split up, but she's my daughter."

"OK, don't get excited."

"I ain't excited. You'll know it when I get excited." Cullen rose and walked off into the night. He detested Kovach. Ten, fifteen years ago, he would have provoked the other man, and then decked him, but brawling was in his past. He didn't do it anymore; he had no taste for it.

The moon was up, three-quarters full, and it cast a silvery glow on the airstrip, and that and the starlight made it possible to walk at this late hour without stumbling over objects. Cullen found himself at the shed where the priest was kept. The guard was asleep. A sleeping guard, found by one of the officers, would be beaten half to death. Cullen shook him awake.

"Volvi a hacerlo," the guard moaned.

"Look, none of my business. My lips are sealed," Cullen managed in bad Spanish. The guard was no more than seventeen, small and frail. Cullen patted his shoulder and went into the shed. A single candle burned, and Father O'Healey was on his knees in prayer.

Cullen sat down on a packing case and waited. After a few minutes, the priest stretched his arms and climbed to his feet. "I'm not sure," he said, not facing Cullen yet aware of his presence, "that kneeling is the best mode for prayer. I have an old aunt, past eighty, who still fusses with her tiny garden on her knees, and she tells me it's a result of practice with prayer, but the way I feel, in ten years it will be a miracle if I can kneel or get to my feet after. What can I do for you, Joe?"

"Hear my confession."

"Come on, Joe, come on—do you believe in God?"

"No."

"Then I can't hear a confession. What good would it do? I can't give you absolution."

"All I want is confession."

"Joe, Joe, use your head. What in hell does confession mean! You're going to tick off your sins? For what? You don't even know what your sins are."

Cullen shook his head. "That's not so," he said. "You're wrong, Padre. I know what my sins are."

"Easy, easy, Joe." He sat down, facing the pilot. "I am going to tell you about sin—very simply, no fancy clerical thinking, no theological trapping, just the story of one small black woman in our parish in San Francisco. She had five children, and a husband who was a bum and walked out on her. She worked two jobs as a maid, she fed the kids, she raised them as good decent kids. We had them in the parish school. The oldest was sixteen—then down to five years old. Five years old was a little girl; she was the most enchanting little five-year-old I had ever encountered. Her name was Daisy, and I taught her the song about the bicycle built for two. She was so bright! She said to me, 'Father, you will look so comical on a bicycle built for two with your robes flapping, and I am going to braid my hair so it sticks out straight behind me.' Can you imagine a five-year-old saying that? Now, the sixteen-year-old freaked out, as they say, on crack. We don't know how much he had, but it was a hell of a lot, enough to make him completely crazy, and with a kitchen knife he killed his mother and the four siblings. He was a big strong boy, and there was no way they could stop him. He cut the throat of his five-year-old sister. Was this something you were going to confess to me, Joe?"

Staring dumbly at Father O'Healey, Cullen shook his head and whispered, "I didn't know about that case."

"Of course you didn't. You bring enough cocaine in every week to make thousands and thousands of kids crazy. A few years ago, a

Catholic bishop was murdered in El Salvador. He was murdered by a death squad supported with money and guns by our State Department —with the same American guns you now run to the contras. My colleague and blessed friend Father Jesus Consenta was murdered by the contras. It happened in a tiny village where he had gone to baptize some children. The contras took this undefended village and put everyone there to death. They cut off my friend's penis and put it in his mouth. Were you going to confess to that? Shall I tell you about the nuns who were murdered—"

"That's enough!" Cullen shouted.

"Anger. Are you coming alive, Joe Cullen?"

"Fuck you!" Cullen shouted, and then stormed out of the shed, and then once outside came to a halt and stood rigid, his back to the shed.

"*Qué pasa? Qué pasa?*" the guard said.

Cullen silenced him with a look, and then turned around and went to the entrance of the shed.

"Can I come in?"

"Sure. Come on in, Joe."

"I'm sorry. I never used that kind of language to a priest. I'm sorry, Padre. Please forgive me."

"Nothing to forgive. Come in and sit down, Joe."

Cullen sat down on the same packing case that had been his chair before, nervously clenching his fists. "Padre," he said, "do you want to escape? If you want to escape, I'll manage it."

"No. If I escape, Joe, it'll give them an excuse to hunt me down and kill me. I don't know this country."

"There's one guard sitting out there. I could gag him, and our 727 is ready to lift off. We're gassed up and ready to go—just waiting for the dope. Yeah—they can eat it. It's night and they're either asleep or drunk, and anyway those Honduran officers don't walk around at night. There's nothing to stop me flying you out."

"And what happens to you, Joe? You think you'd live to talk about it if you stole their plane?"

"I can take care of myself."

"No, I'll let them send me back to the States. I haven't been back in three years. A few things I must do, and then I'll return here. As a matter of fact, I hear arrangements have been made to fly me down to the main contra base tomorrow."

"I know. I'm taking the chopper down there."

"Can you fly a helicopter?"

Cullen laughed. O'Healey loved Cullen's

smile, Cullen's laughter. It was unpremeditated and appeared like the ghost of another man, an unworried man, a man who lived in humor and delight. "Can a duck swim?" Cullen asked. "I am the best, Padre. It's the only thing in the world I can do better than most."

"That's reassuring, Joe. Do you know, I'm looking forward to it. I have never flown in a helicopter. It must be very exciting. Joe, do you like to fly?"

Cullen nodded—as always, at a loss for words when a question was posed that he had never considered. In all truth, no one had ever asked him this question, not as O'Healey asked it, not lightly or offhandedly, but as part of a search that the priest was conducting. Cullen had a sense of this and it placed an obligation upon him. "It's not that I like to fly—I have to. It's like getting drunk," he said slowly, searching for terms to describe what he felt, "but better. Because I don't slow down, no loss of function. I'm airborne. I'm at peace. I don't want anything, because I have everything."

"Everything?" the priest asked curiously. "What is everything?"

Cullen shook his head.

"You used the word," Father O'Healey insisted. "Look into yourself."

"I can't look into myself. Goddamnit, what are you doing to me!"

In the dim candlelight, Father O'Healey saw the tears running down Cullen's cheeks, and then Cullen slid off the packing box on his knees facing the priest, his head pressed into the edge of the priest's robe, his body racked with sobs. O'Healey put his hands on Cullen's head, and said softly, "Who saves a human life saves the whole world."

Cullen awakened with the dawn, and he felt wonderful. He felt absolutely wonderful. Nothing bothered him, not the mosquito netting that shrouded him, not the stickiness of the morning, not the heat, not even the presence of Oscar Kovach in the tiny canteen, where Cullen had a breakfast of coffee, fried eggs, and fried beans.

"It's nice to see you with a grin on that ugly face of yours," Kovach said. "What did that priest do for you—set you up in heaven?"

"Don't be a horse's ass."

"Good. That's the old Cullen. I'm glad he didn't reform you."

"I told him I'd have to ask Kovach. After all, I haven't enough brains to piss without permission from Kovach."

"You're a joy to be around," Kovach said. "I hear you're taking the priest out of here on the chopper. We're loading at noon and I want to take off by one o'clock. So don't decide you want to get laid down there."

"I'll be back. Don't worry. On the other hand, you can drop dead. Surprise me."

"Very funny."

"We're both funny, Kovach. You and me, we're a couple of clowns."

Still, this did not disturb Cullen's pleasure in the morning. He hadn't touched the controls of a helicopter in years, but a copter was a copter, and he had no doubts on that score. As he broke away, Kovach quickened his pace to stay with him, and said, "Come on, Cullen, so I kid a little."

"OK with me."

"No hard feelings?"

"Not here. I'm used to your shit," Cullen said.

"You see—you see, I try to be decent and where does it get me? What is it with you, Cullen? You were broke, and I gave you a job. Doesn't that count for something?"

Kovach was small and wiry. He had a habit of hunching his shoulders and sniffing. He had taken up with a girl in Vietnam and fathered a child and bugged out on both of them. That was not what Cullen held against him, but Cullen used it as excuse to himself for detesting the man. Yet the truth was the truth. He was aware of what he owed Kovach—which made him even more touchy. Now he gave Kovach a friendly pulled punch on the arm, and said, "It counts."

Kovach did not respond and Cullen said, "It counts. Of course it does. Nobody has to tell me what it feels like to be broke and out of a job."

"Thanks," Kovach said. "Tell you something else, Cullen—I don't leave without you. Without you come back safe and sound, that plane sits on the ground."

Cullen nodded. Kovach wanted desperately to be liked. He envied Cullen's superior height and strength. The girls always turned to Cullen. It didn't matter where they were or what nation or color or nationality the girls were. When they saw Cullen's smile, they responded with delight.

"You know," Kovach said, "we're just two of us down here with the spics. We got to stick together, Cullen."

"You got something there. You carry a piece, don't you, Oscar?"

Kovach regarded him suspiciously. "You're not going to do something crazy?"

"What, for instance?"

"Maybe I should take the priest down?"

"You want to play with a Sikorsky? You're no chopper pilot."

"Come on."

"OK, you can fly. You ever been in a Sikor-sky?"

"All right. I got a thirty-eight revolver. I keep it under the seat. You can't walk around in shorts and a shirt in this heat and hide a gun."

"You wear shorts. I don't."

"What the hell difference does that make?"

"Look, Oscar," Cullen said patiently, "if I want to hide a weapon, I strap it on my leg. Only an asshole hides a gun anywhere else. Now calm down. Nothing's going to happen, but I don't want to be sealed in a damn chopper alone in a situation."

"What situation?"

"I don't know. You been around these clowns long enough to know that anything can happen."

"You want me to come with you?" Kovach asked.

"Shit, no! We're in a strange place under very strange circumstances and I ask to borrow your piece and you make a federal case out of it."

"OK, OK. Don't bite my head off. Walk over to the plane with me. I got a thigh strap that can probably hook it on to your calf."

They climbed into the big jet, Cullen feeling that hell couldn't be much hotter, and Kovach pulled the gun out of its hiding place. Cullen checked it. The cylinder was loaded.

"You want some extras?" Kovach asked him.

"What am I going to, a war? No—thank you, Oscar. Do you know who's coming with me?"

"Sanchez, I think."

"That loathsome bum?"

"Show respect, Joe. He's a West Point graduate—which is more than you and me ever came up with."

"You mean West Point educates these lousy fuckers?"

"That's what I hear. I only know what I hear."

"Let's get out of here before I die," Cullen said.

Back on the ground, they were both pouring sweat. The gun on Cullen's calf was a hot, uncomfortable nuisance. His whole leg began to itch. "Tell me something," he said to Kovach. "Do you think they're going to kill O'Healey?"

"Why should they kill him? They're Catholic."

"Oh, Christ, Oscar, dry your nose. They're as much Catholic as Billy Graham. Do you know how many priests they've wasted down here?"

"How do you know?"

"Because I talk to the padre, and he knows. And not only priests but nuns—American nuns—and a bishop. Now that's no small shit, a bishop."

"Yeah, I heard about that. Well, it's their turf. Let the mothers tear it up."

They were at the shed now, and Father O'Healey was standing at the entrance, next to the guard. Kovach took off, calling back to Cullen to take it easy.

"Your friend doesn't like priests," O'Healey said, putting out a hand to welcome Cullen.

"He's not much of a friend."

"I'll be in San Francisco for at least a few weeks. My mother's still alive, bless her soul, so I'll be with her—Mrs. William O'Healey. You'll find her in the telephone book if you ever get out there."

"That's not impossible," Cullen said. "This is my last trip down here, and then I'm through with those mother————. Forgive me—it's the language I speak in the places I go. God knows, they tried to make me literate, but I forget. An officer and a gentleman was not my style."

"Perhaps it was. Are you going to throw up this job, Cullen?"

"Yes."

"When did you decide that?"

"Last night, Padre. About four in the morning."

"A good time for grave decisions. May I thank you, Joe Cullen?"

"For what?"

"For helping me."

"If you want it that way. I can't keep asking you what you mean." Standing with the priest in the shade of the shed's overhang, Cullen felt uneasy. He wanted to say something that he could not put into words, something of great importance. He tried to put the words together in his mind and failed, and as he stared dumbly at the priest, his eyes were wet.

The Honduran guard, indifferent to the conversation between two North Americans in a language he did not understand, now stiffened his stance and whispered, *"Señor, el capitán."* Cullen turned and saw Sanchez approaching the shed. The captain was dressed in an impeccable, perfectly fitted olive-drab uniform, trousers that appeared to have been modeled after a New York motorcycle cop's whipcord pants, brown boots polished until they glittered, and a front-tilted visored cap, seemingly styled after the headgear worn by the Nazi general staff. There was no hint of moisture anywhere on the uniform. A Sam Browne belt completed the costume, along with the pistol that hung from it in a polished leather holster and a set of leg irons dangling from the captain's hand.

"The bastard doesn't even sweat," Cullen whispered.

"Just watch him, Joe, and watch yourself. He's a snake."

119

"Lieutenant Cullen," the snake acknowledged as he joined them. "Father O'Healey." His English was almost without an accent. "If you'll just snap on these leg irons, Father, we're ready to go."

"What in hell does he need leg irons for?" Cullen demanded.

"We follow regulations," Sanchez said.

"Where's he going? We're in a chopper."

"Our regulations state," Sanchez said, irritation beginning to show, "that when a prisoner is being moved from one location to another, he must wear leg irons. I will thank you not to interfere, Lieutenant."

"Let it go," Father O'Healey said. "I don't mind the irons, Joe."

The guard helped O'Healey put on the irons, and as they started slowly toward where the helicopter was parked, the priest said, "And Eugene Aram walked between with gyves upon his wrist."

"What?"

"I don't know. You came up with the word 'gyves.' A line of poetry, and I can't even remember who wrote it. I love poetry, Joe, and my mind is a jumble of lines and quatrains and sonnets and couplets, all of it like clothes packed at random."

"Where's your luggage?"

The priest broke into laughter and said,

pointing to his sandals, "These and my robe and my beads are my worldly goods. I shaved with your razor day before yesterday, if you remember, and as for my toothbrush—gone when they took me. I'm not pretending toward Saint Francis; it simply happened that way."

"I wouldn't buy it so easily," Sanchez said. "He came here uninvited and joined the rebels, those murderous *Indios* of ours, and it's all very well for him to talk about poetry when the truth is that he supports godless Marxists and even takes up arms with them against us."

"Not arms, sir," the priest responded in Spanish. "Not arms. And the *campesinos* don't even know that Marx exists."

Unruffled, Sanchez shrugged, and no one spoke until they were at the helicopter.

Then Cullen stiffened, held back, beads of sweat on his brow. Wrong, wrong; he remembered the feeling. "I want Kovach along. I want a navigator."

"One hundred miles." Sanchez shrugged.

"I'm a lousy navigator," Cullen lied. "Kovach is good. I want him with us."

"No need for a navigator." Sanchez was smiling. "Only one hundred and eighty kilometers. I'll watch the ground."

"Joe, let's get on with it," Father O'Healey said. "Let's get out of here."

The guard led the priest onto the helicopter.

Sanchez followed. As Father O'Healey turned to glance at Cullen, the pilot made a circle of thumb and forefinger. Cullen strapped himself into the pilot's seat, told the others to buckle up, and then sat motionless for a minute or so, familiarizing himself with the controls. He loved the feel of a chopper; there was nothing in the world like it, nothing like the tip forward and then the soaring climb, as a bird climbs—so absolutely different from the roaring climb of a fixed-wing plane. He took off. Over the airstrip and away—and then he heard the sounds of movement behind him.

"Buckle up!" he shouted, and then swung around to see Father O'Healey struggling with Sanchez and the guard, Sanchez bursting into a stream of profanity. Then, very quickly, in no more than five or six seconds, the drama was over. Sanchez drew his pistol and fired. The shot was directed at O'Healey, who was struggling with the guard in the open doorway of the helicopter. Cullen tipped the chopper, and as Sanchez fired, the guard was between him and O'Healey. As the guard spun back from the shot, Sanchez kicked the priest. The guard fell headlong through the door, knocking the priest off balance, and another kick from Sanchez flung O'Healey out of the helicopter, the priest screaming in horror as he fell.

Cullen tore at his seat belt. Sanchez shouted at him, "Fly the plane, you bastard!"

The priest's scream faded, and Cullen, realizing that it was too late for him to be of any use to Father O'Healey, flew the plane instinctively while his mind raced like a stone rattled aimlessly in a tin can. A man he had come to love and cherish, the only man he had come to love and cherish in all of his adult life, had been murdered in front of his eyes, and he had not prevented it or done anything to prevent it —or could he have prevented it, the awful hell and horror of falling from a plane, a hell and horror that threaded the minds of all war pilots? As if he were drained of blood, the blood replaced with ice water, he felt his whole body go cold with horror at the thought of this cheerful, wise, pink-faced man falling eight hundred feet to the most horrible of deaths.

"Just stay in your seat and fly the plane," Sanchez yelled, "or I'll put a bullet in your head."

Time passed, seconds, minutes, and then Cullen turned around, a devilish grin replacing his lovely smile; and as he turned, he drew Kovach's revolver from his leg holster. Sanchez was standing by the open door, one hand clutching a rail, the other holding his made-in-the-U.S.A., army-issue, forty-five-caliber automatic pistol.

"And who will fly the plane then?" Cullen asked, his voice breaking as he spoke. Then he turned the helicopter abruptly, and as Sanchez fought for his footing, Cullen shot him, squeezing off shot after shot, as carefully as if he were on a shooting range, until the gun was empty. He swung the plane wildly, rocking it like a carnival fun ride, until Sanchez's body slid through the open door. Then, weeping, Cullen flew back to the base.

It was a strange land where the hot sun created a stillness, a slowing of action that made Cullen feel he was rushing through a turgid river of air where nothing but he was in motion. He found Kovach in his tent, sprawled on his cot and puffing happily on an exceedingly long Nicaraguan panatela.

"Hey, man," Kovach said. "You just left."

"Are we loaded?"

"What happened?"

"Sanchez killed O'Healey. Threw him out of the plane. Then I shot Sanchez and dumped him and brought the chopper back."

"Are you crazy?"

"Maybe," Cullen said, "but if we don't get into our plane and out of here before they discover that Sanchez didn't come back with me, we are finished. Cooked geese. Shit. So move your ass, buddy, or I take off without you."

And Cullen turned and started to walk toward the runway where the 727 was parked.

Kovach joined him. "We'll never get away with it. Never. You crazy bastard—why'd you have to shoot Sanchez?"

"You're walking too fast," Cullen said. "Nobody walks fast at this time of day. They'll notice and start looking for Sanchez."

"They're probably looking for him right now." Kovach moaned.

"Who? He's the boss. He looks for people; they don't look for him. They try to avoid him. Slow—" Two guardsmen walked by, carrying a roll of bedding and netting. They grinned at the two Americans, and in Spanish, "Find a girl—we got the bed."

In front of the plane, a guard was usually stationed, except that at this moment he was in the shade of a wing, talking to a pretty neighborhood girl. Cullen and Kovach climbed into the plane, and with the first roar of the motors, the guard and his girl tumbled out of the way. As the big plane rolled down the runway, Kovach asked Cullen, "What do we do when we get to Texas?"

Cullen didn't answer until they were airborne, and then he said, "Texas—fuck Texas!"

"What does that mean?"

"I'm through. When we land in Texas, I'm

collecting my pay and then taking off, and I don't stop driving until I reach New York."

"And where does that leave me?"

"You go your way—I go mine. Dump on me, Kovach. I did it. Tell them I moved you at the point of a gun."

"What about the gun?"

Cullen handed it to him. "Throw it out."

"Why?"

"Because that gun killed Sanchez. It's evidence." They were gaining altitude now, and already Cullen could see the ocean in the distance. "Drop it in the water, and then we're out of it clean."

"You got to be crazy. When they discover Sanchez missing, first thing will be to call Texas."

"Look, Oscar," Cullen said gently, "the only wheel in the place was Sanchez. The others went to Tegucigalpa. The chopper's back. Who's going to worry about Sanchez? The guards hate his guts and are scared shitless of him. So nobody's going to call Texas, even if they know how to get through to Texas, which I don't think they do. I think all the connections are made in Tegucigalpa, maybe in the embassy there for all I know. So just work easy."

Cullen was correct in his predictions. Three and a half hours later, they touched down at

Salsaville, and before dark, Cullen had collected his money and was in his car, bound for New York City. In the hours between Texas and New York, he tried to work out the question of his own responsibility in the death of Father O'Healey.

He came to the decision that he himself was responsible for Father O'Healey's death.

The District
Attorney

B EING INTERVIEWED ONCE, and asked about things that annoyed him, Harold Timberman mentioned that under the pervasive influence of TV and films, millions of people believed that places like New York and Chicago were represented by a single person as district attorney. Timberman, district attorney for Manhattan, had a staff of over three hundred assistant district attorneys working under him. He felt that figure should be known so that the enormous reach of crime in the cities would not be glossed over.

Timberman took crime and punishment very seriously. He had the reputation of being incorruptible—some of it due to the fact that he came from an enormously wealthy family who for the past hundred and fifty years had dedicated themselves to public service. They were an old German-Jewish family who had changed their name from Timmerman to Timberman—for reasons lost to the present generation.

Timberman himself was slender, gray-haired, and most elegant in his attire. He had a long narrow head that was usually set erect and aware, a thoughtful face, and dark eyes behind gold-rimmed glasses. He was a serious man of small humor, who thought seriously, moved seriously, and considered matters seriously. He had an astonishing knowledge of the criminal justice system in New York, and he could recall that he had met Lieutenant Mel Freedman somewhere and that Freedman was head of detectives in a small and unimportant precinct on the Lower West Side. Thus, when a TV tape came to him by messenger marked PERSONAL AND IMPORTANT, with Freedman's name on it, he decided to honor the policeman's request and view it himself. He had no free time on the day he received the tape, and he took it home with him to view on his own VCR.

His wife, Sally, had planned a small dinner party, and Timberman convinced her that he could be excused by ten to look at the tape. "They're not late people," he said to her.

"At our age, not many are."

That surprised him. He was sixty, his wife ten years his junior. She rarely mentioned age. He was somewhat distracted when she asked him what was on the tape.

"I really don't know. I would have shunted it off on one of my bureau chiefs, but I remember Freedman. He got Carlione to become our witness, and he busted the whole Zambino family. He said personal."

He rather regretted that later. One of the guests at the dinner table was Professor Ralph Cibrini of the Massachusetts Institute of Technology, professor of economics and one of the nation's leading authorities on the drug crisis. He was a small, cheerful man, with a halo of white hair and piercing blue eyes. After dinner, with the coffee and brandy, the conversation focused on Professor Cibrini. Another guest, the editor of a very successful magazine, was condemning Cibrini's use of economic determinism. "It always reminds me of the hopeless rigidity of Marxism," the editor said. "Life doesn't function that way."

"It troubles your illusions," Cibrini said. "You want a world of pure free will. No way. And to think that you can fight this drug disease with guns and the U.S. Army on our borders is one very dangerous illusion. It happens that life does function that way. The moving force in our society is money, and it just happens, quite naturally, that the people with the most money set up a variety of institutions for the single purpose of convincing millions of citizens that money is not the moving force. Yet it is, believe me. So long as drugs are the source of vast wealth for the importers and the dealers, the drug trade will only grow. That's an irresistible force. In Asia and South America, whole communities exist on the production of drugs, and it's been that way for hundreds of years. It cannot be changed."

"Then what can be changed?" Sally Timberman asked.

"The law and the approach. Legalize the drugs and then wage an enormous campaign against the use of drugs. It's like working with tobacco, which has an agricultural and regional base of production here. Drugs don't have that, so it's a better shot."

"It couldn't be worse," Timberman agreed.

Nevertheless, at ten o'clock, the guests still involved in a fascinating discussion, Timberman excused himself and went into his study to play the tape that Freedman had sent him. He watched and listened to the tape with unswerving attention, and when the interview was over, he reversed the tape, took it out of the VCR, and then dropped into a chair and sat there, staring at the tape.

His wife came into the study and told him that the guests had departed. "What on earth could have been so important?" she wondered.

"More important than I imagined."

"Do you want to talk about it?"

"I'm not sure that I do," Timberman said slowly.

"Oh? That's new. I've been a sounding board long enough to feel hurt. I hear the president keeps nothing from Nancy."

"I'm not the president."

"I wish you were. I'd sleep better. So I don't get to know what you have on that tape?"

"Not right now. Not because I don't trust you in the matter of confidentiality—"

"Oh, thank you, sir. I love lawyer talk."

"—but because I don't want to listen to any opinion until I've slept on it and brooded over it."

"Your mind to you a kingdom is, which is OK with me. I'm going to bed."

In the morning, he greeted his wife cheerfully and, between sips of his orange juice, said to her, "Suppose you had a notion that the CIA was flooding the country with thousands of pounds of cocaine?"

"Is that on the tape? Are you going to trust your wife with a spot of confidentiality?"

"Answer the question, please, Sally."

"You came off with a *suppose* question. Suppose they are. Nothing surprises me any-more."

"What would you do if you thought this could be happening?"

"If I were you? Or if I were me?"

"If you were me."

"Good. Now we have it straight." She leaned back and closed her eyes for a long moment. Then she attacked her plate of scrambled eggs.

"Well?"

"Yes—yes. You don't really want me to an-swer that question?"

"I certainly do," Timberman said with irrita-tion.

"I don't have your sense of public duty, and I also don't like to squabble with you at break-fast. On the other hand, I have three children and five grandchildren, and I would not like to wake up some morning and find that I'm dead, or that one of the kids is dead."

"You're not serious. That's hogwash, and you know it. The CIA does not go around killing people."

"Oh? Then they run all that dope, and they never have to kill anyone? That is absolutely marvelous."

"Bad movies and bad TV and bad books. Why do you accept that garbage?"

"Because it scares me to death, and anyone

who is not scared to death in this year of 1987 is either a total numskull or sound asleep."

"I am not scared to death."

"You're a lawyer."

"And what does that mean?"

"It means that I won't squabble over breakfast, and if you want to show me that tape, I'd like to see it, and if you don't, then let's forget it."

He did not play it for her, deciding that instead he would come home in the evening with a box of a dozen and a half long-stemmed roses. His chauffeur-driven limo was sitting on Park Avenue in front of the building and thereby in front of the eight-room apartment which he owned. Although he was a fanatically honest man, he was also in the circumstance of being born very rich, a position he tried earnestly to consider and understand. In the morning coolness and unclutteredness of Park Avenue, he made a construct in his mind of his country, the United States, and his city, New York, being torn apart and turned into a jungle through the sale and use of cocaine and heroin. For this, men robbed and murdered to feed a habit, and having fed the habit, then frequently turned to madness and killed wife, mother, child, making a history of murder horrible and inhuman such as the planet had never seen before. None of this changed the broad, clean avenue on which his car traveled downtown, and if the people who lived in the high cliffs of apartments that lined this avenue desired cocaine, they did not have to rob or kill, but bought it at a high price from those who did rob and kill. All of this was stuff he had considered before, indeed many times as the endless procession of the killers and thieves marched in and out of the courts, prosecuted by one or another of the hundreds of assistant district attorneys under his command. He lived at the center of the vortex where life was so cheap that the city morgue lacked room for the bodies and where the rewards to the dealers and importers were so large that they could be counted in the billions.

All of this, and the tape.

Once in his office, he put the tape into the VCR that had become a usual part of the furnishings for such an office, but did not play it at the moment. Instead, he asked two of his bureau chiefs to join him in his office. Virginia Selby—Ginny to those who knew her—tall, skinny, good features under black hair, and long legs, thirty-two years old, was the youngest bureau chief. She had come out of Columbia Law; she was New York poor and streetwise, and Timberman considered her the smartest lawyer, man or woman, in his organization. Morty Cohen, fat, smoking two packs a day in yellow fingers, fifty-one years old, tired and cynical, was almost as smart. He regarded the small plaque on Timberman's desk, which said NO SMOKING, sourly. He had seen it many times before, and it made any meeting in this room an ordeal.

"Sit down," Timberman said to them. "Make yourselves comfortable. If you want to smoke, Morty, one cigarette. It's a gesture of humanity on my part. Please save it until you begin to twitch."

"Thank you, kind sir."

"Duly noted. Now, I am going to run a video of a curious confession that took place up in Chelsea."

"The West Side precinct?" Cohen asked.

"Right. That little hole in the wall where nothing happens."

"Why there?"

"The confessor lives near there. Now suppose you just watch and listen."

Timberman then ran the tape that constituted Cullen's confession. Both of his bureau chiefs watched and listened intently, nor did Cohen light a cigarette until the tape was finished. Then silence prevailed. Timberman watched his two bureau chiefs as the seconds ticked by.

"Cat got your tongues?"

Cohen puffed deeply and gratefully and said, "Well, if they were to delegalize tobacco, as they seem intent on doing, it might come to the same thing. What the hell—I don't know. I don't know anything anymore. If the Pentagon could corner the whole dope market, they wouldn't have to ask for taxes."

"Do you think this Cullen character is telling the truth?" Virginia Selby asked Timberman.

"Do you?"

"I think I do—mostly. I'm Catholic, so I can sort of sense what got into him. O'Healey must have made one hell of an impression on him."

"And saved his soul and turned him around and led the sinner to grace," Cohen said. "Ginny, I'd sure have to be Catholic to believe that. I remember reading about the O'Healey case, and I'm ready to accept the fact that he was killed in Honduras, murdered or otherwise, but as a confession this is worthless. How come if Cullen witnessed this, he got out of Honduras alive? Do you believe that cock-and-bull story he gave the detectives?"

Ginny shook her head. "No, he fiddled with that and I suppose he fudged a lot of his story. But he's not one of those nuts who parade in every time we have a fancy murder. What do you think, sir?" she asked Timberman.

"I want more of what you think."

"I can't see any reason to arrest Cullen," Cohen decided. "Even if it happened the way he tells it, he's not involved. Anyway, there's no proof of the priest's death. We have no body, we have no jurisdiction, we have no complaint —and as for Cullen, well, we're not in the absolution business. Let him find a Catholic church and get it out of his system."

"You know what he can't get out of his system?" Ginny asked.

"What's that?"

"The fact that some part of the government of this country is neck-deep in the business of bringing in cocaine."

Cohen snorted. "What else is new?"

"And what does that mean?"

"Come on, Ginny. Anyone who's looked at a newspaper over the past twenty years knows that the CIA has long fingers. They fight wars and they move drugs. They did it in the Golden Triangle and they did it in Afghanistan, and you don't think they could have set up this neat little war of theirs in Honduras and Nicaragua and put together a parcel of bums like the contras without a payoff in drugs."

Still Timberman listened without offering any comment of his own thinking.

"What goes around," Ginny said seriously, "is one thing. What we saw on that tape is something else. Here's a man who ferried the drugs and witnessed—again, according to the tape—the involvement of men in uniform. I know that's no hard evidence, but put him in front of a congressional committee and you'd have something."

"He has a terminal disease," Cohen said. "He knows too much."

"Come on, Morty, who do you think is moving the drugs?"

"That's it. We don't know whether anyone is moving the drugs you refer to. We don't know one damn thing about this Joe Cullen—not one damn thing. We could run an investigation. There are plenty of ways to go: find this Oscar Kovach, ask around the saloon—I know the place—question Cullen, send someone down to Salsaville, track down this feller who, according to Cullen, runs the operation at Salsaville. It's all there, but we also got a docket bigger than anything we ever had before, and all this *maybe* stuff is none of our business, because we have no crime on our turf and no real reason to try to invent one."

"You don't have to invent a crime, Morty. What we do have on our turf is a man self-confessed to one of the biggest drug operations I ever heard of. And if that doesn't involve us, I'm crazy."

"How? What do we charge Cullen with? If the boss here wants to order an operation big enough to find evidence against Cullen—and

he's just a small cog, even if there's substance
to his story—by what right do we move?
Where's our jurisdiction? You want to go down
to Salsaville and stir up the county law, which
is probably some slow-moving reasonably corrupt sheriff? Damnit, we got our hands full
when we step into the Bronx or Brooklyn."

Virginia Selby sighed and shook her head
and then turned to Timberman.

"Nothing else, Ginny?"

"I'm just disturbed as hell."

"So am I," Timberman said, "but Morty's
right. I guess I'll send the tape down to Washington and let the FBI break their heads over
it."

"And what happens to Cullen?"

Timberman shook his head. He was already
putting together in his mind what he would
and would not tell his wife. Not physically, but
in some ways his wife was not unlike Virginia
Selby. If he kept the contents of the tape from
Sally, she would worry about it and make his
life miserable for at least a week. On the other
hand, if he told her the story, it would result in
the incipience of a new crusade on Sally's part.
Somehow, he had to deal with this.

"Ginny," Cohen said, "men like Cullen don't
grow old. He doesn't have much of a future,
and there's not a damn thing we can do about
it."

Timberman thanked them both, told Ginny that she could go, and asked Cohen to remain a moment. After Ginny had left his office, Timberman asked Cohen whether he saw any alternative.

"You could dump the whole thing. File the tape. We don't have to go out looking for work."

"Would you do that, Morty?"

"No," Cohen admitted. "I'm a coward and I love my kids and I'm used to my wife, so I remain impeccably honest. Aside from that, I'm not a Catholic. I'm Jewish, so I'm a little uneasy about accepting the sinner's return to grace. Anyone who pushed a helicopter in Vietnam has enough killing on his conscience to make this latest caper of small consequence."

"He did his duty," Timberman said. "Don't fault him for that." His sister's son had died in Vietnam. He had problems of his own dealing with the war.

"On the other hand, I don't believe his story of what happened in that helicopter. How in hell did he walk out of there alive and how in hell did he walk out of Texas alive?"

"We'll let the FBI worry about it."

"You really think they'll admit what's happening down there and make the connection public? You know, that's what they'll have to do if they take action against Cullen."

"It's their ball."

"I know you're not a betting man, sir, but I'd give you twenty to one that the Feds put it away and bury it."

Timberman shrugged and indicated that the interview was over.

At dinner that evening, just Timberman and his wife at the table, she said to him, "I've lost interest, just in case you are consumed with curiosity as to why I don't ask you about the tape. I've decided that it opens up something rotten in Washington or at City Hall, and ever since you told me that two very important New York judges were being paid off by Roy Cohn, you clam up whenever you turn over a particularly disgraceful rock."

"You're usually right," the district attorney admitted.

"On the other hand," Sally said, smiling over her small victory, "if you should wish to run the tape and have an intelligent point of view to refer to—well, you might persuade me to watch it."

"Too late."

"What do you mean, too late?"

"I sent it to Washington."

"Without making a copy?" she asked incredulously.

"Well—I did make a copy—"

"Then it's not too late."

"Well—yes and no. *No* means that I intend to have it destroyed tomorrow. I feel I had no right to copy it."

"Well," she said, "well indeed. If you destroy it before you let me see it, I shall never forgive you."

They went on with their dinner in silence for a while, and then Timberman said, "I'll have to think about that, won't I?"

"I would think about it," she agreed.

Virginia Selby

BETWEEN her growing up and her professional experience, Ginny Selby could say that if she hadn't seen all of it, she had certainly touched base with most of it. She was the offspring of an Irish father and a Puerto Rican mother. When she was three, Jack Selby walked out of their tiny apartment on 117th Street, just off Second Avenue, and disappeared. Maria Selby insisted to her dying day that "poor Jack" had been abducted and done away with, but the local cops knew Jack Selby as a bum no one would trouble to do away with, and since he was six feet two inches tall, his body would not be easily disposable. They figured that he simply walked out and took off, and since his brain had been stewed in alcohol for most of his adult life, he could very well have forgotten the way back.

But somewhere in his genes there was intelligence, and Maria Selby, who, if the truth be told, was happy to be rid of him, was no fool. The tall, long-limbed Ginny inherited brains if nothing else. At age nine, she was helping her mother do sweatshop piecework in their tiny apartment; at age seventeen, she graduated from high school and took advantage of open admissions at Hunter College, meanwhile holding down a job waiting tables in an Italian restaurant on Third Avenue in the Eighties. At twenty-one years, she graduated from Hunter summa cum laude and won a scholarship to Columbia Law School; and at graduation she was offered jobs at two fairly prestigious law firms. She had grown into a fine-looking, slender woman, unaware of her own attractiveness, fluent in Spanish, street-smart, and full of a carefully concealed rage at poverty and the people who impose it. She turned down the prestigious law firms for a job at half the pay in the district attorney's army of lawyers, determined to carry on her own war against the thugs and hoodlums who preyed on the poor of Spanish Harlem. She had also decided that it was a good road toward political office, something she had placed in her future. Now, eight years later, she was a bureau chief at

fifty thousand a year, unmarried, discon-
tented, and sick to death of the whole spec-
trum that was called justice. Three months before, she had broken a relationship with a man
whose tenderness and endearing qualities had
washed out under a vicious switch of character; and when he struck her, she struck back,
and then came to believe that he would have
possibly beaten her into unconsciousness or
death had not her purse been within reach and
thereby the gun it contained. "Just leave," she
had said to him, "and don't ever come back. I
don't just carry a gun, I know how to use it."

In light of that, it was all the more astonishing to her that she couldn't get the picture of
Cullen out of her mind. "Is it," she asked herself, "that I'm always attracted to these macho
bastards because I have a character flaw? Is it
my mother's experience? Is there a gene that
says, lady, destroy yourself." She told herself,
concerning Cullen, "He's a bum like all the
rest of them." Then why the attraction? Then
why couldn't she get him out of her mind; why
couldn't she stop thinking about him? Likely
enough, he was a killer. Nobody came out of
Vietnam with clean white hands, and his story
about the priest was just the kind of a senseless story she had heard a hundred times from
perps who were defending themselves and trying to talk their way out.

But his guilt puzzled her. Nothing Morty Cohen had said went to the question of his guilt and his pleading for some kind of absolution, for forgiveness and punishment. "And the son of a bitch is a dope runner," she told herself. "No guilt for that—not even a sense that he had done anything wrong." This was a particular kind of a sociopath, a man whose only remorse could be awakened by the murder of a Catholic priest.

"You're not being fair to him," she admitted to herself, and then asked herself angrily why in hell she should be fair to him. Whereupon she reached across the desk for her telephone directory. It frequently occurred to her, during the lean nights when she hopelessly resigned herself to the glass tit on which all her countrymen and women sucked, that if the characters engaged in the mindless dramas of violence that television lived by would either call the cops or look in the telephone directory, their problems might be solved immediately. At that point, however, nothing would be left to separate the commercials.

"Why think?" she wondered. "Few do, and the world goes along." As it would now, and she brushed aside her reasonably intelligent brain and opened the Manhattan white pages. Under C—and not as many Cullens as she would have expected, no more than sixty of them. Probably all originated in the same bleak and hungry Irish village. Names fascinated Ginny. She had always believed that Selby was an Irish name, and then she ran into someone with the same name who said his people came from Holland, and then someone else who was a Selby and was Jewish.

And now, here it was, Joseph Cullen, West Eighteenth Street, 555-8721. She said to herself, "I have to know why I am doing this. I will not do it until I know why I am doing it."

"Very well," she replied to herself, "I will tell you, Ginny Selby, why I am doing this. I am not only bored shitless but I want desperately to be with a man and I'm going to meet him and find out what that damn confession means." And she dialed the number.

The voice on the tape answered the phone, and even though Ginny had listened to the tape only a short while before, the voice surprised her. This time, of course, she was thinking of the man and, in that sense, listening to the voice differently. His speech was good, well-controlled mid Atlantic, the Rs dulled only slightly in the New York manner.

"Is this Joseph Cullen?" She had an official voice and tone. You don't work years at the DA's office without picking up an official tone.

"That's right. I'm Joe Cullen."

"My name's Virginia Selby, and I'm a bureau chief at the Manhattan district attorney's office. Just a short time ago I finished watching the tape you made at the precinct over on the West Side."

She paused, and Cullen said, "What does that mean? Are you going to arrest me?"

"No. Oh, no." She took a deep breath, and continued, "It only means that I want to talk to you and clear up some points in your statement."

"That's OK. Do you want me to come downtown?"

"No. This isn't that official. It would be simpler for us to have lunch together, and I thought if you're free today . . . ?"

"I'm free."

"Do you know where Denby's is, on Fourteenth Street between Seventh and Eighth?"

"Yeah. I know the place."

"Suppose we meet there—at, say, one o'clock."

"How will I know you?"

"I'll know you. Remember, I've just seen the tape of your statement. And understand, the lunch is at my expense. That's a rule I have to live by."

"I understand," Cullen agreed.

Actually, the rule referred only to her own lunch, and the whole venture was so out of line that she had to fight to restrain herself from calling Cullen back and canceling the whole foolish gesture. Instead, she underwrote her whole position by assuring herself that she was not going to sit by and ignore one of the biggest drug-running operations ever put in motion. That put her on the side of the good guys at her uneasy forthcoming lunch.

Cullen was bigger, broader than the TV screen showed him to be, but Ginny had expected that. A TV screen diminishes things. People are always smaller than life on television. But what Ginny had not expected or anticipated was Cullen's smile. She had marked Cullen as another bum, another Irish bum—as Ginny's mother had always characterized her father's friends—a large, brainless man who went where he was led. She should have known better. A man of Cullen's background doesn't fight his way through college unless he's something better than brainless. His smile shattered all her preconceptions, and she tried not to feel that she would trust a man with such an open, delightful, and innocent smile.

Denby's was one of those nonethnic restaurants that served ordinary, decent food: roast chicken, roast beef, pot roast, meat loaf, lamb chops, mashed potatoes, spinach, string beans, and one brown gravy for all occasions. Bacon and eggs and omelets were presented almost apologetically, and all the vegetables were overcooked. But lunch could be had for seven or eight dollars, and there were clean table-cloths and good bread. They knew Ginny because it was close to her apartment on Eleventh Street, and they gave her a quiet table in the rear.

Cullen moved her chair when she sat down. He would have done it anyway, but he had a thing for tall, dark women, and he had a sense, as Ginny had, of another street-smart person. She asked Cullen whether he wanted a drink, and he shook his head. She mentioned that she didn't drink on duty and she was still on duty. She ordered poached eggs, and Cullen had a roast beef sandwich. Then Cullen asked her what a bureau chief was.

"Timberman runs a big operation," she said, "over three hundred district attorneys. We're divided into bureaus, and a bureau has a bureau chief."

"Makes you a cop?"

"No, just an assistant DA. Look, let me tell you right off, Cullen, that you can walk out of here if you want to. I'm only sticking my nose into this because I watched the tape the cops on the West Side made of your confession. You know that you're not being arrested or accused of any crime."

"I know that. I don't know why."

"There are reasons. For one thing, no body,

no witness, no way to know whether you're telling the truth. For another, this is sticky as hell, and when something gets this sticky, people don't want to mess with it."

"You're messing with it."

"That's true." She pointed to his sandwich, which had just arrived. "Eat."

He grinned at her.

"Nothing's funny, Cullen. I don't think you know what the hell you're doing. You've turned over the biggest rock I ever heard of, and you don't seem to have enough brains to be frightened. And don't think I'm friendly. You're a dope smuggler, and to me that's shit."

She was fighting his grin. Inside, she was saying, Ginny, you're so fucked up you could write a book about it.

"Why should I be frightened?" Cullen asked.

"What's with you?" she demanded in a fierce whisper. "What in hell is with you?"

"Look, lady," Cullen said, "I don't owe you one goddamn thing. I don't even know why I'm sitting here and talking to you, except that I don't have anything better to do today. I smuggled dope. I helped kill the best man I ever knew. Are you a Catholic, lady?"

"Call me Ginny. Understand? Ginny? Am I a Catholic? I was born one, and I haven't set foot in a church in twenty years, and what's it to you?"

"Nothing, nothing." He devoured his sandwich furiously, and asked, through the bites, "You're not hungry?"

"How much of that confession was true?"

He chewed and swallowed what was in his mouth, and then said, "Most of it."

"This Sanchez character threw the priest out of the helicopter?"

"That's what he did."

"And what did you do?"

"I flew the helicopter back to the strip."

"This priest was the best man you ever knew, and you watched Sanchez kill him and you did nothing to Sanchez?"

"I was piloting the chopper."

"And this Sanchez bum let you walk away?"

Cullen stared at her for a long moment, and then he said, "Lady, what do you want?"

Ginny sighed and shook her head.

"I'm not going to call you Ginny, Miss Selby," Cullen said. "I think you came here to set me up."

"You're wrong!" she exclaimed.

"Maybe. Maybe not. Let me tell you something. When I took this job of bringing guns down to the contras, I figured I was doing something with the government behind me. I didn't know dope was part of it. I'm not very smart, lady. If I was smart, I wouldn't have been in that crazy Nam killing, and it wouldn't have taken me so long to learn the kind of shit runs this country. Now let me put it to you straight and neat. I knew that this contra thing was a scam to make money for someone, but I needed the job and I figured it was legal. I am no goddamn moralist. When I learned they were shipping dope, I didn't fall down surprised to learn that some kind of Feds were involved. What else is new? You want me to smell out a job that's clean? Lady, I'm a pilot. The only damn thing I know is how to fly a plane. But I was involved. Something happened to me when I met Francis O'Healey. Maybe I felt no damn different than you about the church. I couldn't call him Father; I called him Padre. I don't think you know what the hell I'm saying, but listen. You want to separate shit from shit. I can't do that anymore. The Feds paid me to take a gunship and wipe out Vietnam villages. You ever see a baby child chopped into hamburger by fifty-millimeter shells? You want to separate things and tell me that's legal and running dope and guns is a crime? No way, sister. You know what O'Healey gave me? He gave me grace. You remember what the nuns used to talk about in school? So now figure it out. Thanks for the lunch." And with that, Cullen got up and stalked out of the restaurant.

Ginny fumbled in her purse, found the bills

she wanted, dropped them on the table, and then bolted out of the restaurant after Cullen. He was already halfway down the street toward Seventh Avenue, and she had to break into a half run to get close enough to call out to him.

"Cullen! Cullen!"

He turned, saw her, and waited while she walked toward him with long, easy strides. "Why?" she demanded as she came face to face with him. "I was trying to help you."

"Yeah?"

"I was. I didn't set you up. Do I look like that to you? It would have been stupid. Do you really think I'm wired?" She opened her purse to show it to him. Her coat and jacket were open, and now she pulled up her blouse to show there was no wire on her waist.

He grasped her arm. "Come on, let's walk. You don't want to stand here on the street undressing."

"Walk downtown. I have to get back to my office."

"OK." They turned down Seventh Avenue.

They walked a block in grim silence, and then Ginny said, "Cullen, did you ever do something and find you couldn't explain to anyone why you did it, and perhaps not even to yourself?"

He thought about it for a while, and then he

nodded. "Yeah, I went into a cop station and confessed that I had killed a priest and that I ran drugs."

"You couldn't explain that to me—why you made that tape?"

"No. Except—"

He swallowed the words and walked on. He had a long stride. Ginny had to move to keep up with him.

"Except what?"

He stopped abruptly, turned facing her, and snapped, "What the hell are you after? Who are you? What do you want of me?"

"You can't explain and I can't explain," Ginny said miserably.

"OK. Let's leave it that way." He swung around and crossed Seventh Avenue, leaving Ginny standing on the corner, thinking to himself that there was no reason why he should tell her anything, and it would have made no sense whatsoever to try to explain that before he spilled out his guts onto a piece of electronic tape, he was dead, and that now he was alive. That was feeling and consciousness and there was no way in the world that he could put it into words; except of course to come up with *grace*. He had said *grace* because it was the only word of mystery that he possessed.

Ginny spent the remainder of her lunch hour walking downtown to her office. A nasty

November rain began to fall, less rain than a cold mist, and Ginny wrapped her thin coat tightly around her and endured the discomfort as a fitting punishment for her foolishness. Like so many Catholics who have left the church, she functioned within her own set of sins, guilt, and punishment.

Later that afternoon, shortly before five o'clock, she was summoned into Timberman's office. Cohen was already there, fingering a package of cigarettes, lacking the courage to light one. Without preamble, the district attorney said to them, "I've heard from Washington, and they've put a top-secret lock on that tape we saw this morning. You are not to discuss it with anyone, and I want no leaks, because if it does leak, I'll know where it came from."

"That's hardly fair," Ginny protested. "How about the West Side cops?"

"I spoke to Freedman up there, and I told him that if he didn't put a lock on it, I and others would be very displeased. I think he'll listen."

Cohen said, "I'm sorry, sir, but I think I speak for both of us when I state my belief. You can't lock that story, no way. It's going to leak, and when it does, I think you should accept the fact that Ginny and I are not involved."

Timberman thought about it for a moment, and then nodded. "Fair enough."

It was a gesture of dismissal, but at the door, Cohen paused and asked, "Was there anything else in the way of explanation? Forgive me for being curious."

"You're forgiven," Timberman said shortly.

Outside in the corridor, Ginny said, "Thank you for covering my ass."

"What do you think of all this?"

"It's business as usual, and sometimes the shit hits the fan. This is the most corrupt administration in the history of these United States. Half of the damn Executive is either indicted or on trial, and if there were any way to put some muscle behind it, the whole damn White House would be in jail. I don't mind that they steal and turn the Pentagon into a money machine. That's old hat and we're used to it—but to go into the dope business and compete with the Mafia, that's new."

"Nothing's new," Cohen said. "During Prohibition, they were in the pockets of the mob for all they could get. Indignation, Ginny, is self-imposed neurosis, and I got enough neuroses floating around not to want any more. Be thankful that we're running an honest operation here in Manhattan, which is a miracle in itself. There was a time when there was a payoff price on every crime that existed—including murder."

Back in her office, Ginny opened the *World Almanac* and read, "Nicaraguan and Honduran forces clashed near their common border, and, for the second time in 1986, U.S. helicopters transported Honduran soldiers to the vicinity of the fighting. On Dec. 4, Nicaraguan soldiers overran a Honduran border post in pursuit of Nicaraguan contras who opposed the leftist Sandinista regime in Nicaragua and who had established a base inside Honduras . . ." She read on until darkness fell, and then came to herself with a start. Time to go home. Time to end another day, having accomplished nothing more than she had accomplished the day before.

"I am bored, I am tired, I am sick of this wretched job, which consists of indicting drug dealers and pushers and importers and wholesalers and finding them back on the street or replaced by two where there had been one, and everybody talks and nobody really gives a damn or does anything intelligent about it, and I take my pay and I am lonely and sick of the whole damn thing," and having said all this to herself, she felt better, put on her coat, slung her bag over her shoulder, and left her office and walked down the long, dismal hallway that led to the wet streets.

And on the way, she asked herself, "Would I? Would I leak this lovely story? I was admonished, but I didn't give my word, and Morty, bless his heart, has covered my ass. So, would I?"

She mulled it over and over in her mind and came, finally, to the conclusion that she would. When the proper time arrived.

The Meeting

THEY NEVER TOOK the big plane to Washington. They had a corporate jet that they flew to El Paso, and from El Paso, they took a regular airline flight to Washington. General Swedenham and Colonel Yancy sat together, and Swedenham gave Yancy a whispered lecture on *looseness of operation.* "It's the way the whole goddamn military is," Swedenham said. "They never work anything out. They always go off half cocked—and they are nothing for us to imitate. Now look at the way they carried out that stupid operation in Iran, going in there with a rabble of fucken helicopters, with no support and no cooperation." Swedenham was a man gone to fat, with a hoarse whiskey voice.

"Yes, sir," Yancy whispered.

"Yes, sir, yes, sir—don't give me any more fucken yes, sir, because I'm not asking for agreement but for a little common sense. On what basis did you hire this man Cullen?"

"His record checked out. He's an old pro, and Kovach went down the line for him with no holds barred. Kovach says—"

"Look," the general said, his whiskey whisper like a knife in Yancy's side, "you pay off. Not Kovach, not anyone else. What in hell do you think we're into? Do you think we're playing games? What are you putting away, Yancy, a million dollars a month? Is that play money?"

"Well, Senator—"

"Stop!" the general said. "You stupid bastard. Never, never mention that name in public. Never. Not that name, not the name of the undersecretary."

"Well, sir—"

"Oh, shit, don't argue with me, Yancy. If we blow this, that forsaken Congress of ours will burn the flesh off our bones. You don't understand one goddamn thing about this country. You can have everyone from the president down running a scam with you, and if the bubble bursts, you are alone."

"Not alone," Yancy thought, "because if this bubble bursts, let me tell you, my fat friend,

Colonel Yancy will cover his hide." But he bent his head in agreement, reminding the general of the dog in a dog fight who accepts defeat by rolling over on his back with all four paws wagging in the air. He had never been fond of Yancy; he mistrusted men who were strikingly handsome, and Yancy was very handsome indeed. People said of Yancy that he looked like a film star, and he irritated the very devil out of Swedenham by wearing every ribbon he possessed, including his Good Conduct ribbon, every time he put on his uniform. Swedenham himself was retired, and he had the feeling that Yancy paraded his army active-duty status at every opportunity. Swedenham considered it senseless and provocative, and he discouraged it, knowing, however, that he could not forbid Yancy to be in uniform. Yancy's superior officers had only the foggiest notion of what his special duty consisted of, and certainly they were unaware that he was involved in the process of turning himself and others into multimillionaires by selling guns and taking payment in kind in a white powder that was very marketable. Swedenham himself had happily lived his life without guilt or conscience, and while he had never thought of himself as a sociopath, he had in his time given himself many a pat on the back for his ability to make hard decisions without blinking. In Vietnam, he had been an eager supporter of the body-count publicity and of such things as the use of Agent Orange, and in his practical manner of looking at things, he had always accepted the mercantile dictum "Buy cheap and sell dear."

Yet he had no desire to disaffect Yancy, who was stupid but useful; and now he soothed his feelings by telling him they were facing some hard decisions that would require stiff backbones.

"Into combat!" he said to Yancy, squeezing the colonel's arm.

Monty met them at the Washington airport and led them to a black stretch limousine, and all the way to their destination at the safe house, he said nothing. The general understood that. You don't talk in a car, no matter what, and Yancy was kept quiet by the grim expression on Monty's face. Yancy knew who Monty was and that Monty was short for Dumont, but he also knew enough to ask no questions about him. Monty was elegant, he was handsome, his manners were exquisite, he was blond and tall, and he had the ability to look at Yancy as if Yancy were a tolerable insect. Monty was West Point.

And Dumont Robertson was other things as well. In the three-hundred-acre Berkshire Mountains estate—land that the Robertsons had purchased in 1832—he was the local mirror image of Ted Kennedy, standing firmly against whatever Ted Kennedy stood for and contemptuous of the fact that the Kennedys did not play polo. In the Berkshires, people like Monty practiced snobbery rather than socially packaged inclusion, but in New York, it was quite different. If the Berkshires were a place for the Robertson children to bring swain and mistress and screw and get drunk and sniff white Bolivian powders, New York demanded another set of rules. In New York, Monty was ready to break the ass, as he put it, of any of his four kids who might step out of line, and since they turned up in New York only on school holidays, his command was not challenged.

The point being that Monty was a reigning prince of New York society. Not that Monty was fool enough to believe that there was such a thing as *society* in the classical sense. He had read enough about London and New York society at the turn of the century to know that the word did not quite apply—yet it was related, and the pack of stock manipulators, merger experts, crooked brokers, real estate kings, media stars, and billionaire lawyers who made up the current New York social mix were the only proper constituency he had. His was old money; theirs was mostly new but there was a lot of it, and Monty accepted the situation with grace. There were still Vanderbilts and Astors and Depews enough to decorate the edges, and there was his wife, a six-foot beauty with a shock of yellow hair that was envied as much as her social position. She needed her rank more than Monty did, although his was decently helpful.

This helpfulness was a rather odd thing, for what Monty desired most eagerly was respectability, not the respectability of the middle class, but the respectability of an honored titled gentleman in London, a man whose name being linked with any devious or sub rosa project would elicit snorting disbelief. It was Monty's simple wish to be both good and evil too, although in his mind he dealt not with evil but with necessity; and where the necessity arose, he dealt with it himself. He sent no other to run his errands, and because he buried his own dead in his own way, the creeps and misfits and scoundrels who abounded in government honored him and respected him.

The general had known Monty for years—as had the others. Only Yancy was kept in ignorance, and when he attempted to make his own relationship with Monty, he had been met with a cold wall of resistance.

"I don't like that snotty son of a bitch,"

Monty had once said to the general, "and I don't trust him." But the general assured Monty that, since Yancy's ass was in the same sling, there was no need to worry.

At the safe house, they were ushered into a conference room, where Fred Lester and Reynaldo Perez and another man, distinguished, white-haired, and nameless, were waiting for them. The white-haired man was addressed only as "sir," and that in great deference.

The conference room was tastefully equipped. Instead of the modern furniture that most boardrooms contained, this centered on a large eighteenth-century table with ten comfortable Chippendale chairs. On the floor, an Aubusson rug glowed with age and beauty, and on the walls a flocked wallpaper that was either the real thing or a fine imitation. On one wall, a portrait of Nathan Hale, that revered spy of the American Revolution, and on the facing wall, as a nod to the British cousins, a painting of Major André. In theory, the room was as safe as anything could be in this age of the new technology, but the general always maintained a sneaking suspicion that there was a microphone somewhere. Well, be that as it may, one functioned as best one could, and the reputation of this room was certainly the best.

At the side of the room, a butler's tray held Scotch whisky and bourbon and the various mixers. Ashtrays and a humidor with several sizes and shapes of Cuban cigars. The humidor was passed around. No servant entered or left the room.

They took their seats in silence. Monty chose a Romeo and Juliet, clipped it with a gold cutter, lit it, and then opened the meeting bluntly with "Gentlemen, we have a difficult situation as a result of pure stupidity. I am being blunt because this meeting requires bluntness. Suppose you explain the situation to our friend here," Monty said to the general, indicating the white-haired man.

"On the recommendation of Captain Oscar Kovach, reserve, we hired as his copilot Lieutenant Joseph Cullen, also reserve. We needed a copilot and navigator desperately. Kovach is a poor navigator. Kovach described Cullen as a fine pilot on multi-engined planes and an excellent helicopter pilot as well. He also had a bad record of behavior in Vietnam. If not for his skill, he would have been busted on several occasions, and once it came to the edge of a dishonorable discharge. Air force records revealed a troublemaker and a brawler. He had a bad experience with an upper-class Vietnamese woman in Saigon, and she charged him.

However, there was no criticism whatsoever of his courage and skill as a pilot, and when Kovach brought us his name for consideration, we felt we had found a good man. He was being well paid and was promised a bonus of one hundred thousand dollars at year's end. He also knew that he was covered and that his own risk was minimal."

"That's a justification," Monty said, "not an explanation. But there's no point in blame. The plain fact of the matter is that the situation exists." He turned to Perez. "Your opinion, Colonel?"

Colonel Perez resembled a bookkeeper more than a fighting man. Plump, pink-skinned, wearing gold pince-nez, his thin hair the color of corn silk, his trim gray worsted suit eminently proper, his white shirt and maroon striped tie totally conservative, he could have passed anywhere as an unimportant cog in some large corporation. He had just the slightest Spanish accent, and his tone was crisp and businesslike. "The operation must continue," he said flatly.

"Ah, well," Monty said, "I think we must have some agreement on that. General?"

"Certainly."

"Colonel?" to Yancy.

"I agree—if it can."

"And Mr. Lester?"

Lester was a large, large-bellied, easy-man-nered, easy-speaking Texan. He wore boots hand-made for him in Mexico, and outside on the coat rack he had left a very expensive Stet-son hat—in fact, four hundred and twelve dol-lars worth of hat. He enjoyed expensive things. His silk shirts cost six hundred dollars plus, his string ties eighty-one dollars, and his Mexi-can boots, embossed with silver, and in spite of the devaluation of the peso, fourteen hun-dred dollars a pair. He wore a diamond pinky ring of thirty carats, perfect and unsullied, and he never apologized for his love of the expen-sive. He was married to a gorgeous twenty-three-year-old blonde who, as he put it, cost him forty million dollars, settled on her with the marriage contract.

His opinion was to the point. "Son, it's a damn sight better than the oil business. In fact, today the oil business stinks."

The white-haired man said to Swedenham, "General, you engaged in an indiscretion. A man's military record is neither a reliable nor even an approximate picture of what he was or might be in civilian life. Did you trouble to find out whether he had a police record? Whether he was religious? What his religion was? Whether he was a man of guilts, compas-sion, whether he was innocent of the rape charge or what went on there? What his education was? What other pilots thought of him?"

The general shook his head. "No, sir."

"Very well. Water over the dam. Monty, tell us what we face. Put it all on the table."

"Yes, sir. This is in terms of all Cullen's contacts to date. Fortunately, we are dealing with a tight-lipped man. His first contacts were made in Sullivan's saloon on Ninth Avenue. We know that he let no one into his confidence there, and while he left with a prostitute whose name is Sylvia Mendoza, according to her own statement he never mentioned the priest until they were in her apartment. Of course, she'll not mention it to anyone else. At the Church of Saint Peter the Rock, there was a bit of a problem. The church is served by an old priest and a younger curate. We had an operative, female, quite old, go there posing as Cullen's mother. Of course, she understood that the confession was privileged; she only desired to ask the priest's opinion as to the state of her son's health, or some such thing. It was the old man, Immelman. He is dead of a heart attack. He was in fact suffocated, so there is absolutely nothing to indicate other than a natural death. He was a very old man."

The white-haired man interrupted at this point with a question: "Why didn't you take Cullen out at this point?"

"Yes, sir. Very stupid on our part. He disappeared—that is, for a few hours. We had a man on him, but we should have had two. He walked down to the river and out on an old pier, and he sat there for hours. Our man had to piss, and the damn fool went into one of those portable toilets that had been set up for repair work on the pier. When he stepped out, Cullen was gone. He swears that Cullen had no notion that he was being tailed, and I'd guess that was the case. That's how he came to walk into that West Side precinct without our knowledge."

"And when did you pick him up again?"

"Not until the district attorney had the tape. He didn't go home and he didn't turn up at his apartment. He went to his bank and cashed a check for nine hundred dollars, most of it in fifty-dollar bills. We should have thought of the bank, but we didn't. Remember, sir, at this point he hadn't made the tape and we felt that we could control the situation until we had some exchange with you and Mr. Lester. We also wished to get a proper handle on the death of Father O'Healey. That was something I did not learn about until a few days ago."

"Not only stupid but sloppy."

"Yes, sir," Monty agreed. "I admit that, sir."

The white-haired man then said, "It presents

us with an untenable problem and possibly an impossible one."

"Nothing is impossible," Fred Lester said, smiling, the first smile since they had come together in the room. "Son, you got the money and the clout, and nothing is impossible. You got impediments, remove them. That's the way I see it."

"Impediments," the white-haired man said softly.

"Spell it out," Perez said to Monty. "Put it on the table. We will see what we have."

"We have problems," Monty said. "At the precinct where the tape was made, we have five men: Lieutenant Freedman, three detectives—Jones, a black man, Leary, a fat old Irish cop, and Ramos, Hispanic, probably Puerto Rican. Then there's a young uniformed cop, Lefty O'Neal, who ran the tape. Thought is that they've been close as hell about this, but who knows? Five New York cops present a problem. Unique."

"Are any for sale?"

"We don't know yet. We'll know by tomorrow or the next day."

"On the other hand," the white-haired man said, "New York cops take all the shit that's coming down, and nothing surprises them." The word *shit* came oddly, wrongly, from the elegant, soft-voiced man, whose speech, like

181

his dress, was impeccable. "They've passed this along to Timberman, and I understand that Timberman has been told that this is a most delicate federal matter, and that it will be handled as such."

"He has two assistants who also saw the tape."

"Did he tell the cops that this is an absolutely top-secret matter?"

"Well, we must think about this. I would prefer that there be some way of handling that end without violence."

"I don't know." Monty waited a long moment before he continued. "Two of his top people saw the tape, bureau chiefs. Names of Morton Cohen and Virginia Selby. They are old pros and, as I hear it, smart. On the other hand, I am told that no lawyer with drive and ambition remains with the DA's office for more than a few years."

"Which adds up to what?" the general asked.

"Possibly to the fact that we have here two defeated people who have given up on what every good American wants most."

"For sale?"

"Who knows?"

"The DA warned them to keep their mouths shut?"

"As I understand it."

"Which leaves Harold Timberman. Tell me something about him, Monty."

It was a thing of Monty's that he never referred to notes. A lifetime of training had given him a mind like a computer filled with softwear, and it was said that he had burdened his brain with so many facts that there was never room for art or philosophy, although he knew a good many artists and writers through their files in the reference rooms of his organization. He felt that he was properly equipped for his work, and that both guilt and conscience were what Fred Lester referred to as impediments. If he questioned himself, it was to tell himself that, like any other scientist, he dealt with facts.

He spelled out the facts concerning Harold Timberman. "German-Jewish background, fifth generation in America, father and grandfather in public service, plentiful old money out of cotton mills and finance in the 1880s, nominally religious, attends Temple Emanu-El in New York, Park Avenue address, and a reputation for being unreachable."

"Which is the trouble with the goddamn old money," Fred Lester said. "They've lost ambition."

"No man is unreachable," the white-haired man said. "Where is he vulnerable?"

"He has three children, five grandchildren."

"Worth considering. Now, tell me, Monty, is there a duplicate of the tape?"

"Absolutely not. We've checked that every which way. There is no duplicate."

"The tape must be destroyed immediately."

"Agreed." ·

"And Cullen must be taken out immediately."

"Oh, yes. Certainly."

"And Kovach?"

Here, the general intervened with a snort of disagreement. "Hold on! Pilots do not grow on trees."

"No, they don't," Monty agreed. "Kovach should not be eliminated; he should be involved."

"And how do you bring that about?"

"There are ways."

"We'll leave that in Monty's hands," the white-haired man said. "The Feds?"

"I trust you, sir. They have known about the operation for months now, and indeed they were involved, very deeply involved."

"Nevertheless, we will be thorough. I want no documents here. Shred whatever you have —except . . ." He left the thought unspoken, but it was communicated. Any document that provided a connection with a person of power was a source for blackmail, and blackmail, after money, was the most useful weapon. The white-haired man, like Monty, was not given to panic. He was not flustered, and Monty could follow his thoughts without difficulty. Everyone had a past, and in everyone's past was something that would not bear scrutiny.

"Meanwhile," the white-haired man said, "the operation must continue. I do not often invoke patriotism, but the contras must be supported and maintained."

"Yes. Agreed."

There was a chorus of agreement.

"We need a navigator," Monty said. "If he's a good pilot, so much the better, but our plane can't go out with one man in the driver's seat. Actually, we need two men."

"I have a lad working for me who says he's a first-rate navigator. Air force trained, dishonorable discharge, rape and theft. He has some brains and no damn common sense, but he knows that if he fucks me, I'd put him down without a quiver. Mostly his problem is women. If the colonel here"—turning to Perez —"can provide women . . ."

"No problem, Mr. Lester."

Lester chuckled. "For want of a hooker, a war was lost. We can't have that, can we, sir?"

"We need another pilot."

"I can provide that," Colonel Perez said. "The man I have in mind is an army officer and dangerous. When the operation is completed, he must be taken out."

"Agreed," Monty said.

"What in hell do you mean—when the operation is finished?" Lester demanded.

"When the contras have taken over the government."

"Hell, man," Lester said, "that ain't anything we're going to see in the near future, and as for patriotism"—turning to the white-haired man—"you got your ideas and I got mine. I go along with old Cal Coolidge, who said that the business of America is business. I don't see a hell of a lot of difference between drinking yourself into an early grave and making shit out of your life and your family's life, or smoking something that sure as hell's going to give you lung cancer, or sniffing a harmless white powder that puts a piece of joy into the lousy pisspot that life is for most folk. I got almost thirty million dollars in this operation. I bought the protection you give me, and I'm sure as hell not going to fold my tent like an Arab and silently steal away."

The white-haired man smiled and said, "You're quite a character, Mr. Lester. I would not be perturbed, if I were you. I'm sure we look forward to a long and prosperous business relationship."

"Good. Now if there's no loose ends to pick

up, the general and I have a plane to catch at Dulles."

"There are always loose ends," Monty said comfortably. "Trust me to find them."

"Son, I always trusted you," Lester said.

Father
Immelman

LIEUTENANT FREEDMAN's lean figure accentuated his height. He was six feet under curling orange hair and a high-bridged nose that suggested a bird of prey. He had pale blue eyes behind glasses, and often a look of anger when he was not angry at all. He was not an angry man. Frustrated, often annoyed at the shortcomings of the men who worked with him, but not angry, lonely and in love—all of that made a better picture of the man than the simple declaration that he might have been more if he had not become a cop. Born in 1946, son of a semi-invalid soldier and a mother who whined and whimpered her way through a short life that ended with cancer fifteen years after his birth, he had not exactly been overwhelmed with opportunity. He finished high school with high marks, served a stretch as a medic in Vietnam, came home whole, went to City College, fought his way through two years of it washing dishes and waiting tables and doing whatever else might keep body and soul together, and then gave it up to be a cop.

Along the way he met Sheila, and the alternate phases of heaven and hell began. Now he had entered a phase of moderate Eden. She was tolerating him again, and this might last for a day, a week, or a month. It served to make him, who had no real religion aside from being born Jewish, more tolerant of everything Catholic—since Sheila was such, though hardly in good standing—and ready to listen to Father Paul White, a young priest from the Church of Saint Peter the Rock. Under other circumstances, he might well have turned Father White over to Leary, good Catholic that Leary was, and let him deal with whatever had to be dealt with—which in this case was rather far-fetched.

Father White, very young and pink-cheeked, admitted that he did not have very much to go on. "Not much more than a feeling here," touching his chest. "The thing is, Lieutenant, that I was with Father Immelman when we went over to Saint Vincent's for our physicals.

Well, they made such a fuss over the old man. They said that at seventy-three he had the heart and circulatory system of a man half his age. And you know, he didn't do much exercise. Dr. Kelly, who examined him, called in two of his colleagues, Dr. Levy and Dr. Hotsinger. I mean not for consultation, but simply to check the condition of a man who did not exercise and ate everything bad for him—he loved junk food, hamburgers, frankfurters, that sort of thing. And sweets—oh, yes, he loved sweets. And then, two weeks later, he dies of a heart attack. I simply don't understand it. I don't believe it."

Thinking about the little church, only a few blocks away, that had come to their attention once before when the poor box was robbed, Freedman nodded sympathetically and asked whether Immelman had been under some sudden stress.

"No. Oh, no. You know, he was such a gentle person. One of those old-fashioned priests, almost saintly."

"Where did this happen? In his sleep?"

"No. At the altar. He was in prayer, very relaxed."

"And, of course, the doctors agreed?"

"The ambulance took him to Saint Vincent's. I insisted that he be examined there."

193

"Why did you insist?" Freedman asked curiously.

"Because the whole thing disturbed me so. Not simply his death. Of course that was a dreadful shock, but he had lived his years and he was a good man . . . and . . ." He went off into his own thoughts. "I don't truly know how to put it, Lieutenant."

"You mean you have no reason to say he was murdered, and if you do say it, you'll feel like a fool coming here with no more than a gut feeling. But I would guess you have something else. What is it?"

"Well, a few days ago he asked me an odd question. He had heard a confession, and it troubled him. I could see that. In some ways, he was childlike, in the sense of innocence, and the question he asked me was this: Could a person truly know whether or not that person believed in God? Then he put it another way: Was not belief in God an absolute in every person's being? For him, this was an astonishingly radical thought and outside our teaching. You're not Catholic, of course?"

"Jewish," Freedman said.

"Ah, yes. Well, I don't think such a construct exists in Jewish theology either, but coming from Father Immelman, it was absolutely amazing. I probed at it. I should have left it with him, but I was intrigued, and then he told me of the confession he had heard that day. Now you understand, Lieutenant, that the contents of a confession are sacred, so he told me nothing of them; but he did say that the man in the booth desired absolution desperately yet refused to admit a belief in God. This troubled Father Immelman, because he had to deny the man absolution. It occurred to me that if I had heard the confession, I would have reasoned with the man that only a belief in God could have brought him to our church in search of absolution, but Immelman was rather rigid in that respect."

"Tell me," Freedman said, "how do you see this absolution? I mean, I understand the word, but how do you think of this in your religion?"

"We think of no sin that cannot be forgiven. This is in our doctrine of the soul. The priest acts as the vicar, the spokesman of Christ, and it is Christ, as the merciful Son of God, Who grants forgiveness."

"Even of murder?"

"Yes, of course, if the humility and sense of sin are present."

"Then why on earth," Freedman wondered, "would a man who doesn't believe in God confess and desire absolution?"

The priest shrugged. "Thus the question."

"Did Father Immelman say anything about

this man—age, size, appearance, black, white?"

"He could not. It's forbidden."

"Did anyone else see the man? It was a man?"

"Yes, a man. Well, I don't know. Now, there's only myself and Mrs. Dougherty, who is the rectory housekeeper and happened to be in the church."

"Did you ask her?"

"No, it never occurred to me."

"Then let's go over there and ask her. And by the way, did they perform an autopsy on Father Immelman?"

"I asked them to. They found nothing to suggest that he had died of anything but a heart attack."

Downstairs in the precinct house, Ramos was making time with a pretty blond cop by the name of Thelma Grady. Freedman pulled him away and introduced him to Father White, and while they walked the few blocks to the church, he gave Ramos the few facts they had concerning Father Immelman's death.

"How thorough was the autopsy?" Ramos asked. "Did they test for poison? Pinpricks, injections—that sort of thing?"

"Oh, come on," Freedman said. "That's far-fetched crap, and if you set out to kill an old man, there are easier ways to simulate a heart attack."

The street had trees. It was one of those streets where the owners of the old Chelsea brownstones had taken up the city's offer to plant trees, and while it was November, the trees still held a few brown leaves. It moved Freedman to reflect on the intensity with which living things clung to life, even in this strange, throbbing, bursting, and agonizing city. It was a sharp, chilling day, and already a homeless man was stretched out over a grate, but his thinking would have to change, and the man was no longer the bum in the simple manner of his childhood but someone homeless, poverty-stricken, and often enough crazy —schizophrenic, paranoid—or conceivably dying of AIDS; and here he was, Jewish, following a young priest to a church that was mostly an empty shell, because an old priest had died of a heart attack—which the young priest doubted. His thoughts kept returning to Cullen, and possibly it was his listening to Cullen's confession that prevented him from telling White to go home and let the dead rest in peace.

"Easier ways?" Father White asked. Murder shocked and horrified him. He had come out without a coat, and now he drew his thin jacket tighter. Some wise teacher at the seminary had told him that reality was not only more wonderful for one who believed in God, but more terrible. Infinitely more terrible, he might have added.

"A pillow will do it. Hold it over the victim's face until he suffocates. It will pass as a heart attack."

"I don't know," Ramos said. "I mean, Lieutenant, if they were looking for something at the autopsy, they might think about the condition of the heart. Look, Father," he explained to the priest, "even if first-rate doctors at Saint Vincent really loved you and the old man, they wouldn't have done the autopsy. It would be done downstairs in the pathology room."

Freedman shrugged. It made no damn sense whatsoever for someone to engage in a sophisticated hit to take out an old priest, yet once inside the church, he could not help noticing how handy several pillows were. If the priest had been kneeling in prayer, it would have been simple for the killer to pick up a small cushion from a front pew and get the old man from behind.

"I'll find Mrs. Dougherty," the priest said. "Will you wait here?"

The church was empty except for a single old woman who sat silently on one of the rear pews. It was warmer inside than outside. "At least it's a place they can sit and warm up,"

Ramos said. "It begins to fill up as the winter sets in."

Father White returned from the rectory with the housekeeper, a small, gray-haired woman in her late sixties, nervous, full of the feeling of having done something wrong.

"She came here from Belfast, where the troubles are," Father White explained. "She saw too many bad things, and it's hard for her to relax with the police."

"Ah, Mother," Ramos said with a sweetness that surprised Freedman, "I'm Catholic myself, and the lieutenant here is a Jew, so we're as unlike the Belfast cops as night from day."

Poetic, Freedman reflected, and who would have thought it from this hard-assed Puerto Rican? And aloud, he added his reassurances. "Just a few questions, Mrs. Dougherty."

"But the poor old man died of a heart attack."

"Yes, we know that. Yet a few days ago he heard the confession of a strange man, I mean someone who wasn't a regular here." Freedman was uncertain as to whether membership was a practice in a Catholic church.

"Yes?"

"Did you see this man—the man who confessed?"

"There was only one I didn't know. I never saw him before."

"But you saw him when he came to confess?"

"Sure and I did, Officer." Then she added, "It was I that directed him to the confessional. He sat down in the booth, and then I went for the good father, may he rest in peace."

"Good. What did he look like? A tall man?"

"That he was, tall and built strong and Irish."

"How do you know he was Irish? Did he tell you his name or talk about being Irish?"

"Would I need his name to know a lad's Irish? Black Irish, with the blue skin and the dark hair."

Ramos and Freedman exchanged glances.

"Did he smile, Mother?" Ramos asked suddenly.

"No." She shook her head. "He had too much sorrow."

"Well, thank you, Mrs. Dougherty. You've been most helpful."

"I have no wish to hurt him. He did not have the look of a bad man."

Outside, on the steps of the church, Father White said, "You both know something, don't you?"

"Not really."

"You don't want to talk about it?"

"I wish," Freedman said, "that I could ask

Father Immelman who came here and asked him about the confession."

"I know of no one—"

"Of course you don't."

"And my suspicions?"

Freedman shrugged.

"Did someone kill him?" the priest insisted.

"I'm not sure."

"Is one ever to know?"

"In time. These things tend to iron themselves out in their own good time."

They walked down the street, leaving the priest standing somewhat forlornly on the steps of the church. The weather had turned colder. Ramos shivered and suggested that they stop for a cup of coffee, and neither of them said anything until they were seated in an old German bakery on Eighth Avenue, drinking coffee and eating apple crumb cake.

"You put your finger on it," Ramos said. "Someone came into the church and talked to the priest."

"Where was Mrs. Dougherty? Where was Father White?"

"Mostly you walk into a church daytime, it's empty. He could have been there alone."

"And what led him to the church? Do you know what kind of a witches' brew we're cooking here? The hell with it. The old man died of a heart attack. Old men do."

"He wasn't so old," Ramos said. "Seventy-three isn't old."

"It's a goddamn lot older than you or I will be if what we're thinking is so."

"The man who confessed was Cullen," Ramos noted. Freedman nodded. "That's what the old man asked White about."

"I suppose so," Freedman agreed. "I hate a situation where people know things they're not supposed to know."

"Why don't we talk to Cullen?"

"I had that in mind," Freedman said. "But goddamnit, why would Cullen kill him?"

"Why would someone else kill him? You know we got nothing. So let's push it."

They walked to Cullen's apartment on Eighteenth Street, and Freedman considered how it was with a cop. You didn't phone ahead or announce your coming. You just walked in, and right now, when Ramos persisted, "You think he did it?" Freedman turned on him angrily and snapped, "No, I don't think he did it, and it's a fucken piece of insanity."

"All right. Don't bite my head off. I only asked."

"We'll ask him."

Cullen was at home. He buzzed them in and opened the apartment door for them without hesitation. He was in his undershirt, smoking a cigar, and had been watching the six o'clock news on his TV. A bottle and a glass half full of beer stood on the end table near where he had been sitting. He turned off the television and motioned for them to sit down.

"Beer?" he asked them. "It's all I got."

Freedman felt a sense of warmth in the room, the striped covering of the couch, a day bed with pillows and a flowered spread, a bookcase with three shelves of books, and on the floor a rug with a design of an American eagle. Freedman often regretted that he had no measures of taste. He liked certain things. He liked the pictures on the walls of Cullen's room, even though he recognized them as the kind you buy in stores that sell cheap oil paintings. Cullen had been well paid and he had money, but Freedman couldn't blame him for hanging on to his money. He was at the end of a road, and maybe there was a turning point and maybe there wasn't.

Ramos shook his head to the suggestion of beer. Ramos was angry, and Freedman was intrigued by the reaction of these two men to the murder of a priest. In fact, Cullen had not murdered the priest, and Immelman might not have been murdered at all. The younger priest, Father White, was also angry and felt betrayed by Immelman's death. Perhaps he loved Immelman more than he realized or perhaps he was frightened by the prospect of being alone in the church. All of these were surmises; this was not Freedman's place or background. How would he have felt about the murder of a rabbi?

"Sit down," Cullen said. He was not impatient or troubled; he had made his peace with these two men.

In the ordinary course of things, there would be a line of questioning. Where were you at the time of Immelman's death? What did you say to Immelman that differed from what you said to us? Why did you go to the Rock to confess? Wasn't there a church you went to when you went to church—which you must have done at one time?

But this wasn't the ordinary course of things, and Freedman said bluntly, "Father Immelman is dead. We think he may have been murdered. We want to know whether you had anything to do with it. You don't have to answer any questions and we got nothing to make an arrest. We're just asking you."

Ramos was furious. He felt it was the wrong line and a lousy line to take, and as always, when anger arose between him and the lieutenant, he told himself, "That damn Jew doesn't know where he's coming from," and Freedman became a Jew. A few minutes later, Freedman the Jew disappeared and Freedman his friend who had saved his life twice returned, but Freedman sensed the content of the anger and bore it bitterly.

Cullen's response was unexpected. He stared at them a long moment before answering, and then he said, "Who the hell is Immelman?" Yet he had heard the name, and it lay uneasily at the bottom of his memory, and as he sought for it, he remembered how the old lady in the church had asked him to wait. Was it Immelman? Did she say Immelman?

Ramos had swallowed his anger. The two detectives remained silent and watched Cullen.

"Give me that name again," Cullen said.

"Immelman." Freedman spelled it out.

"Is that the old priest at the church on Twenty-first?"

"You got it."

"He's dead?"

"You got it again," Ramos said nastily. "He's dead."

"Murdered?"

The two detectives said nothing.

"He was an old man. Who the hell would shoot him? This city is crazy."

The detectives exchanged glances in spite of themselves.

Ramos said, "You said you saw it done."

"Hell, man, yes! But not here. That's a jungle down there. That's the asshole of creation.

This is New York City. What the hell is this? Are you both nuts? You think I did it? You think I went back there and shot the old man?"

"No, I don't think you did it," Freedman said, pressing Ramos's arm in a gesture that said, "Trust me." Cullen was on his feet. "Sit down," Freedman said. "You, too, Ramos. The old man wasn't shot, he was smothered, and sure you could have faked that, Cullen, and that would make you either a great actor or a brilliant poker player, but in my book you don't rate twenty cents as a poker player. What kind of a cigar is that you're smoking?"

"A Nicaraguan Royal."

"Is it any good?"

"Not as good as a Cuban. Try one."

He offered cigars. Freedman shook his head. Ramos accepted and lit up. Ramos softened and admitted that this was a very good cigar, and Freedman told Cullen about Father White and his suspicions. It gave Freedman a peculiar feeling to sit here and talk like this to a man who had been part of what may have been the biggest cocaine-smuggling operation in the history of drugs, and if he could have made a case, he would have put the cuffs on Cullen and brought him in. But others had said to keep his hands off, and he had no case for drugs. Murder in his own precinct, on the other hand, was something else. He had a feeling that Cullen's time would come, and he was content to wait. But murder?

"I don't know," Cullen said. "You think someone put a pillow over his face and smothered him—"

"Was he a big man?" Ramos asked.

"No, a skinny little fellow. You could knock him over with an electric fán. But there's got to be a reason."

"There is," Freedman said. "He heard your confession."

"Come on, come on," Cullen said. "That's crazy. You're telling me he was maybe killed because he heard my confession?"

"What did you tell him?" Ramos asked.

"What I told you. Only, part. Goddamnit, that's none of your fucken business, what's between me and a priest."

"It is now," Freedman said. "Who else did you tell your story to?"

"Nobody."

"Nobody? Come on, Cullen—you were exploding with it. You were in Sullivan's place the other day before you came to us, weren't you?" It was a shot in the dark. Freedman couldn't remember whether Cullen had mentioned being in Sullivan's place except when he met Kovach.

"Yeah," Cullen admitted.

"Who did you talk to there?"

"I talked to Sullivan, but not about Father O'Healey. I never—what in hell are you after?"

"You might say nothing at all," Freedman answered sourly. "You come in off the street and tell us that you watched a priest thrown out of a helicopter in Honduras and that you were part of the biggest drug operation in history and that you were working for the CIA or something or some part of the goddamn army, and it was all legal and set up in Washington or wherever in hell they set these things up, and you ask us what we're after? Let me tell you something, Cullen. I don't like you, I don't believe you, and most of all I don't like priests being murdered, and sure as hell one day I'll get to the bottom of this, because this old man wasn't knocked over in Honduras but right here on my turf."

He finished, and then the three men were silent as the minutes ticked by. The room thickened with smoke. Ramos puffed on his cigar.

"One other person," Cullen said finally. "She's a hooker, name of Sylvia."

"Sylvia who?"

"She said her name was Sylvia Mendoza."

"And what did you tell her?"

Cullen sighed and shook his head and said, "One day you look at yourself and you realize how stupid you are. God Almighty."

"What did you tell her?"

"I killed the priest. I told her I killed Father O'Healey."

Freedman shook his head and looked at Ramos, who was staring at Cullen as if he had never seen him before.

"Just this hooker? No one else?"

"No one else."

"You really think you killed that priest—I mean Father O'Healey? You really think you killed him? You see, I want to know what you are. Are you crazy? Or were you on crack? Because if you think you killed him, maybe you did kill him, and all the rest of what you tell us is pure, unadulterated horseshit."

"I'm not crazy," Cullen said stubbornly. "I could have stopped it. I had control of the chopper. But I didn't, and I don't do dope, so just drop that angle."

"All right." Freedman spread his hands. "Maybe yes, maybe no. Meanwhile, where does this Sylvia live?"

"Not far from here. Couple of blocks, not far."

Ramos took a long pull on the cigar, admitting to himself that it was a very good cigar, at least two dollars, which was more than he could afford for cigars. He took out his notebook and asked Cullen for Sylvia Mendoza's address.

"I don't remember. I can take you there."

"Good. I was beginning to think you should. It's just after five, which is a good time to find a lady at home."

Cullen put on a jacket, and then the three men walked to the apartment house. They went up to the seventeenth floor, a detail Cullen remembered, after the doorman had assured them that Miss Mendoza was home, with a grin that was a snicker and that made Freedman calculate how much she had to pay the doorman. Freedman hated the process of payoff, everyone paying off someone else, and all of it hanging over the city like a sickness.

At the apartment, they pressed the door button and heard the chimes tinkle inside. Ramos pressed it again and again, but no one came to open the door and there was no movement or sound from inside. Freedman told Ramos to go down and get a passkey from either the doorman or the super, and if anyone got snotty about a search warrant, to tell him that they had probable cause to believe that a crime had been committed in the apartment. As he said that, Freedman felt a tickle of gooseflesh across his body. With Ramos gone, he said to Cullen, "You haven't seen her since then?"

"No."

"Did she turn tricks here?"

"She said I was an exception. I felt like shit warmed over, and she must have responded to it and felt sorry for me. She said she never took anyone upstairs—"

Which would be a dumb thing for him to say, Freedman realized, if he'd had anything to do with what might or might not be inside.

"—but she made an exception for me. She said she worked the uptown hotels, the Plaza and the Pierre and such places, which could have been the truth, because she was a beautiful woman."

The super came back with Ramos. The super was a short, dark, heavyset man with a black beard. He had a scowl that defended him against the world, and Freedman realized that no one was himself anymore, but in this world of endless television tripe everyone was a piece of bad art. "I knew she was a tramp," this particular piece of bad art said as he opened the door with his passkey. "He"—the doorman —"says she's inside." Shouting, "Miss Mendoza, are you in there?"

"Cut the yelling," Ramos told him, leading the way into the apartment. Somehow, Cullen saw her before anyone else, pointing. "Oh, Jesus," he whispered. "Oh, Jesus God!" She lay on her back in one corner of the room, behind a big armchair that was covered with bright chintz. She wore a kimono over a brassiere and lace panties, and all over her body were round, uneven spots of blood, some larger, some smaller, some with trickles of blood like the legs of gross spiders.

The super stayed by the door. Ramos and Freedman walked to the body, Cullen close behind them.

"Ice pick," Ramos said.

"Twelve times."

Ramos touched her wrist. "Cold."

Her eyes were wide open. Cullen stepped forward and bent over her. Ramos pushed him away.

"What the hell are you up to?" Freedman demanded.

"I want to close her eyes."

"Don't touch her," Freedman said more gently, and to Ramos, "Call it in."

While Ramos used the telephone, Freedman stared thoughtfully at the body. Cullen dropped onto the couch, his face in his hands. Freedman then turned to the super and told him to go. "Just stay in the building. We'll call you if we need you."

"The troops are on the way," Ramos said as he put down the telephone. The super left reluctantly. Freedman pointed to Sylvia Mendoza's body. "Does it ring any bells?"

"Tony Carlione." He shook his head.

"Tony Carlione. Always twelve times."

"The Feds put him away five years ago after the big trial. You know the routine. New name, new location, new life, big bonus."

"I know. I read the papers."

"Still and all," Ramos mused, "why should anyone else want to lay it on Tony?"

"Why indeed. And is Tony stupid enough to leave his signature?"

"He takes stupid pills. They all do."

"Pride in his work," Freedman said.

"For Christ's sake," Cullen exploded, "that was a woman, a human being! Don't treat her like shit!"

Ramos looked at Cullen and nodded. "Interesting. I hear you drove a gunship in Nam."

"Take it easy," Freedman said. "I don't know what's between this dame and you, but for God's sake, Cullen, if we got emotionally involved with every stiff, there'd be nothing left of us in a couple of weeks. Pour yourself a drink."

"I'd like to get out of here."

"No, I'm afraid not. The big wheels from Manhattan South will be here any moment, and they'll want to know how you figure in this."

"What do you tell them?" Ramos wondered. "The word from downtown is that we never made that tape."

"Beautiful. How I hate those bastards in Washington."

"Gets us nowhere. How did we get here?"

"Cullen's a john. She promised to meet him here. He kept calling her and he got nervous. So we came here."

"No way." Ramos shook his head. "You could only flush that down the toilet."

"All right. She called Cullen at his apartment. Told him she was scared shitless. He tried to call her back. No answer. So he called us."

"That might wash," Ramos admitted.

Freedman shook his head. "Lives, jobs, pensions—" He whirled on Cullen. "Did you hear that, mister? We are going to cover you with that story. She called you. You called us. You fuck up, so help me God I'll see you put away for the rest of your life."

"Fair enough."

"Now let's go over it again."

They had it down pat by the time the homicide people arrived, but Freedman had the hopeless, miserable feeling that they were helping to weave a net that would never be untangled.

"What I don't understand," a lieutenant of detectives from Manhattan South said, "is just what your relationship to this broad consists of."

"I liked her," Cullen said. "That's allowed. Maybe I loved her."

"Freedman here tells me she's a hooker."

"You can't love a hooker?"

"Sure, sure."

"She's a beauty," someone else said.

"Sure, she's a beauty."

"You get a full statement from him," the lieutenant of detectives said to Freedman. "Who did you say killed her?"

"Tony Carlione."

A younger man from Manhattan South said, "What the hell is it with you guys? You seen it done? What have you got with this Tony Carlione? His calling card."

"Johnson, shut up and don't be an asshole," the older detective said. And to Freedman, "Are you convinced that you make him?"

"He was the most important ice pick man in the mob. They used to call him Twelve-tone Tony. It was his style. He was proud of it. The mob used him on the docks over in Brooklyn, and if you want to have a better rundown on him, talk to the Brooklyn guys."

"You got any notion how he connects with this woman?"

Freedman shook his head. Ramos said, "There could have been something. She's no chicken. She's got a long past."

"Enough to pull him out of the safe harbor

the Feds provided for him? Just showing his face in New York could be his ticket out of things."

Freedman shrugged. "It's what he does. He's a hit man, a professional killer. That's how he made his points. Maybe somebody bought this hit; maybe it was his own score to settle."

"We'll talk to the Feds," the lieutenant from Manhattan South said. "They know where Carlione is or where he's supposed to be."

"Good luck."

"Maybe you got class," Ramos said sourly. "It takes class to talk to the Feds and have them talk back."

"My guess is," Freedman said as a parting shot, "that wherever Carlione is, it's where he's supposed to be, and he's got a nice tight alibi to prove it."

"We'll see."

Freedman and Ramos and Cullen walked back to the precinct house, where they worked out a statement by Cullen that would satisfy everyone concerned. At least they hoped it would satisfy everyone concerned. Cullen signed it, and then they told him that he could go home.

"But stay in the city," Freedman said.

"You know," Cullen said, "I told her to call me Culley. I told her that's what my friends call me. Friends. My God, I got no friends."

"Go on home. And lock your doors tonight."

"You know," Cullen said, "I don't like to appear dumber than I am, but if Father Immelman was murdered, only one thing links him to Sylvia."

"We thought of that," Ramos said.

"People like Monty and Mr. Lester—they just don't give a fuck, not one little bit."

"Go home, Cullen."

He left, and the two men sat for a while in Freedman's tiny office, the lieutenant behind his desk, Ramos on the single old chair that stood beside the desk, and after a while of silence, they got tired of trying to figure things out. Ramos asked Freedman what he was going to do tonight.

"I thought I'd call Sheila."

"She's not your wife these days."

"Yeah, which seems to make it better."

"My friend, Inez, she says she's got a friend who's an absolute knockout."

"Not tonight."

"Yeah, Well, I said I'd meet her at seven. It's almost seven. You know, they'll kill Cullen."

"You got too much imagination, Ramos."

"I wish I didn't. All they have to do is kill Cullen and burn the tape."

"You know," Freedman said, "if you want to find two here and two there and put them together and do the counting yourself, it always makes four. There isn't a shred of evidence that the old priest died of anything more than a heart attack, and as for the hooker, who knows? Maybe she was something to Carlione. Maybe he had his own reasons for leaving his safe hole and cutting her up."

"It's like me getting up at five in the morning to be a cop without pay. Contract killers kill for hire."

"Go ahead," Freedman said, standing up. "Knock yourself out. You'll go nuts."

"Yeah. How about you and me and Jones and Leary and Lefty? We all saw the tape. We made the damn tape."

Freedman dropped back into his chair and said, "Get out of here, Ramos. Go home. Take a hot shower. I don't want to think about this."

"Could be you're right."

"Leave on that happy thought."

Ramos departed, and Freedman dialed the number of Cornich, where Sheila worked, but the place had closed and there was no answer. Freedman thought about the place for a while, the three floors on Seventh Avenue, the glitz and glamour of the showrooms, the little theater where they did their own style shows, the young middle-aged men in their Italian suits, the flow of money charged to the perks, and then he looked through the glass door to the squad room, where the green paint was flaking off the walls and where two dull-eyed detectives sat at ancient desks, typing out reports on twenty-year-old mechanical typewriters.

He called Sheila at home.

"I knew you'd call," she said.

"All right, you know me. Are you pissed off because I called?"

"Not right this minute. Come on, Mel, you want to talk, talk sweet."

"I'm sorry."

"OK. Begin again."

"Let me take you to dinner—please. I'll go home and shave and put on a tie. Please. I'll take you to a good place. I'll call the Four Seasons. You can always get a reservation there if you're a cop."

"Sure."

Just like that. Her response silenced him for a few moments.

"Mel?"

"About eight o'clock," he said weakly.

"I'll be ready."

Freedman put down the telephone and held out a hand. It was trembling slightly. He was as excited as a kid on his first real date with his first love. He left the precinct house like a somnambulist, his thoughts searching a chest of drawers for a white shirt. He was certain he had a clean white shirt, but he then decided that a striped shirt might be better. He grinned and nodded. The men she knew around Seventh Avenue would wear striped shirts. His own trouble was not that he dressed poorly, but that he simply did not dress at all. As often as not, he didn't wear a tie. It is true that he had paid three hundred dollars for his sports jacket, but he wore it every day, as he did his gray flannel trousers. Sheila hated the way he dressed, but tonight he turned himself out very well indeed, pale blue striped shirt, dark blue silk knit tie, navy blazer, and gray flannel trousers, not the daily pair, but new ones worn for the first time.

Sheila smiled and nodded immediate approbation as she opened the door for him; and as for Freedman, he looked at her and melted. She wore a long-sleeved silk-jersey blouse, black, and a long, swirling skirt of heavy black silk, and on the black silk of her blouse, the strand of pearls he had given her before they were married. Her black hair was cut shoulder-length and curled inward, and her only makeup light-colored lipstick.

They were welcomed royally at the restaurant, no new thing when he was with Sheila, and Freedman ordered a dinner of asparagus vinaigrette, sliced white veal rump roast, tiny boiled potatoes, French beans, and fresh raspberries with cream for dessert, and a bottle of the best white Burgundy on the wine list.

It was a dinner of the things Sheila liked best, and Freedman couldn't care less about a check of almost two hundred dollars. Sheila gave him his head, only remarking once that this was not anything a police lieutenant would do every night.

It was at her suggestion that they went home to her apartment, and it was in a way at her suggestion that they went to bed. And after they made love, since he couldn't sleep, she made coffee and she took out a box of his old cigars that had sat in the refrigerator for months. They sat in her tiny kitchen while he filled it with cigar smoke. She didn't complain. She liked the odor of cigar smoke. It was the first cigar Freedman had smoked in months. Well, conditions had changed. Other vows were also broken.

Freedman thanked her. He groped for words to tell her how he felt. "You been so damned kind. You were the best thing ever happened to me, and I tossed it away."

"We're good, but not with marriage."

"Yeah."

"And you've got to see," Sheila said, "that with all this great night together, you're still depressed and miserable."

"Yeah."

"Still the priest in Honduras. You know, Mel, you're Jewish and that's why you give this priest so many points. I grew up Catholic, the whole schmear, parochial school, priests, nuns —and let me assure you, Mel, I've known priests I wouldn't give you twenty cents for."

"Yeah."

"That's all you got to say, yeah?"

"Look at it the way I do, Sheil. I'm nobody. I'm just a cop in a mean little precinct. I got no big opinion of myself. Sure I dream that maybe you and me, we'll get together again, and maybe a couple of kids. But I got enough sense not to push that, and I got enough sense not to lie to myself. All right, like all cops, I live in shit, I work in shit, but no matter how lousy it gets, I tell myself that it's better than anywhere else, that I live in a country where everyone has a shake. But look at it. I don't give a damn whether that priest in Honduras was a saint or some worthless bum. The fact of the matter is that he was murdered and nobody did a damn thing about it. I got an eyewitness to the murder, and I'm told to keep hands off him and forget it. I got an eyewitness to the biggest drug operation in history, and I got every reason in the world to believe that it's carried on by some government bureau in Washington, some part of my government, and I'm told to keep my mouth shut and forget it and leave it alone. The DA tells me that it's jurisdictional, the chief inspector tells me it's out of my hands, and now I could have two murders that flow directly from it, and I have to lie to those shitheads at Manhattan South or else get bounced out to Staten Island or Jamaica Bay or some such place, and I got a thick-headed Irishman who's maybe next on this crazy slaughter list, and I can't do one damn thing about it."

"Mel, for Christ's sake, let's go back to bed and sleep," Sheila begged him. "I'm too tired to think and too old to be scared. And you're scaring me."

Oscar Kovach

THE FOLLOWING DAY, Harold Timberman, the district attorney, lunched at the Harvard Club with the governor of the state.

Timberman cautiously raised the question of cocaine, as pertaining to Cullen's tape. Because he could not plunge right into the pivotal question that the tape raised, he tiptoed around it with talk about the broader drug scene. "Of course, I remember Prohibition," he said to the governor. "I'm a bit older than you, I think. I was just a kid. Nevertheless, I watched it tear the country to pieces and turn honest men into crooks and rip morality to shreds. That was the real beginning of organized crime."

"I guess it was. Do you feel the same process working today?"

"I do."

"As bad?" the governor wondered.

"Worse—much worse. Now it's kids, sometimes kids as young as nine or ten years. Crack turns them into lunatics. Two days ago, a ten-year-old murdered his father and mother—shot them, his father's pistol."

"I know. I read the papers."

Their talk led to the question that such talk always leads to, with Timberman saying, "There has to be a way to get a handle on this."

"So I am told. What else is new?"

"Tell me something," Timberman said, feeling that this was the proper moment, "is it thinkable, is it possible, that some part of the government is in this up to the neck and is running drugs?"

"Possible? Anything is possible."

"That's pretty vague."

"So is your question," the governor said, smiling. "Why don't you tell me what's on your mind, Harold?"

"Do you remember that during the Vietnam War there was talk of the CIA making a deal with the opium lords in the Golden Triangle north of Thailand, and in exchange for bases, buying their drugs and running them into the United States?"

"During the war you heard all kinds of things."

"Come on, come on," Timberman said. "My nose is in court, but you hear things. You must. Now what about this contra thing? Is it guns for drugs?"

"This is very unlike you, Harold," the governor said. "Your life is dedicated to proof, hard evidence. You really can't expect me to feed a rumor mill."

At the same time, in Sullivan's bar, Cullen was saying, "Bobby, you can't expect me to keep putting out, and whatever I put out goes right up your nose."

Bobby was a thin, sickly looking man, yellow skin with a parchment texture, blue blood-shot eyes, a shaking hand that touched Cullen's arm tentatively.

"Culley, we were both there," he said pleadingly.

"We were—almost twenty years ago."

"I'm dying, Culley."

"Oh, shit," Cullen said.

"If you're broke, Culley, forget it."

"I'm not broke and I can give you the hundred. I could also burn it."

Billy Sullivan, listening to them, said, "Bobby, you come in and eat whenever you're hungry. I never turn you away. I got a place in back where you can crash. If Culley wants to give you the hundred, take it, but don't piss it away on a trip to Washington. What are you going to find on that goddamn black wall?"

"Harry Brown, the black guy. He saved my life."

"I know. Sure. Harry was a beautiful guy, but you won't find him on the wall."

"Why?"

"He died last year."

He turned to Cullen and said, "Like I'm dying of the Agent Orange shit. I won't have no name on the wall?"

"I don't know, Bobby." Cullen turned to Sullivan and shook his head slightly. Then he took out his wallet and handed Bobby two fifty-dollar bills. "Take the Washington bus up at Thirty-ninth Street."

"God bless you, Culley."

When Bobby left, Sullivan said, "He'll blow it on happy dust. You know that."

"Let him have his white soldiers," Cullen said. "Maybe he'll go to Washington and cry over the black stone. It makes no damn difference, Billy. He'll be dead in another few months, the same way Harry Brown died."

"They fucked us nicely."

"Flag and country. What the hell difference does it make? Sooner or later, they'll blow us all to hell with atomic bombs."

"You're in a great mood."

"Yeah."

"Another hamburger?"

"Why not?"

He yelled over his shoulder, "Put one on for Culley. Well done and onions. You want tomatoes?" to Cullen, who shook his head.

"No tomato."

The men who ate lunch at Sullivan's were an early crowd. Mostly they were men who worked in the neighborhood, an area of a hundred different small industries, or they were construction workers or people from the waterfront. They worked early, ate early, and left early, and now, except for Cullen, Sullivan, the cook, and the girl who waited tables, the bar was empty. "I turn around to the booth over there," Sullivan said, "and half expect to see Sylvia. She got a bad rap. I liked her."

Cullen nodded.

"She had a kind of class. Did you make out with her?"

"Not really," Cullen said. "I didn't try."

Sullivan shook his head. "That was no boat to miss. When I saw you leave with her, I figured it would take your mind off things. And can you imagine—some crazy bastard cutting her with an ice pick twelve times."

Cullen was thinking of his wife, Frannie, the thought interlocking with the picture of Sylvia Mendoza lying dead on the floor of her apartment, a beautiful woman. He could have loved her. How desperately he wanted to know a woman he could love. That was the awful hole in his being, lovelessness, emptiness. He could have loved Frannie, but she hated his guts and had grinned with delight when the divorce came through. He never contested anything she said, the lies she told at the custody hearing—which gave her Sarah, their daughter. Sarah was only three then. She'd be five years old now. Who knew whether she remembered him? Frannie had disappeared out to the West Coast.

Sullivan interrupted his reverie. "Do you know why Bobby wants to go down there and look at the black stone?"

"Harry Brown?"

"Yeah, I remember Harry Brown, built like a brick shithouse, but dependable. He carried Bobby, poor bastard. No, it wasn't him, it was Oscar Kovach."

"Kovach? What the hell was he doing here?"

"Well, he was telling Bobby about the black stone, how he saw it in Washington—but that wasn't why he came in. He missed you by about thirty minutes. He was looking for you."

"Did he say why? What for?"

"No. He was asking where you lived."

"Did you tell him?"

"Culley, I don't know where you live, and if I

did know, I wouldn't tell that cocksucker. I remember where you lived when you were together with Frannie. That was a nice place."

"She's gone to the Coast. What else did Kovach say?"

"He said he had some money that was coming to you."

"Yeah, he always was a philanthropist." Cullen dropped his voice. "Billy, I need a favor."

"Just say it."

"I need a piece."

"Ah, come on, Culley," Sullivan said. "You don't want that kind of shit. You need money—"

"Billy, I don't need money. I got seven hundred in my pocket and enough in the bank. I'm scared, period. I'm neck-deep in stuff—and I'm scared. I can't explain it. It's just too damn complicated."

"Tell me about it. Maybe I can help."

"Nobody can help. I want to stay alive, that's all. I need a gun. If you can't help me—"

"Did I say that?"

"I don't know. If it has a number, then I can't take it. So maybe the best thing to do is to forget that I asked."

"All right. Just listen. I got a big forty-five army issue that I keep under the counter, and that's registered with a permit. I can't give you that. But I got one of those little .30 caliber

Saturday night specials, with no number and not registered, and I can give you that. I hate to."

"I know."

"Jesus, Culley, nobody knows better than us what kind of shit a gun is."

"I know."

"OK, as long as you know and think about it." He went into the back room and returned with a small parcel in a paper bag. "It's fully loaded. I don't keep extra ammo. I took it in trade from a wino, a guy I used to know. Figured he'd live longer without it. You finish with it, chuck it into the river."

Culley thanked him. "I won't forget, Billy."

"Forget it. This is something I don't want either of us to remember. If you got a brain in your head, you'd throw it into the river right now."

Cullen shrugged. But he didn't throw it into the river, and at home that evening he examined it carefully, unloaded it, tried the action, and then reloaded it carefully. He had a tremendous respect for weapons, along with hatred, along with compassion for the ground soldiers in Vietnam who'd had to use the weapons, the marines and the other enlisted personnel who had been combat foot soldiers. Too many of them ended up with one sickness or another, and he had no delusions about what would have been his own fate if he had been among them. He was crazy enough just looking down from a helicopter.

He slipped the little gun into his pocket and he considered the possibility of going out for his dinner. He couldn't face the thought of another Billy Sullivan hamburger. He didn't want to drink, and he hated to eat alone in a restaurant quite as much as he hated the food served at the small bars and hamburger joints. A cafeteria filled him with a special kind of lonely misery; it was not the process of eating or the food, but the loneliness, the sense of being unnoticed and totally uncared for. He decided on a bottle of beer from his refrigerator and the remaining half of a ham and cheese sandwich he had bought three days ago, and he turned on his television set and watched the six o'clock news as he munched the dry bread of the sandwich. He was prepared for the doorbell to ring, and when it did, he turned off the TV and opened the door without asking who was there. That it should be Oscar Kovach was no surprise to him.

He motioned for Kovach to enter, closed the door behind him, and then went into the kitchen, calling back, "Sit down, Oscar. I got cold beer. No liquor in the house."

"Beer's fine," Kovach said.

Cullen came out of the kitchen with a bottle

of beer in his left hand. His right hand was in his pocket, grasping the handle of the Saturday night special. Kovach was standing at the doorway, an automatic pistol, silencer attached, in his hand; and in the fraction of a second it took Cullen to see and respond, Cullen flung the beer bottle at Kovach and Kovach flinched enough to sear Cullen's side as the bullet tore through his shirt. Cullen dived behind a big armchair and Kovach delivered his second and third shots into the chair. Cullen had the gun out, and he shot Kovach as Kovach took two strides to get around the chair. The bullet struck Kovach in the chest. He dropped his big pistol, fell on the floor, rolled over, and then sat up, a bewildered expression on his face, and he managed to say, "I think you killed me, Culley. I got a hole in my chest." Then he fell back.

Cullen shook him. "Come on, Oscar, come on! What did you want to shoot me for? For what? For who? Come on—was it Monty? Or that son of a bitch Fred Lester? Tell me!"

Then Cullen realized that Kovach was dead, and that he would tell nothing to anyone ever again. His eyes were wide open and staring, and when Cullen felt for a pulse, he found none.

"You son of a bitch," Cullen said. "You killed me too. I'm sitting on a murder rap."

For once, Cullen regretted that he did not keep a bottle of booze on hand, for he desperately wanted a drink. He had never been classified as alcoholic, as so many of his buddies had been, and he could forgo hard liquor. He had a real need for it only in the small hours of the night, when terror would come whispering to him; and he felt that way now as he stared at Oscar Kovach's body. He had fired only one shot, and the Saturday night special was not loud. Probably it had not been heard. The old brownstone he lived in had one apartment on a floor, and at this hour most of the other tenants might well be out.

He sat down on the couch and stared at Kovach. If only he had not met him; if only he had not been in Billy Sullivan's saloon when Kovach appeared and offered the job. Eventually, he would have gotten a job. If only he had told Kovach to go to hell. Now he had killed him. Self-defense? Try to prove that in a city court. Then what do you do? Call Freedman?

No, no—no way.

Dump the body? Get rid of it?

Impossible. Totally impossible. He didn't have a car. After he had driven from Texas to New York, his car was burning a quart of oil every two hundred miles. The car was seven years old and not worth the price of a New York garage. Cullen had sold it for five hundred dollars. What was he to do? Hail a taxi and ask him to drive him to the river to dump a body? Or walk the body a quarter of a mile to the river. Nothing made any sense, except that he was in a trap with apparently no way out.

He thought about the guns. He could tell a straight story: Kovach had come here to kill him. He had fired once and seared Cullen's side—and the reminder brought pain there. His shirt was sticky with blood. He went into the bathroom, thinking that he could show the two—or was it three?—bullet holes in the chair. But who was to say that the heavy automatic belonged to Kovach or that Kovach had come there armed? He had his shirt off now. The wound looked and felt as if someone had dragged a rough file across his ribs. It was only a surface wound, the blood oozing out of it, but it was painful. He took a clean handkerchief, saturated it with rubbing alcohol, and swabbed out the wound. He had a kit of bandages, and the largest in the kit just covered the wound. Not much of a wound and nothing to worry about. He had had worse in Vietnam without being pulled off his chopper. He rolled the shirt into a ball, put it in a plastic bag without cleaning it, and squeezed it onto a shelf in his medicine cabinet. It was the only evidence he had that Kovach had fired at him, but it was no evidence at all as to who had fired first. He could have put the shots into the chair himself.

He put on a clean shirt and then went back into the living room and sat down, trying to think the things through. It was not likely, he realized, that the bullet had gone entirely through Kovach's body, so possibly there was no blood on the floor—although what difference that would make he couldn't imagine. He kept thinking that this apartment was his home, but it was no longer his home. He contemplated taking both guns to the river and throwing them in, but after a little thought, that seemed senseless. What difference could it make if he disposed of the guns? But he did have his wound; and what difference did that make? It could have been self-inflicted. It could have been the result of both of them firing at once. The more he thought about it, the more hopeless it appeared. He was cold, tired, and miserable. He thought a cigar might help, and he went into the kitchen to the refrigerator, where he kept his cigars. There were three there, three of the fine Cubans that Fred Lester handed out at the Salsaville strip. He pinched the end off one and lit it as he went back into the living room, and then he said to himself, "I'm crazy, sitting here like some stupid asshole, smoking a cigar and staring at Oscar Kovach's body."

He took another puff on the cigar, and then he placed it in an ashtray, picked up his telephone, asked Information for the number of the precinct house, and then punched it out. A voice on the other end responded, and Cullen asked for Lieutenant Freedman.

"Freedman."

"Lieutenant, this is Joe Cullen."

"Yeah. Cullen. What can I do for you?"

"About a half hour ago, my doorbell rang. When I answered it, it was Oscar Kovach. You remember the name."

"I remember the name."

"The same guy that flew with me to Honduras."

"Yeah. Go on."

"The moment the door was closed behind him, he pulled out a forty-five with a silencer attached and began to shoot at me."

"What? Say that again, clearly."

"He pulled out a gun," Cullen said slowly, "and began to shoot at me."

"Were you hit?"

"In the side. Just a scratch. He grazed me."

"Where's Kovach now?"

"He's here."

"What do you mean, here?"

"He's dead."

"You're telling me that Kovach is dead—in your apartment?"

"I'm looking at him right now," Cullen said miserably.

"Are you sure he's dead? I can have an ambulance there in ten minutes."

"Lieutenant, I was in Nam. I know dead."

"OK. Now listen to me. Just stay right there, and don't open the door to anyone but me. I'll be there in five minutes."

"That's no good. Listen to me, Lieutenant. There's no way I can prove that Oscar attacked me and that I shot him in self-defense. I called you because you been decent to me and I didn't want to leave a stiff here on my living room floor. But I'm not going to jail for this one. That son of a bitch walked in here to execute me."

"I believe you. Will you listen to me, Cullen! I believe you. I don't want you to run."

"Lieutenant," Cullen cried, his voice rising, "I got to run! I'm in something up to my neck, and I don't think my life is worth two cents. Look at it, I'm a drug runner and a murderer—"

Now Ramos, sitting in the squad room, picked up his phone and switched in. Freedman's voice carried.

"What the hell is that?" Cullen demanded.

"Sergeant Ramos switched onto the line. We're both listening but that makes no damn difference. Now listen to me, Cullen, and for once in your life do yourself a favor. Don't run! Don't be a horse's ass. Just do as I say. Lock the door and wait for us to get there."

"I can't."

"You damn well can!" Freedman shouted.

"No, I can't."

Freedman slammed down the telephone, grabbed his jacket and coat, and bolted out of the office, calling Ramos to follow him.

Kovach Dead

THE TYPE OF converted brownstone that contained Cullen's apartment usually has a front door controlled by a spring lock, which in turn is activated electronically from the various apartments. Such houses for the most part do not have resident superintendents. In some cases, there's a superintendent for a number of such buildings, three or four; in other cases, a landlord lives on one of the floors and rents out the others, and himself acts as superintendent. But at Cullen's address there was no apartment number marked SU-PERINTENDENT. With a choice between ringing the bells of other tenants until he got a buzz, indicating that the door lock was open, or picking the lock, Freedman chose to pick the lock—a task he allocated to Ramos.

"Do the Jimmy Valentine," he said to Ramos.

Ramos, who had never read O. Henry, would not give Freedman the satisfaction of being asked who in hell was Jimmy Valentine; he simply took out his ring of picks and went to work. Meanwhile, Freedman was pressing Cullen's call bell in the vague hope that Cullen had listened and had not run.

It took Ramos about thirty seconds to pick the lock. "Upstairs will be harder. A kid could spring these buzzer locks."

Upstairs, after they had climbed three flights of stairs, was harder. There were two locks, and one was a Segal, which, as Ramos pointed out, was one of the very best.

It took him about five minutes to spring the locks, and then they went into the apartment and saw Oscar Kovach's body. Cullen had left the lights on, and he had not altered anything that had happened in the living room. The body lay as it had been, eyes open. A small chair was overturned, and a beer bottle lay in a wet puddle on the rug, the smell of spilled beer heavy in the air. Two guns were on the floor, not moved since Cullen had fired and dropped his. Freedman stopped at the door, closing it gently behind him and then standing silently, studying the room, while Ramos prowled through the bedroom and the kitchen.

"Nothing," he said, looking into the fridge.

Freedman had noticed before that the place was decently furnished—a couch, day beds, a television set with a twenty-one-inch screen, a good rug. In one corner, leaning against the wall, was a banjo. An odd instrument for a man like Cullen. Few men understood the possibilities of a banjo, of a technique like Scruggs's picking, and Freedman wondered about the relationship of a man like Cullen to the instrument: chords that he could sing to? Or the mercilessly difficult process of using it as a complete instrument?

"Odd," he said.

Ramos was bending, as if to pick up the guns, and Freedman warned him off. "Leave it the way it is. Let the hotshots at Manhattan South mess with it."

"Oh?"

Freedman walked to Kovach and touched his face. "Cold as a flounder. Cullen got him in the heart. One shot."

Ramos was examining the chair. "Bullets went through. That son of a bitch is a heavy weapon." He looked behind the chair and found a bullet.

"Let it lay," Freedman said.

"You believe him?" Ramos wanted to know.

"Sure I believe him. Why not? He doesn't have the mentality to set anything up. He's not a criminal or a killer. He's a poor stupid bastard who believed that even shipping white shit was all right as long as those pisspots in Washington were involved. He got involved with a set of murderous lunatics and never had the brains to know it until it was too late."

"Maybe. Why the confessions?"

"That's your line. I'm not Catholic. Ask me about Jewish guilt and I can tell you something. Catholic guilt is not my line."

"And what do we tell the homicide boys when they come?"

Freedman laughed. "I don't know what to tell myself, Ramos. So help me God, I don't know what to tell myself. Off the top of my head, I have to think that those tinhorn lunatics running the guns and dope are sending us a message. Forget the tape. Cullen is dead, the priest is dead, the hooker is dead—now forget about the tape. It doesn't exist. It never existed."

"Cullen's alive."

"Yeah. He has a problem."

"And the scenario makes no sense—you, me, Jones, Leary, Lefty, not to mention that the story's all over the place. What do they do? Kill everyone?"

"No—just enough to send up a message.

What the hell, stories like this have been all over the place for years. Back during Nam, there were stories about the CIA running dope out of the Golden Triangle, and there are stories going around that the government has been working hand in glove with a bum called Noriega, paying him off with guns and running a steady stream of dope into this country, with the excuse that Panama has to be kept quiet, and you don't see nobody waving the flag and yelling that this has to stop."

"They killed two cops last week," Ramos said. "This city is a battlefield and there are more dopers and they're a lot better armed than we are. I still don't know what we tell the homicide guys."

"We tell them that Cullen telephoned with a story, and we hotfooted it over here and here we are."

"What story?"

"Kovach came to the door and tried to shoot him."

"Why?"

"How the hell do we know why?" Freedman said.

"Same guy mixed up in the murder of the hooker."

"So?"

"Jesus God, Lieutenant, they only have to talk to some uniform at the precinct house to hear about the tape—if they don't know about it already."

"So they know about it."

"And what the hell do we say?" Ramos demanded.

"We tell them to talk to the DA. The DA said to forget about the tape. It was sent to Washington."

"And what was on it?"

"Ask Timberman."

"How many years did you say you had to your pension?"

"I didn't say. I got years. I'd like to make captain."

"I'd like to make lieutenant," Ramos said.

"All right, there you are. We can call ourselves typical samples of the American drive toward upward mobility—or some such shit—and meanwhile, watch our step. I'll do the talking if you want me to." Then Freedman picked up the telephone and called Manhattan South.

It was the night shift, and the man in charge was Lieutenant Brady, a tall, thin-faced, good-looking man who had been told on numerous occasions that he looked like Clint Eastwood. Before that, he had switched to Marlboro cigarettes because he had been told that he looked like the cowboy in the advertisements, but lately he was smoking Camels once again.

But not now. Now he stood in Cullen's apartment, his notebook out, staring sourly at Freedman. "So you think it was self-defense?" he said to Freedman, not asking a question but denying a statement.

"That's what he told me on the telephone."

"Why did he call you?"

"You'd have to ask him that," Freedman replied.

"Did anyone ever tell you we're on the same side?"

"I certainly hope so."

Lieutenant Brady snapped at the fingerprint man, "Don't waste your time. Just get what's on the guns and the beer bottle."

"He's been dead about an hour—just a guess," the ambulance man said.

A man from homicide was drawing a heavy chalk mark around the body.

"Take it away when he finishes," Brady said.

"The word is," Brady said, "that he came to your precinct house and made some kind of confession about killing a priest."

"Cullen?"

"No, Jack the Ripper."

"Yeah, that's clever," Freedman said sourly. "Jack the Ripper. You know something, Brady, if you got anything to say, come out and say it and don't fuck around with how smart you are. You're right. Cullen came to us."

"And said what?"

"Call Mr. Timberman and tell him you'd like to know what Cullen said when we taped him in our precinct house. I'm sure he'll oblige you. But since he instructed us to keep our mouths shut, and since the chief inspector underlined that, we got nothing to talk about."

"Goddamnit, Freedman, this is a murder case."

"Yes."

"And it connects with the murder of Sylvia Mendoza."

"That could be."

"And you have pertinent information that you refuse to share with us."

"No! Absolutely not! You call the DA and get his agreement, and I'll give you everything I got. Meanwhile, I am following orders given to me by a superior."

"I will do that."

"Fine. And now Sergeant Ramos and I will go about our business. I'm finished for tonight, but I'll be at the house in the morning. You can reach me there."

Going downstairs, Ramos remarked that there were no media on the scene.

"There will be, but what's the difference. They won't print anything."

"Why?"

"Come on, Hosea, what are they going to

print? That a pilot for a gang of drug importers who are highly connected took a contract to waste another pilot for the same company who got pissed off because some Honduran thug threw a priest out of a helicopter? God Almighty, Hosea, we got an army of four thousand men down there in Honduras, and the whole shtick is to keep the contras going so that the arms-dope combine can stay in business. You want the *New York Times* to print that—a nice headline like this, for example: Two murders and one attempted murder organized by General Carl Swedenham, so that the profits of his drug operation can be maintained. Come on, come on, this stuff doesn't go in the media."

"Where does it go, Lieutenant?"

"Damned if I know."

"You believe Cullen?"

"Don't you?"

Ramos shrugged. "I don't make sense of it—not your way, Lieutenant. To my way of thinking, the old priest could have died of a heart attack, and hookers get snuffed every day. It goes with the business. I can't believe that someone is knocking off people to cover their operation. You just said it. They don't have to cover their operation. Everyone knows and nobody knows. That Golden Triangle affair came off years ago, and nobody even got a wrist slapped."

"And Kovach?"

"The way Cullen told it, he hated Kovach and Kovach hated him. How much Kovach hated him, we don't know."

"Or how much Cullen hated Kovach."

"Right."

They were outside now, and a cold, thin rain was falling. Ramos hunched his shoulders and shook his head. "Ever been to Puerto Rico, Lieutenant?"

"Not yet."

"Warm. Sweet. One of the sweetest places on earth. The sun shines. The people are nice. Gentle, sweet, nice people, not like the bums who infest this place. Why the hell my father had to leave the place and come here, I'll never know."

"You can go back."

"You can't go back. You never go back. Could you go back to wherever your people came from?"

"No way. So you figure maybe Cullen evened up some old grudges?"

"It could be."

"No, no way," Freedman said. "You can knock off, Sergeant. We're on overtime."

"What are you going to do?"

"I think Cullen went over to Sullivan's place.

I think he's there right now. You know, a man like Cullen, he doesn't lie much. They come off either as saints or dumbbells, but they're not saints and they're not dumbbells. They're simple."

"I'll hang in with you tonight," Ramos said, trying to sort out what Freedman had said and see whether he could make some sense out of it. "Should we get a cab?"

"It's only a few blocks. We'll walk—what the hell, it's not much of a rain."

"Yeah, they're simple. Do you know much about the saints?"

"Not your saints. Hell, a saint's a saint. Where did you go to school, Hosea?"

"I came down from East Harlem to Eighty-fourth Street to go to a Jesuit school."

"Smart cookies."

"You can say that again. What do we do, arrest Cullen?"

"He shot someone. They tell me that's against the law."

"Jesus, I am confused," Ramos said. "I been confused before, but this is real high-class confusion."

"So is life," Freedman said.

Working people in the neighborhood would eat Billy Sullivan's hamburgers and fried potatoes for lunch, but the dinner hour was flat, and aside from a couple of men at the bar, the place was empty. Billy recognized Freedman and Ramos. Sullivan's had been robbed three times in the past few years, and both detectives had been at the place.

"Can I give you something?" Billy asked them. "On the house."

"Behave," Freedman said.

"It's after hours."

"So it is, so it is. The sergeant and I are working overtime, and you wouldn't want it to get around that we could be humanized by a couple of free beers."

"Not me, Lieutenant," Sullivan said.

"We're looking for Joe Cullen."

"Who?"

"Joe Cullen. You don't know him."

"I'm trying to recall the name," Sullivan said.

"Try harder," Freedman said. "You're in the way of being a public servant, Billy, and how in hell could you be a public servant without a liquor license?"

"Are you threatening me, Lieutenant?"

"Naw. Would I threaten you? But let me tell you this, Billy: it would be a lot friendlier to let us poke around the place than to wake up some mean judge for a search warrant, which would make us a lot meaner than we are."

"Poke around the place." He seemed to be listening. "Well, sure. I got nothing to hide.

Come along." At the end of the bar, a door led to the area behind it. There was a small office with a desk and a metal file cabinet, the kitchen, inhabited now by one old man who was cleaning pots—pots, dishes, and a stove and refrigerator—and a door that led to the bathroom. The bathroom window was wide open, a cold wind blowing through the kitchen.

"I told you to keep this door closed," Billy Sullivan said to the old man. "I got to get back to the bar," he told the detectives.

Freedman and Ramos went to an Italian place on the next block, where Ramos ordered fried red snapper while Freedman settled for linguine, with garlic and cheese.

"You eat too much pasta," Ramos said.

"Why? What difference does it make?"

"You need protein," Ramos said.

Benny Contina, their waiter, said, "I'm sorry, Sergeant, but that's not what they say today."

"What do they say today?" Ramos asked sourly.

"Protein. You got enough of it."

"And how do you know that?"

"I read it. Maybe I heard it on television."

"Will you bring him the damn red snapper?" Freedman said.

Contina said, "You're sore at me?"

"We love you," Ramos said.

"Can I talk to you?"

"As long as we can eat."

The waiter pulled up a chair. "I got a sister—ah, you don't want to hear it."

"Tell us," Ramos said more gently.

"She married a bum." He paused. A long pause.

"It happens," Freedman said. "My wife could say the same thing."

"I don't mean it's a guy who fools around or drinks or don't bring home a paycheck. A real bum. He beats up on her and twice she had to go to the hospital, and it's bad for the kids to have to see. So I tell her to call the cops. She calls the cops, and they come and tell her there's nothing they can do, it's a family matter."

"Yeah, that's what a lot of them say."

"So what do I do? Wait until this bastard beats my sister to death?"

"Where do you live?" Freedman asked him. "What's the precinct number there? Do you know?"

"It's the Ninth—you know, down on Fifth Street."

"Yeah. All right, I know McCormick, he runs the squad there. I'll call him, and maybe he can put the squeeze on the crumb."

"I don't know how to thank you, Lieutenant."

Freedman made a notation in his book. "Forget it. *De nada.*"

When he left to get the food, Ramos said, "McCormick won't lift his ass to help his own mother, and *de nada*'s Spanish, not Italian."

"Aside from learning Italian, what should I do? Tell him to fuck off?"

"You're right. What about Cullen?"

"He'll turn up."

"Dead or alive?"

"God knows."

"Do you want to put out a bulletin?"

"They'll do all those good things at Manhattan South. The advantage of being a very small precinct is that while the hotshots downtown are figuring ways to merge you somewhere else, they take a lot off your hands."

"Yeah."

"You're pretty sure they'll try to kill him?"

"Sometimes yes," Ramos said, "sometimes no. Sometimes I think about it and believe him, sometimes I don't. There's one thing I know."

"What's that?"

"That no matter how much cocaine we pick up, no matter how many ships we search, no matter how many busts we make, there's always more around than yesterday."

The food came.

"Eat your fish," Freedman said.

Between bites, Ramos asked, "Seeing Sheila tonight?"

"Goddamnit, we're divorced!"

"Well, don't bite my head off. I just asked."

"Sorry."

"What's with you, Lieutenant? You're full of anger. That's no way for a man to be, not in our job. No, no, a cop should never be angry."

"My father was always angry," Freedman said. "You know, he was one of the first Jewish lieutenants on the force. Then he joined up in World War Two—didn't have to, you know, being a cop—and he was shot in the belly and lived in a wheelchair. That's why he was always angry."

"Poor man," Ramos said.

"Yeah, you can say that. What are you doing tonight?"

"I figured I'd go down to Fourteenth Street. They got a new Spanish picture there. I like to brush up on my Spanish."

"Enjoy."

It was the wrong word. Ramos was the loneliest man Freedman had ever known. He never spoke about his wife, who had taken a year-old little boy to Puerto Rico after the divorce. Ramos had been there twice, and then he stopped going there, and he never spoke about either his wife or his child. He was a very tall, handsome man, well educated and well read. After dinner, the two men parted, Ramos turning downtown while Freedman walked back to the precinct.

Ramos loved women, and women returned the affection. Freedman had seen him talk to women in stores and once on the street, not prostitutes but women about their own business, and the women almost never pulled back or away from him. He was charming in a way that few men are, at least in New York, yet he couldn't make it with his wife, and he was afraid, Freedman felt, to try to make it with another woman—at least to the point of something more than a one-night stand. Well, it was an occupational hazard with cops; Freedman knew that as well as anyone.

At the precinct house, nobody raised an eyebrow at Freedman's appearance. They were used to his turning up at odd hours; but he, in turn, was always surprised at how different things became when another shift took over.

He sat down in his tiny office, put his feet up on the desk, and tried to work out in his mind exactly how he felt about Cullen. There was little doubt that Cullen would be destroyed. Even apart from outside forces, Cullen lived on a route toward destruction. In this case, he wished that he could protect Cullen, but he would have to find him first.

But of course *they* would find him first. A man like Cullen might be very hard to find, unless one was on him all the time, and if they had sent Kovach to kill him, there would have been a backup outside to see what happened, and when Cullen came out of the house instead of Kovach, they would have known what had happened. Cullen had gone straight to Billy Sullivan's saloon, and then out the bathroom window when he and Ramos walked into the bar; but if Cullen had a tail on him, the tail would still be on him.

All of this on Freedman's mind. Why should he want to protect Cullen? Cullen was not simply a criminal—or was he a criminal at all in this strange year of 1987? "I took a job," he said. "I did what I was told to do. Who doesn't?"

He liked Cullen. He might not be able to put the reason into words, but he liked Cullen. He was intrigued by Cullen. He was intrigued by the idea of a Catholic priest who would go down to Honduras barefoot—his only measure was his vague knowledge of Saint Francis —and cast his lot among the poor peons who were fodder for the murder squads, armed so well and neatly by the United States. He even sort of understood that force which made Cullen confess to a murder he did not commit; for Freedman believed Cullen. Still, he was a small-time cop and no more than a small-time cop; and in a world where the murder of Father O'Healey could provoke only a few inches of speculation in the *New York Times* and practically no speculation or indignation anywhere else, a small-time cop mattered not at all.

His world had crumbled a long time ago. He was an honest cop, and he ran an honest squad in a world where honesty was a bad joke, and where the dope pushers and the local political leaders occupied adjoining cells, where dollars were no longer counted in millions but in billions and trillions, and where thousands of men and women in the same city that contained the countinghouses slept in the streets, over grates, on the floors of railway stations and armories, in cardboard boxes, and in piles of rags and waste.

"Screw it," he said, becoming judgmental at last; and then he left the precinct house and walked tiredly to the furnished room he called home.

Virginia Selby

CULLEN knew that he was being followed. He suffered from the Vietnam syndrome, not as much as his friends, some of whom had the sensitivity of hummingbirds, an awareness so sharp and agonizing that it was the edge of madness, but he had part of it. The world was a place of death, any moment, any hour, any day. You walked like a hunted animal, watching, listening. He was a pilot. A tired, begrimed, and wretched rifleman might say to him, as many had, "Man, you got it made up there in your lousy chopper"; but the chopper would come down, and when it did, it was his turn.

He walked quickly, slowed up, turned corners, and then decided that there were two of them. He signaled a cab on Sixth Avenue and told the driver to head uptown. They had not ignored that possibility. A car took its position behind them.

"Where to?" the driver wanted to know.

"The Hilton. On Fifty-fourth Street."

"They haven't moved it."

As they slowed to turn into the driveway of the Hilton, Cullen gave the driver a five-dollar bill, stepped out of the cab, and bolted into the hotel. He didn't turn to see what had happened to the other car, but strode quickly through the hotel, out through the garage exit, north on Seventh Avenue to Fifty-seventh Street, and then into a cab that was just pulling up to discharge a fare at Carnegie Hall.

"Madison Avenue and Seventieth," one place being as good as another. He paid the cab at Seventieth, looked around for a tracking car, found nothing that he could put a finger on, and then walked west on Seventieth Street to Fifth Avenue.

When he reached Fifth Avenue, Seventieth was empty behind him. He drew a slower, easier breath as he walked downtown; and a block downtown, looking back, he saw the corner still empty. So much for tracking a man in New York City; yet his heart was still pounding and he was filled with fear. They wanted him dead. He didn't worry about the cops, and when he had crawled out of the bathroom window in the rear of Billy Sullivan's saloon, warned as the cops came through the doorway, his terror was that someone who wasn't a cop would be watching the back of the place. He got through a maze of backyards and fences without seeing anyone, but when he emerged, a man was waiting, and then he knew that they were on to him and had picked him up once more. Not too mysterious; they had had Sullivan's place spotted from the front and from the rear.

But it was New York, and you can't hold on to someone in New York, not with twenty operatives, not if the victim knows the city.

No cabs now; he decided to walk and to pick up nothing that could be a lead to him, and so he walked on, down Fifth Avenue, across Fifty-seventh Street, and down Seventh Avenue, all the time racking his brains for a plan, a direction, a place. By now a bulletin would have been put out, all media, all points, a man wanted for the killing of Oscar Kovach. Between the city police and the nameless group that desired him even more fervently, there was no rest, no refuge, no hole to crawl into. Every hotel would be covered, every bus station, every airfield. He thought of the subways, but he would still be in the city, and the thought of being trapped underground chilled his blood.

It was all right for the moment. The streets were filled with people. But later on, as the streets emptied, that refuge would disappear. To be alone on the streets was to be marked, and sooner or later a prowl car would find him. There were places by the river where he once could have found an empty shipping carton to crawl into, but now they were the homes of the homeless. Cullen was of the company. He could never return to his apartment. Whatever it might be to others, to him it was his cave, his shelter against the world. It was barred to him forever. He had almost six hundred in cash in his pocket. It was his whole resource; he could not cash a check or go to the bank. He kept asking himself, "What do I do? Where do I go?"

He kept walking, grateful that the rain had stopped and that the night was not too cold. He had left his apartment dressed in old flannel trousers, a sports jacket, and a London Fog raincoat. Decently dressed; there were hundreds and hundreds of men passing by dressed no different than he.

He was at Forty-fifth Street and Seventh Avenue when the idea occurred to him, a place of refuge, at least for a few hours, that could not be connected. He went into a huge, garish drug store and began to thumb through the Manhattan directory, through the S pages. What had she said her name was? S, he knew, S-E-L, possibly, telling himself, "Cool, Cullen, cool and think. You're in trouble over Kansas, you sort out the possible fields, you always keep a place in mind if you have to come down, come down as best you can, but cool." Of course: Selby. She hadn't spelled it for him, but how else could it be spelled? Ah, there, his finger on it: V. Selby. That's what a woman did who lived alone, and she, being a DA, should have had more sense. It's a giveaway, but people fall into a pattern, and she'd probably listed it that way since she first had a phone of her own.

He punched out the number, and a woman's voice answered.

"Miss Selby? Is this Virginia Selby?"

Doubtfully: "Yes?"

"Miss Selby, this is Joe Cullen."

A long pause at the other end. He could almost feel her breath being drawn in, and then her words came slowly and carefully: "Mr. Cullen, where are you?"

"I'm in a telephone booth in midtown, and if you don't know, I'm wanted by the cops for a killing and I'm also wanted by the crowd that moves the dope."

"I know."

"It's not the cops, it's the other crowd. I think they want to kill me. I'm tired, I'm frightened, and a man tried to kill me tonight, and I swear to God I have no place to go, and if you'll only let me have an hour of your time —after that, you can turn me over to the cops."

"Can you get here, to my apartment?" she asked.

"If you want to turn me in, that's up to you."

A long silence now, and then she asked, "Are you armed, Cullen?"

"No."

"All right, I'm on West Eleventh Street." She spelled out the number slowly and carefully, only two digits, but slowly and carefully. "That's between Fifth and Sixth Avenue. Now I want you to understand this, Cullen: after we've talked, I will have to turn you over to the police. But I want very much to talk to you. Is it too far to walk?"

"No, I can walk."

"Yes, that would be better." She hesitated, then, "Cullen, we're being ridiculous. Walk over to Fifth Avenue and take the bus. It should be perfectly safe. No cabs."

"I'd rather walk," he said.

"All right, if you're not too tired."

He was too tired, terribly tired, but as he walked on downtown, he felt a little better. A door had opened up, a slim, precarious door, but a door nevertheless, and a few minutes ago there had been no door at all. He had no feeling about Virginia Selby that he could express: he didn't like her, he didn't dislike her; he had been suspicious of her and suspicious of her motives in approaching him, because as far as he could see, her motives made no sense. Yet, desperate, he had turned to her.

He remembered that he had once been part of a family, a father and a mother, an only child—odd in an Irish family—uncles, an Uncle Henry, Uncle Bert, Aunt Mary—there were cousins once, a grandmother—and now it was gone and all the connections were gone and he could hardly remember their names, and suppose he called one of them and said, This is Joseph. I've just killed a man and left his body in my apartment, and I need a place to hide and rest, a hole to go to ground—then what would be the response? Not hard to imagine: We know no Joseph, we'll call the cops, leave us alone.

The hell with it, he told himself, because everything had been turned on its head, and let's see what happens, and if I had any sense, I'd walk over to the precinct and turn myself in to Freedman, and in the end she'll do it for me.

It was one flight up in an old Village brownstone, and as she opened the door and ushered him in, he was taken aback by the bright, col-

273

orful, feminine quality of the room. As in many of the old brownstones, the main room was large and square, facing the street in this case, eighteen by eighteen feet, with a twelve-foot-high ceiling and beautiful old plaster molding, all of it painted white, as were the walls, and the main furniture being two large couches upholstered in bright flowered chintz on a yellow rug, and on each of two facing walls, large nonobjective paintings. There was color all over the room, and it held him, and to Virginia Selby there was something totally childlike in the manner of his standing inside the doorway, entranced by the room itself.

She said, "Sit down. You must be very tired."

"Yes, now that I've stopped moving."

She had a drink prepared. He took off his raincoat.

"Just drop it on the chair there."

He sat on another chair, not on one of the couches.

"This is brandy," she said. "I have coffee on the stove. Are you hungry?"

He shook his head. She handed him the glass of brandy and he tossed it down, choking a bit over the raw fire in his throat. Virginia went into her kitchen—in the passageway between front room and back room—and came back with a tray loaded with coffeepot, cream, cups, and a plate of cake. She set it down on a table near one of the couches.

"Sit here," she said, indicating the couch. He rose and moved slowly. She poured the coffee and then seated herself opposite him.

Cullen looked at the poured coffee and shook his head.

"I have beer. Would you rather have beer?"

He nodded, and she went into her kitchen and returned with an opened bottle and a glass. He poured the beer himself, with Virginia Selby sitting quietly and watching.

"You're not afraid of anything," he said, a note of respect in his voice.

"I'm afraid. But I'm not afraid of you, if that's what you mean."

"I guess so."

"Do you think I should be afraid of you?" she asked gently.

Instead of replying to that, Cullen said, "What can a DA do? I mean, can you arrest me?"

"I suppose I could. As a matter of fact, anyone can make a citizen's arrest. I'm not going to arrest you or call the cops."

"You said you might."

"That's what I said. I've changed my mind."

"Why?" he asked.

"Can't you just accept the fact that I've changed my mind?"

"Sure. But I don't want to accept anything anymore. I'm on their list, but until they get to me—"

"All right. I'll tell you why I changed my mind, Cullen. I'm at a point where nothing makes sense anymore and the shit is up to my ears. I've wanted to talk to you—no holds barred—since I saw the tape. Talk—and only to me, no tapes, no witnesses. I want to talk to you and I want you to talk to me. No holds barred, do you understand?"

"I'm trying."

"Where do you come from?" she asked gently. "I don't see you pushing dope. Dope is for pigs. You're not a pig."

"Why not? I went to a priest to confess. I'm a fallen Catholic as low as you can fall, and this was my first confession in damned many years. I started to confess to Father O'Healey, but in the situation there, it would have been just dumping on him, and it wasn't so important then, and it only became important after Father O'Healey died. You're a Catholic, you said?"

She nodded.

"You ever think about the saints?"

She shrugged. "Not enough to write home about, Cullen."

"Like me—until I met O'Healey. Then I began to ask myself, is he a saint? Now that's stupid!" he exclaimed.

"Not so stupid."

"No? Let me tell you something, Miss Selby—"

"I told you—Ginny."

"OK, Ginny, I'm trying to make a point." His mouth was dry. He took a long drink of the beer. "I'm trying to make this point—that I never talked like this to anyone in my life, and the only reason I do is because if I don't get this out of my system, I'll go crazy, because I'm not that different from all the other poor bastards who were in Nam, and I'm not asking for absolution."

"Oh, the hell with absolution, Cullen. We're talking. We're trying to exchange something."

"I know, I know, but I was full of this rotten feeling that I had murdered O'Healey, and you can take a man out of the church, but you don't take the church out of him, so I walked into Saint Peter's and tried to confess. There was an old priest in the booth, and I told him that I had murdered a priest—"

"You told him that?"

"Yeah, that's what I told him. I know I told it different on the tape, but in the confession booth, I just said it flat, because that's the way I felt, and I felt that if I tried to doctor it up or explain the details of what really happened,

the confession would become a lie. Do you understand that?"

"I think I do," Ginny agreed. "But wasn't he
upset? My God, you tell a priest you murdered
a priest—"

"I know. Yeah. But he was old. It didn't rat-
tle him. He only wanted to know whether I
believed in God, and he said that he couldn't
give me absolution unless I believed in God."

"Nothing like the church."

"Funny thing, I can't lie in the confession
booth. I can lie anywhere else. But I step in
there and that smell hits me, everywhere, it's
always the same smell, it's a smell as old as
time, as old as my time anyway, and I'm not
sure how that mixes with the fact that I'm not
lying there . . . Do you believe in God?"

"Sometimes," Ginny said, smiling.

"I did—until Nam. Even in Nam, up to a
point. You're scared enough, you don't believe
in God, you're just facedown in the mud,
scrabbling for your mother's tit and pleading
with whatever might be there not to let your
ass be cut to shreds by Charlie's rapid fire—no,
you don't believe or disbelieve, you're just
scared as shit. But we cut up a village with a
gunship I was flying, and then we put down
there and I walked through the place."

She wondered whether he was conscious of

the tears on his cheeks. "You don't have to talk about it. It was a long time ago."

"When I dream about it, it's now." He spoke slowly, as if he were clutching for each word before he spoke it. "There was nothing left alive in the village, and then I saw a little girl, maybe five or six years old, and I thought she was alive because she had a smile on her face and her eyes were open, but her dress was bloody, and when I lifted it, I saw that the rapid fire had cut her practically in half. You know, I have a daughter," he went on, flowing one thought into another. "She's five—I don't know, I haven't seen her in two years—God, I don't even know whether she remembers me or knows who I am."

"Lighten up," Ginny said. "We all have garbage that we carry—"

"No, no," he protested. "I'm trying to connect some things, and as much as I try, I get lost."

"Well, that happens. How many of us ever try to look inside ourselves and make some sense out of what we are and what we do? It's not easy."

"What I'm trying to say is that after I spoke to the old man at Saint Peter's—well, the next day I spilled it all out at the precinct house. It had to come out, because after I left the church I went over to Billy Sullivan's place and I got drunk. I'm not a good drinker. I saw too much Irish drinking when I was a kid to feel good about it, and after I finished air force training and became a pilot, I never touched the stuff. But I got awful damn drunk at Billy Sullivan's, and the same thing happened to me that always happens when I drink too much. I fell asleep and then I woke up and my stomach felt like the pit of hell and I vomited. And then I crawled out of the bathroom and I must have been totally zonked, because there was God or Jesus or something looking at me, and He said, "Report!" not angry but very firmly. So I said that I killed people. I went to a place that I had never been to or heard about even, and they put me into a gunship and I killed. I can't even count how many I killed and mostly they were village people in these lousy little hutches, women and kids and old people, and it was a lead-pipe cinch to knock them over, and there was always some stinking, motherfucken officer screaming at me to give him a good body count, and I don't give a fuck, he'd tell me, whether it's six days old or a hundred years old, you put it in the fucken body count. And that's how I came to go to the precinct house the next day and make the tape."

They sat in silence after that for a minute or so. Ginny felt as close to Cullen as if she had known him a lifetime. She wondered if he had that kind of a feeling about her.

"You don't have to cry," he said.

She hadn't realized that her eyes were heavy with tears. Cullen's remark was so gentle that she had to tell herself specifically that this heavy, powerful man, with his thick sloping shoulders and his thick neck—a football player's neck in her book—was neither a brute nor a fool, but a human being wounded so deeply, so terribly, that for him there could be no absolution or peace ever.

She shook her head. She hadn't realized, and now she went for a box of tissues.

Wiping her eyes, she tried to explain her tears, but did it poorly. "I'm supposed to be a hard-nosed DA," she said, "and I'm sitting here like a sentimental schoolgirl." She tried to change her approach. "Is the tape the truth?"

"Most of it. Captain Sanchez—he was on the chopper with me—he pushed the priest out, and then I shot him—"

"They let you have a gun?"

"Oscar carried the gun. No one knew he had it—except me."

"All right," Ginny said, "let's go on to another point. According to the evening news, you killed Kovach, called Lieutenant Freedman, and then fled the scene. I want to know what happened."

281

"I had a feeling about things, and I was scared—I mean, I had a sense that they would try to come after me." He told her about Sylvia Mendoza and Father Immelman.

"And you seriously think that they were killed because they knew about you and Father O'Healey?"

"And the dope. Maybe."

"But the tape. The cops saw the tape. I saw it. The DA saw it—OK, we pass that. Where did you get the gun that killed Kovach?"

"I can't tell you that. Anyway, it was a floater. You can pick up a floater any time you need a gun."

"All right, tell me about Kovach."

"There's nothing to tell. He came into my place and pulled his gun. I threw a beer bottle at him as he got off his first shot. He flinched, and the bullet seared my ribs. He threw two more shots at me as I ducked behind a chair, and then I got a clear shot with the Saturday night special, and I killed him. I didn't want to kill him. Oh, Christ, I never liked Oscar; he was a louse; but I didn't want to kill him. I never wanted to kill anyone—even in Nam. I killed, but I didn't want to."

"And what about the wound?"

"Nothing. I cleaned it and put a heavy bandage on it, and then I changed my shirt."

"Why didn't you wait for Freedman? The wound would help in a self-defense plea."

"Ah, come on, lady," Cullen said hopelessly, "an illegal gun . . . Who's to say who fired first?"

"Ah, Cullen, use your head," she begged him. "If your gun fired once and his gun fired three times—"

Cullen shrugged.

"You're giving up your life. Why? Right now, from what you tell me, there's only one safe place for you, and that's in jail. Do you have any money?"

"In the bank—yeah, enough."

"But you can't touch it, because the moment you do they pick you up. By now, they've covered the banks, and by nine in the morning they'll know where your money is. Cullen, Cullen, believe me."

"Why?" he wondered. "Why you—why anyone? Oh, Jesus, I'm so tired." He rolled over and stretched out on the couch, and she noticed how he winced with pain as he changed his position. "Lady," he said sleepily, "you're beautiful and I'm too damn tired to get up and kiss you. Thank you." A moment later, he was asleep.

She glowed with that, telling herself that no one had ever said a nicer thing to her; but that thought was concocted out of the same romantic illusion that had prompted her to put her job, her career, and her future on the line to help Cullen. After all, what did she know about Cullen? Or, for that matter, what did Cullen know about Cullen? He was still struggling out of the morass of war's stupidity, the idiocy of spending a million dollars on a trial to establish the guilt or innocence of a single killer, and then sending an army to kill a nation so that the body count could be measured against the body bags covered with the Stars and Stripes, which so proudly we hail at the twilight's last gleaming.

On the other hand, there was Father O'Healey, who had been thrown out of a helicopter, and was he now a saint in heaven, provided you believed in heaven, which Virginia Selby certainly did not? And what had it meant to a man like Cullen, who had slaughtered with professional ardor, to meet O'Healey, wearing sandals and a homespun robe, and ministering to the poorest of the poor, like a veritable Saint Francis, laying them to rest and closing their eyes after they had been mercilessly slain by clients of the U.S.A., armed with guns from the U.S.A. and an ideology from the land of the free and the home of the brave? Had something exploded in Cullen's mind? Or was it actually Jesus Christ, Son of the Lord God of Hosts, who had shared a living room with Cullen and had said to him, "Explain."

"What a burden to put on the poor sod!" Ginny whispered, and then, seeing how soundly he slept, decided to go out and buy some food for a decent meal. She scribbled a note in case he woke, and then left, closing the door quietly behind her. No one had thought of Virginia Selby as being either romantic or delusional, nor would she ever be able to explain a vague and undefinable feeling that had pervaded her since she saw the tape in Timberman's office. Was the face of Cullen her father's face? She wondered about that, trying desperately to insert sensible reasons into senseless behavior. In so many words, she was harboring a criminal and a murderer—whether he had spoken to Jesus or Saint Francis notwithstanding. Only his word said that he had killed Kovach in self-defense, and all she knew of that killing was what she had heard on a news program. She had put her life and career on the line.

She thought of a delicious steak, one of those fine, triangular cuts of meat, an inch thick, that when cooked melts like butter; but of course the butcher was closed. Henry's Deli was the only possibility, and she had him cut a half-inch-thick slice off the big roast of cold beef that was always sitting in his counter. A box of instant mix would give her mashed potatoes, and she bought a small apple pie and a six-pack of imported beer. Not in a hundred years would she herself eat such food, but the same illusion that led her to shelter Cullen also led her to believe that a man like Cullen would be pleased with food like this. She also bought a small can of gravy. She would warm the slice of roast beef so gently that its taste would not spoil, fix the potatoes, pour the hot gravy onto the potatoes, and warm two water rolls that she had in her breadbox. He would find the meal irresistible—and then?

What then?

There was no *and then.* "Joseph—" She had never called him by his first name, or Mr. Cullen. That was the cop thing, their rule of politeness for a collar. They could pick up the worst bum in the city with a string of priors a yard long, yet when they talked to the media, it became Mister bum. She had always called him Cullen. What had he called her? She tried to remember. He had called her Miss Selby—and then Ginny. She remembered how he had been in the restaurant, hard and tough and distant. Now he was something else. Or was he? Could someone like Cullen invent the sight of Jesus Christ standing in his living room? Drunks saw snakes and devils and things like that.

"Miss Selby," Henry said.

"Oh?"

"That'll be seventeen dollars and eighty cents."

She gave him a twenty-dollar bill. She stared at the change and then dropped it into her purse. She couldn't count; she couldn't focus. Back at her front door, she turned the key and entered quietly. The couch was empty.

"Well, he's in the bathroom," she said to herself as she put the bag down in the kitchen.

"Cullen, it's me, Ginny. I'm alone." When there was no response, she glanced into her bedroom—empty—and then faced the closed door of the bathroom.

"Cullen, are you in there?"

She opened the door and the bathroom was empty. For a long, long moment, she stood and surveyed the room. The toilet seat was up. He had used the toilet before he left, which meant nothing, but it had to be noted. Whenever men were in the place, they lifted the seat but did not replace it. Men were thoughtless that way.

Ginny closed the bathroom door and went back into the kitchen, where she took out of the bag the food she had bought at the deli, laying each item on the cabinet top. Then she picked up her garbage container and swept the food into it.

She went into the living room and sat on the couch where Cullen had sat, and began to cry. "Oh, fuck it," she thought, using language she would not speak aloud, "you're an asshole. You and your goddamn fantasies. Now you're up shit creek, and now you have nothing but grief. Where were you? they ask him. I was with Virginia Selby, who never called the cops. No, he wouldn't do that."

"Oh, my God," she said aloud, "what was I hoping? Sweet Mother of God, tell me."

A Conversation
with the Bishop

"**T**HE POINT IS," the bishop said to him, "that there is such a thing as liberation theology, and it is not anything the Holy Father regards with pleasure."

"No, I suppose not."

"The fact that you volunteer so easily, Father O'Healey, must not be held against you. Absolutely not. You are a man who thinks, and I think you have made an effort to understand yourself."

"I try."

"Do you meditate?" the bishop asked.

"Yes. That began at the seminary."

"In the Buddhist fashion, I presume?"

"Yes. It had taken hold at that time. I was

told that even in Ireland it became a sort of underground mode of prayer."

"Oh?" The bishop was curious. "Then you see it as prayer?"

"Yes. To me, prayer is only to listen, not to demand."

"Then tell me, Father O'Healey, what do you listen to?"

O'Healey smiled. "If I knew that, Bishop—"

"I have never tried it, sitting cross-legged as you do, and I'm not sure that at my age my legs would consent. If I were to ask you whether your meditation connects in any way with your willingness to go to Honduras, how would you answer me?"

"With great difficulty," O'Healey replied, breaking into laughter. "With very great difficulty."

"Of course, you grew up Francis Luke O'Healey. The Irish pull no punches when it comes to naming a poor, helpless child. Have you become a Buddhist? The Zen Buddhists say that he who knows cannot talk, while he who talks does not know."

"No, sir. I'm still a Catholic priest."

"My secretary," the bishop said, "who is infected in a similar fashion, insists that one can be a Catholic Zen Buddhist or a Jewish Zen Buddhist or a Protestant Zen Buddhist."

"There's a point there," O'Healey admitted,

"since the word *Zen* means only to sit in meditation, and I'm not sure that it asks for any more."

"You went to a Jesuit seminary?"

"Yes."

"I thought so. Now let's get back to this business of liberation theology. Let me read you something." The bishop picked up a magazine, opened it, and read, " 'We deal with a question of suffering, which can also be termed a question of pain, and I have never heard a suggestion that a Catholic priest can turn his back on human suffering and pain and remain a priest of the church in anything but name—' "

"I wrote that," Father O'Healey said.

"Of course. Nevertheless, I want to read it to you and I want you to listen to it."

"If you wish."

"I continue: 'Time after time, I have heard the argument that a human being remains a human being, rich or poor; and while I may dispute the absolute validity of such a position, I can accept it generically. We are children of God. I have never doubted that, but I do doubt that pain and suffering among the rich can ever be measured against pain among the poor. The latter is too much to measure against anything but itself. Thus I see the mission to the poor and the oppressed as being the highest calling to which a priest can aspire;

and if the poor are oppressed and if their condition derives from their oppression, must a priest abandon them? Can he still minister to them and not be a part of their struggle against their oppressor?' " The bishop finished reading and looked at Father O'Healey questioningly.

"Unto Caesar what is Caesar's and unto God what is God's?" Father O'Healey asked.

"It is Holy Writ."

"I can't imagine God partitioning things—the Almighty parceling out His turf and responsibility."

"I always have trouble with Jesuits," the bishop admitted.

"Anyway, it's inconceivable to me that Jesus could have said such a thing." Then O'Healey added, "I like you and respect you, Bishop, and I wish you did not find me so troublesome."

"You are troublesome," the bishop admitted. "When you marched with the gays, the cardinal was very put out, and your various speeches in the freeze movement—the media, you know."

"One can hardly scream quietly."

"Yes, but one can pray quietly."

Father O'Healey nodded. He tried to practice humility, but it was not his best thing.

"You must understand," the bishop said,

"that if most of our priests were of your point of view, the church might tremble to its very foundation."

Which might be a very good thing, Father O'Healey thought, but said nothing aloud.

"On the other hand," the bishop admitted, "if I were to send a priest down there who possessed the opposite point of view, he might sequester himself in the Church of the Apostles, where there are always soldiers, as I hear, and very few worshippers. I am not quite a fool about all this, Father O'Healey, and I know that the poor farmers and Indians have fled into the hills, and Father Veste felt that his mission there was meaningless, and that the opposition to the murder squads was Marxist, and he had the excuse of his mother's illness—and of course I want to be fair to him."

"Marxist?"

"Father O'Healey, I am quite aware that the only people in this country who claim to understand Marxism are the Jesuits."

"I did take a course that included Marxism."

"I am sure you did," the bishop said a bit testily, "but I am in no mood to argue the question."

"No, of course not. But please, we must consider how on earth a group of illiterate peasants who have seen their crops stolen, their families beaten and murdered—we must consider how they could possibly be Marxists. They can't read. They have never heard of Karl Marx. They don't know that the Soviet Union exists. They only know that unless they resist, they will die."

"Have you ever been in Honduras, Father O'Healey?"

"No, but I've spoken to people who have been there. I worked in Mexico for a year. My Spanish is excellent. I am not going into this with my eyes closed, but I must be honest with you. I will go where the people are, and if it means being with a guerrilla movement, then I will be there. I don't know how else I can serve."

Rather sadly, the bishop said, "I won't stand in your way. I do wish things were otherwise. Our government has troops in Honduras, and the country is our ally and is ranked as one of the nations of the free world—and this makes things difficult to explain."

"I appreciate that."

"I almost wish you had not told me of your intentions. On the other hand, how can I deny what you say?"

That was eight years ago. Now, eight years later, the bishop was told that a New York City policeman, a Lieutenant Melvin Freedman, was on the phone, calling from New York. The bishop, in his study, picked up the telephone and asked Lieutenant Freedman what he could do for him.

"I have been informed," Freedman began, and then stopped and said, "Do I call you father? Or what? I'm not Catholic."

"Whatever you wish. It doesn't really matter."

"Good enough, Bishop. Now, I have been informed that you had a working relationship with Father Francis O'Healey and that you were at least in part responsible for his going to Central America."

"Where did you get this information?"

"I have an old friend who's a cop, or let us say a detective who is assigned to the cardinal when something needs protection. He got the information through the cardinal."

"I see. Yes, it's true. Father O'Healey and I worked together here in San Francisco. It was clearly his desire to go to Central America, and he was sent there. Certainly, he did not take the step against the wishes of the church, if that's what you're after?"

"No, not that."

"Then you must tell me what your interest is. We've had no word from Father O'Healey for some weeks now, and we are deeply concerned."

"No word at all? Please, sir, I'll explain in a moment what our interest is. If you have any doubts about who I am, you can obtain our precinct number from Information and call us back."

"That won't be necessary, Lieutenant Freedman. I'm old enough and possibly wise enough to recognize the voice of an honest man."

"Thank you. Now, about Father O'Healey—no word at all?"

"No, and that worries us terribly. We made inquiries of the church in Honduras and of the Honduran embassy in Washington. The embassy claims to know nothing about him or his whereabouts, and the church says they heard only that he was back or on his way back to the States."

"Have you spoken to the State Department?"

"Yes. They have no knowledge of where he might be or what may have happened to him. We fear the worst, and your call troubles me. Please—if you know more—"

"In a moment. If you will permit me—about letters, sir. Have you had any letters from him?"

"Oh, yes. Yes, indeed."

"And the last letter? When did you receive it?"

"I think it was September fifth."

"Could you make a copy of it and mail it to me? I'll give you the address."

"Yes. I see no reason not to, Lieutenant. Now please, tell me—is he dead?"

"Now understand that this is hearsay, but we do have some indication that he may have been killed."

"What kind of information?"

"We have a witness who says that Father O'Healey was pushed out of a helicopter to his death."

"God help him," the bishop whispered. "What a terrible thing! Is there any real evidence?"

"I suppose you could say that evidence of a murder is not real until you find the body, and this is probably a body that we'll never find."

"But you believe it?"

"I'm afraid I do," Freedman said.

"Lieutenant Freedman, please understand me. I must press you. This is a man with family, a mother still alive, two sisters—and aunts and uncles. What am I to tell them? If Father O'Healey is alive and I tell them he's dead—that would be a terrible thing, don't you see?"

"Yes, but I think that's up to you. I felt that someone out in San Francisco had to know the truth, inasmuch as there is any truth, and that led me to you. I could imagine the worry and speculation at your end."

"Yes, and good of you. But tell me why. Why would anyone kill him in such an awful way?"

"Well, he was with the poor people, the peons or whatever you call them, and they never get a fair shake, and I guess he pushed too hard."

"But he was only a priest. He didn't carry arms. What could he possibly do?"

"I don't know. Maybe be in the wrong place at the wrong time."

"But Honduras is an ally of ours," the priest argued. "I read that we have four thousand American troops there. Why would we let them kill priests?"

Freedman had no acceptable answers. He knew some answers, but how could a New York cop convince the bishop that his nation, the cop's nation, the bishop's nation, fostered murder squads and armed them with the latest weapons and never interfered with their license to kill anyone who disputed their right to steal, rape, and murder, and in return were paid off with millions of dollars worth of cocaine, brought into and sold in a country where such acts were against the law?

He put down the phone. Obviously, he could not say to the bishop, "That fucken son of a bitch CIA."

But when he repeated his conversation to Ramos, the detective shrugged and said, "I'm sure the bishop knows why. Up there in San Francisco, the church has turned helping those poor bastards in Central America into a religion. I sent them fifty dollars. Funny, but the church is in the center of it. I never thought it would be."

"What spooks us? Are they reds?" Freedman persisted.

"That's what the bullshit says. Reds. Marxists. What the hell is a Marxist, Lieutenant?"

"A Russian, I suppose. A communist—people in Africa. I read there are three or four countries in Africa supposed to be Marxist. The state owns everything or something like that—how the hell do I know?"

"You're a college graduate."

"Yeah, stand up and cheer."

"Father O'Healey's people? Come on, they don't even know what the word means," Ramos said.

Then the copy of O'Healey's last letter to the bishop arrived. Freedman read it, and he passed it to Ramos to read.

"My dear old friend," it began, "I write this with a heavy heart and with no assurance that it will ever reach you. They are making it more difficult each day to send letters out of the country to the States. We have a way to get our mail through, but I cannot explain it. It's a totally new way, and if I described it, it would put certain people in jeopardy. Be it said at least that I can write without restraint, without fear.

"If I say that I have had a tragic day, I also feel that I am repeating myself. I have tried in previous letters not to involve you or the church, but I think that things have undergone a qualitative change. Perhaps the presence of so many American troops here and a sense of America's need for Honduras in its war against Nicaragua have emboldened the worst elements in the government.

"Usually, when the death squads decide to attack a village that they have specified as being Marxist—a totally lunatic term for these poor, illiterate Indians—they act against the men and the boys. If the men are trapped in the village, they are executed, so they have worked out a way of signaling that gives a village advance notice that it is in jeopardy. If the murder squad is not too large, the armed men will fight it; otherwise, the men and boys hide in the bush. Until now, the murder squads have been content with knocking the women about and smashing things and a certain amount of raping, although the most attractive women will hide in the bush with the men.

"The day before yesterday, I was in a village, baptizing three newborn babes, when word came that we were the target of a murder squad. Since there were only three rifles and one pistol in the village, the better part of valor made the men decide to hide in the bush. I went with them, and we took every boy who was over eight years old. We were about a mile from the village, crouched in the jungle growth, when we heard the sound of shooting. Some of the men wanted to rush back immediately; others counseled caution. Everyone was terribly disturbed, and when we felt it was safe to return, the village was silent except for the barking of the dogs. When we came into the village, we discovered that every living soul in the village was dead, old women, young women, boys and girls and the infants I had just baptized. They had been executed by the light rapid-fire carbines that we have flooded the military with. One infant I had baptized, eleven days old, had twelve bullet holes in her tiny body, the little corpse so ripped to pieces that it bore no resemblance to a human being.

"If my hand shakes and my writing is poor, consider what I have witnessed—done to these poor people by the will of some giant power, many miles away and even more distant in terms of their understanding. For a whole day, I gave the last rites and helped to dig graves and then I spent the night in prayer, trying to find God and know what one of His priests should do.

"Yours in Christ, Francis O'Healey."

After finishing the letter, Ramos stared in silence at Freedman. They were sitting in Freedman's tiny office at the precinct house, both of them silent now and looking at each other the way two people at a funeral, both of them close to and beloved of the deceased, might look at each other.

Minutes went by, and then Freedman, burdened increasingly with a sense of this priest who had so strangely come into their lives, said to Ramos, "Why didn't the bishop give the letter to the press?"

"Maybe he did."

"Come on! You tell me no paper would publish this? That's bullshit."

"Then he didn't give it to the press!" Ramos snapped. "What do you want from me?"

"Cool it, Ramos. I'm trying to understand something."

"So am I."

"You're Catholic. I thought maybe you'd know something I don't know."

"What?"

"How the hell do I know!" Freedman exclaimed. "I don't even know what the hell drove him down there."

Ramos shook his head hopelessly. "Yesterday," he said, "I saw a list of names in the paper of kids who went down to Nicaragua.

They're called witnesses for peace. Half the names were Jewish. I haven't been in a church since I was married, and that's more years back than I want to think about. I have bad dreams about O'Healey too, but a cop has bad dreams about a lot of things. I do my work, I draw my pay, and someday I'll take my pension and put a gun in my mouth and blow my brains out, so don't ask me to comment on the condition of society, because I only got one word for it—it stinks."

Lieutenant Freedman found it hard to disagree with that.

Monty

ON THE TELEPHONE, Sheila said to Freedman, "Mel, I got a date tonight. I told you that. I got a dinner date with a buyer from Minneapolis—"

"A buyer!" Freedman exploded, loud enough for the men in the squad room to hear him and pretend not to hear him. "You always said you wouldn't touch one of those bastards with a ten-foot pole."

"Well, there you are," Sheila said, "and now listen to me, Mel. I am not your wife, period. This is why I stopped being your wife. You made me crazy with your goddamn suspicions. Now I am not married to you. I could fuck the whole lousy shmata business, and it's no skin off your back—"

"Can I get a word in?"

"No! Because I haven't finished. It just happens that this buyer is Mr. Sam Ginzberg, and he's seventy-three years old, and he runs the best store in Louisville, Kentucky, and he caters to all that crappy horse crowd, and he still does his own buying, and he does nothing but talk about his damn twelve grandchildren, and he always takes me to dinner so he can ask questions about the New York cops, and he bores the life out of me, but he's sweet, and the boss says if I ever tell him I divorced a crud like you, I'm fired, and we go to dinner at a place called Ratner's downtown, where they don't serve any meat, because he's very kosher, period. Furthermore, we dine—you should excuse the expression—at six-thirty and he's back in his hotel at nine, because in New York he misses his afternoon nap."

"Then you're free at nine-thirty?" Freedman asked pleadingly.

"What!"

Lowering his voice, Freedman said, "What did I do wrong? Haven't I behaved decently every time I saw you? We had fun. We could still take in a movie after dinner. Or just watch TV. Maybe only for an hour or two—"

"Come on, Mel," she said. "You know what happens when we get together. We live in the age of AIDS. I haven't been with another man since we broke up—oh, the hell with it. Better come by at ten. Mr. Ginzberg might be bursting with energy tonight."

Freedman was a reasonably happy man as he left the cubicle he called his office and entered the squad room. George Jones looked up from a report he was writing, and said, "Lieutenant, can you tell us how come that tape Cullen made never hit the newspapers?"

"Or the box?" Leary put in.

"Did you ask the sergeant?"

"Ramos said to ask you."

"He was right. You asked me."

"Do we get an answer?" Jones said.

"No." With that, Freedman left. He had to do things—take a shower, shave, change his clothes, eat something, read the papers, try to work out his continuing approach to Sheila, whom he had every intention of remarrying one day. When the time finally approached and he rang her doorbell, she was wearing a pale yellow robe and her black hair was tied at her neck. She had cleaned her face and removed all makeup. That was Sheila's ploy. Her skin was perfect; she was one of those rare women who looked better without makeup, and being five feet and ten inches in height, she could kiss Freedman on his own level.

"Did you eat?" she asked him.

"Sort of."

"Sort of. You know what kills cops—not bullets but the lousy junk food they live on. Come on in the kitchen."

In the kitchen, she put together a salad of lettuce, cucumber, and tomatoes, toast, butter —the last thing on earth that Freedman desired at that moment. But he forced himself to eat without complaint or demur. Then they sat over coffee.

"You're different," Sheila admitted.

"How?"

"I don't know. You're just different."

"About AIDS," he said, "I want you to know something."

"I don't have to know anything."

"I want you to know it. After we split, I never slept with another woman. I'm not lying. I wouldn't lie about something like this."

"I know you're not lying."

"If I seem a little crazy, it has nothing to do with you and me. It's what I'm up against."

"We talked about that," Sheila said gently. "Give it up, Mel. Forget it."

"You know, I walked into rooms where my feet sucked up blood, and four, sometimes five dead bodies, all cut up the way those demented dopers do it, and I could go home and go to bed. This thing sucks at me."

"Why? What's so different about it?"

"I'm Jewish," he said.

"What else is new?"

"I don't know this kind of shit. I don't understand it. Just tell me something. You're a Catholic. When I told your father that we wanted to get married, he damn near cut my head off. All right, I know I bored you with all this crap before, but try to help me. Here's a priest. I don't know that much about priests, but they live easy. All right, they give up on a wife and kids. A lot of people do. But they eat three square meals a day, they get respect, and nobody can fire them if they do what they're supposed to do. But here's a priest who gives up everything to go down there to the asshole of creation to be with a lot of illiterate peons, no pay, beans when he can get them; otherwise he goes hungry—he gets shot at, nobody gives a damn about him, nobody thanks him, and he ends up being dumped out of a helicopter at eight hundred feet—and my government calls him a red and antes up for the guns that shoot the shit out of these peons of his, and not only that, but Washington supplies the helicopter, which has to cost maybe five, maybe ten million dollars, for him to be tossed out of."

Sheila spread her arms hopelessly. "What do you want, Mel, a lecture about politics, which I don't know a damn thing about?"

"No. I want to know about priests."

"There are all kinds of priests. What do you

313

want me to tell you? There was a priest had his hands up my drawers when I was thirteen years old."

"No, you're kidding. You never told me that before."

"So I never told you. I don't knock priests the way some people do. There are all kinds. You ever heard about Saint Francis?"

"Of course I heard about Francis of Assisi. I'm not ignorant, just stupid."

"You know, it wouldn't break your back to say something nice about yourself. You got a low self-opinion. That's the trouble with you and you don't know it."

"Sheila, please knock that off."

"OK. I'll tell you about Saint Francis. He's a kid who's got everything, comes from a good home, father has money, wears fancy clothes, nothing to worry about—and then he dumps it all, changes his fancy clothes for rags, and dedicates his life to the poor."

"That was a long time ago."

"Seven, eight hundred years."

"This is 1987," Freedman said. "I don't think it fits—not with O'Healey. I mean, it's all too different, Sheila. O'Healey's a priest. I never heard of reds who couldn't live without a priest. You know, you're a cop, you begin to think that everything's bullshit because most of it is, but there's got to be a little left that isn't."

"So ask yourself how it feels to be married to a cop."

"Oh, hell. I'm tired and I love you. That's not bullshit. Maybe that's the only thing in the world that makes any sense. Let's go to bed."

At half-past four in the morning, the telephone in Sheila's bedroom rang. When it was his bedroom as well as Sheila's, the telephone was on his side of the bed. After he left, Sheila moved it over to the other side, and now Freedman had to stumble around the bed in the dark, feel for the telephone, and then knock it off the night table. It fell with a resounding crash. Sheila awoke with a scream of fright, and he had to shout into the telephone "Hold on" while he put his arm around Sheila to reassure her that everything was all right. Then he picked up the telephone, and it was Ramos, saying, "What the hell's going on?"

"Nothing. I dropped the telephone. It frightened Sheila."

"You can say that again," Sheila said, her voice shaking. "I'd almost forgotten the joy of being a cop's wife and waking up in the middle of the night."

"What's up?" he asked Ramos.

"Cullen's dead."

"Oh, no!"

"They caught up to him and put four bullets into him."

"Poor bastard," Freedman said, his voice so mournful that Sheila, who had turned on the bedside light, asked, her voice full of fear, "What happened, Mel? What happened?"

"They killed Cullen."

"Oh, Lord, no," Sheila whimpered, like a little girl. It got to her. It got to everyone involved in the case.

"Where?" he asked Ramos.

"On the sidewalk right outside the church. I think they had the place staked out. They were hunting him, and I think they figured he'd go to the church. Where else could he go?"

"I'll meet you there. Ten minutes," Freedman said.

Freedman was naked, his tall, long-muscled body, with its pale white skin and orange hair, sort of funny, clownish, causing Sheila to smile as he struggled with his clothes, not a graceful man, not at all a graceful man.

"Can I make some coffee?" she asked him.

"No, I got to get over there."

"A few minutes," wondering what difference a few minutes might make. Cullen was dead. She had never seen Cullen, but she had grown up with an Irish father and an Italian mother, so she could visualize Cullen, or create him to her own specifications.

"No," Freedman said, putting his arms around her. "Forgive me, baby." He had always asked her forgiveness when the telephone awakened her in the middle of the night. He bolted out the door and Sheila stretched out in bed, wondering whether she could fall asleep or whether it made more sense to get up and shower and call it a night. It was almost five o'clock.

At the church, Ramos was waiting for him, and there was one of their own prowl cars still there and another from Manhattan South. Freedman had always protested the way prowl cars piled up at the scene of a crime when the crime was finished, and he sent his car away. Ramos had his collar turned up, and he was rubbing his hands and talking to Father White, who was in slippers with a robe wrapped around him.

"It's all in hand," Brady, from Manhattan South, told Freedman. "Four shots, three in the body, and a finish shot in the head. Totally professional."

"Where's the body?" Freedman asked.

"The wagon wouldn't wait. You know how those guys are. Why don't you come over to the house and talk about it?"

"What's to talk? The man's dead."

"Yeah. You know, Freedman, it seems to me that you know a hell of a lot more about Cullen than we do. We're on the same side. Why don't you be a nice guy and share the knowledge?"

"Talk to the zone commander. When he says, Freedman, go share the knowledge, I'll share. Until then, I don't know any more about Cullen than you do."

"That's sweet. That's very sweet."

"I'm a sweet guy," Freedman said.

It was cold and it was beginning to rain. The Manhattan South cops took themselves off, and Father White said, "Lieutenant, why don't you and Sergeant Ramos come inside to the kitchen? I'll cook up some hot coffee and toast some bagels and we'll all feel better than standing here in the rain."

They sat in the kitchen of the old rectory beside the church, a kitchen hardly changed from the way it had been half a century ago, old iron-and-enamel stove, long wooden table, tin sinks, refrigerator crowned by its cooling mechanism, and beautiful Dutch tiles on the floor. The old housekeeper, cross at having been awakened at this hour, put up the coffee in a big enamel percolator and left Father White to do the rest. He toasted the bagels and brought out butter and cream cheese. Freedman, suddenly very hungry, found himself eating the bagels with gusto while Ramos drank black coffee.

"Father White," Freedman said, "would you go down to Honduras or El Salvador or some such place to be a priest for the poor who lived there, even if they were in revolt against their own government?"

Ramos looked at Freedman strangely, and Father White, taken somewhat aback, stared a long moment at Freedman before he answered, "I didn't think—well, I thought you'd ask me about poor Cullen. It did happen here, outside our door. I heard the shots and I got outside as quickly as I could—"

"Quickly? You ought to have more sense than that, Father. If you had gotten outside before they took off, you'd be in the same morgue as Joe Cullen."

"They were in a car, you know," the priest said. "I got outside just as the car was turning the corner. There was nothing else moving on the street."

"He rushed out there, Lieutenant," Ramos explained, "to give the man the last rites."

Freedman brooded over that while White spread cream cheese on another bagel and handed it to the lieutenant. "About Honduras," Freedman said, chewing, his mouth full of food.

"Well, it's an odd question," Father White

said, preferring to turn the conversation back to the crime. "Mr. Cullen—"

"Let's drop Mr. Cullen for a moment, Father. There's nothing we can do for him. About Honduras."

"Well, that's a difficult question. A priest can't just walk out of his duty to fulfill some romantic dream. Have I thought about it? Well, I must admit that I have. After the Maryknoll nuns were raped and murdered by the death squads of El Salvador, I was properly horrified that our government could support the men who did it, and to be truthful, I did have romantic fantasies about going there —especially after the same group murdered the archbishop—and perhaps ministering to the guerrilla movement; but that must have been the fantasy of hundreds of priests, and you see, I am here in Chelsea. But how does this possibly connect with Cullen's death?"

Ignoring the priest's question, Freedman insisted, "Why? Why? Not revenge—you wouldn't think that way as a priest?"

"Oh, no, surely not revenge. But my feeling was that these men and women had sanctified themselves in the service of Christ. Did He not say to go among the poor and lowly to preach His grace? To bring comfort to the dying? If the truth be told, I say a mass on a Sunday, and there are a dozen people in the church—"

Ramos, becoming increasingly uncomfortable at Freedman's insistence, said, "Let's go, Lieutenant."

Outside, they got into Ramos's car, and Freedman said, "What got you, Hosea?"

"You ask for something he can't give."

"What's that?"

"Look, Lieutenant, my father came here from Puerto Rico in 1933. He wasn't some ignorant kid. He finished high school, and he'd had two years of college in Puerto Rico. He majored in chemistry and biology, and even with the Depression, he got himself a job in a medical lab and he was making forty dollars a week, damn good money at that time. Then the Spanish Civil War broke out and he goes and joins the Abraham Lincoln Brigade to fight against Franco. And he wasn't a commie. I ask him why; he can't answer me. It's something deep inside, and it was deep inside that priest, and maybe it's why the good guys don't disappear. Ah, Jesus, I don't like to talk to priests. They make me nervous."

Ramos drove them to the morgue. The first gray hint of morning was in the air. The rain had stopped and the clouds were breaking up. It would be a cold, clean November day, with blue sky overhead.

But not for Cullen, Freedman thought.

"I swear I do not know what the hell we're doing here. I hate morgues."

"I want to see him."

"OK, OK, you want to see him. You know, Mel, you're crazy, I'm crazy. Every cop in this city is crazy. You want to see a dead man. Say hello for me."

"You're in a sweet mood."

"They woke me at four. What kind of mood do you want?"

The people at the morgue were not happy either. It was the end of the night shift at a place where nobody laughed very much. "I thought he belonged to Manhattan South," the morgue attendant said as he pulled out the locker.

"We own a little piece of him."

"Funny," the morgue attendant said. He uncovered the body.

"Forty-five," Ramos said. "Not nice."

Freedman turned away after a single look. Cullen's head was open from the heavy .45 caliber impact. It had been taped together for cosmetic purposes. His face, thankfully, as Freedman thought, was uninjured. His eyes were closed, his skin white as a cotton sheet.

"Seen enough?" Ramos asked.

"I bet there's no claim on the body," Freedman said once they were back on the street. "Did he have any relatives? Did he say? Jesus, what a fucked-up society we are! No families anymore, just bits of flesh floating around."

"Lovely. You're a prince of good cheer. Do you know something? Next week is Thanksgiving."

"Yeah. Let's have some coffee. I'm cold. I rushed out without a coat. I don't know. Did I leave it at Sheila's?"

They went into a lunchroom for coffee and Danish, and Freedman called Sheila. It was seven forty-five now, and Freedman thought surely Sheila would be dressing to go to work. "What time is it?" she asked sleepily.

"Honey, did I wake you? It's almost eight."

"Drop dead," she said tiredly, and cut the connection.

"I'm no good," Freedman said to Ramos. "I'm so tired I can't think straight. Drive me home and I'll get an hour of sleep before I hit the house. How about you?"

"I'm all right."

In his furnished room, Freedman set the alarm for an hour, kicked off his shoes, and fell facedown on the bed, fully clothed. He was asleep in a moment, and it felt like an instant later when the alarm went off. He showered and shaved, put on a fresh pair of gray flannels, shook out his brown tweed jacket in which he had just fallen asleep, and donned a fresh blue Oxford shirt and knitted tie. He was neither original nor creative in his choice of wardrobe. It was nine-thirty when he arrived at the precinct house, and he was properly chilled.

Virginia Selby was waiting in his office, and he nodded and said, "Morning, Ginny." He was not crazy about the district attorney's end of law and order, nor about the personnel who ran it.

"Joe Cullen's dead," she said.

"That's right."

"Last night?" trying to keep her voice even.

"Like four o'clock in the morning."

"Were you there?"

"After it happened. All we can make out of it is that they had the church staked out, and when he turned up, they killed him. Four shots, three in the body, one in the head. The priest in the rectory was awakened by the shots and he ran to the front of the church in time to see the car driving away. To make the time fit, it meant they got out of the car to leave one in his head. That's professional. Also to clinch the ID, and that's also very professional. I don't know what pros are in town because I just got to my office. With things like this, they usually bring in someone from outside." Freedman studied her narrowly. "What's your interest? Did Timberman send you up to talk to me?"

"I saw the tape, Lieutenant. Timberman played it for me and Morty Cohen."

Freedman nodded and waited. He had long ago discovered that when someone is uncertain whether or not to speak, silence is most effective.

Finally, Ginny said, "He went to the church because he had no other place to go. He couldn't go home after he killed Kovach. Do you believe his story about Kovach?"

Shrugging: "What difference does it make now?"

It made a difference to Virginia Selby. She closed her eyes for a moment, searching in her mind, trying to make a connection with the Church of Saint Peter the Rock. "But why did he go to the church? I mean that church."

Freedman spelled it out, the confession and Father White's theory that Immelman had been murdered. Virginia listened, and when he had finished, she sat in silence.

And Freedman waited. He had work to do, cases that were overdue, assignments to give out, and still he waited.

Softly, Ginny asked him, "Can they hear us?" nodding at the detectives in the squad room.

"If we talk loud enough."

Even more softly, "Mr. Timberman didn't send me. I came here on my own."

"Yes?"

"Aren't you going to ask me why?"

"You're an important DA, Ginny. Someday you'll have Timberman's job."

"You think so?"

"A lot of people think so." Their eyes met. "So you'd better consider carefully whatever you were going to tell me."

"All right." She closed her eyes tightly and remained that way, with her eyes closed, for a few seconds. Then she said bluntly, "I felt something for Joe Cullen. Do you understand?"

Freedman waited.

"Nothing that he knew or returned. I just felt something for him, and when I heard this morning that he had been killed, I wept."

Freedman wondered whether in all the world anyone else wept for Joe Cullen.

"That's all," Ginny said, deciding that it was enough and that there was no need to speak of their two meetings. He was dead; it simply did not matter. There was no way in the world that she could explain to Freedman or anyone else that her heart went out to him as it had not gone out to any other man. She could not explain it to herself. Love is something not easily explained on any level, and if Virginia Selby had tried to define the bit of unrequited light that had entered into the world of horrors where she made her life and living, she would have made a total fool out of herself—which, she told herself, she truly was.

"You're wondering why I came here?"

"Sort of—yes."

"I have a lot of respect for you, Lieutenant. I think you're smart and decent and sensitive."

"Flattery will get you everywhere," Freedman said, smiling.

He had a nice smile, Ginny decided, not like Cullen's, but then she had never met a man whose smile danced all over his face, as Cullen's smile did.

"I'll tell you why I came here. Very simple, Lieutenant. I want you to get the man who killed Cullen. I want you to bring him in, and you and I will make one of those unbreakable cases, and I swear on my mother's grave that I'll put him away."

The swivel chair Freedman sat in was one of his precious possessions. He swiveled around now to look directly into the squad room, and then he swiveled back to face Virginia Selby. He had once had a fantasy that if he and Sheila ever had a kid—a little girl, preferably —he would bring her here and spin her in his desk chair. He was sure she would love it.

"That's what you want," he said.

"You can do it."

"Ginny, no one man killed Cullen. You're

not only asking for the impossible, you're asking me to go where angels fear to tread."

"You're not an angel, Mel."

"You'd better believe it. I'm a New York City cop, and if I even look the wrong way or even push one of the scumbags we get in here, I got the zone commander up here beating my ear off."

"My heart doesn't bleed for you."

Freedman grinned. "If I could make miracles and find this gang of high-class thugs who are bringing in the cocaine with Washington's blessing, what on earth makes you think you could prosecute them?"

"Find them and bring me some evidence, and if I can't get a conviction I'll throw in the towel."

"That's dumb. Look, I felt something about Cullen. I've been trying to figure out that whole act—Cullen and Father O'Healey and the peons and the dope and whatever lot of bastards in our government are running the act, the CIA, the White House, the Justice Department, the army, or some bunch of demented mavericks—but whoever it is, it's not one man."

"Then get them all, Mel."

"Bless your heart," Freedman said. "Who knows!"

328

She left, and Ramos came in and asked him, "What did she want?"

"Miracles. She wants me to bring in Cullen's killers. She's determined."

"Why?"

"God only knows. I will tell you something, Hosea: this is not only a world I never knew, but one that I have little desire to know. It is not good for a cop, who is told to wear his uniform so that he can show up at one of those fancy funerals they give a cop who is shot by some crazed drug dealer, to know that his own sweet government blesses the drugs and the dealers."

"Right on. But what makes it personal with her?"

"I'm not sure I understand that end of it. She had something for Cullen."

"She never knew Cullen—or did she?"

"God knows." He glanced into the squad room. It was empty now.

"They're all out," Ramos said.

"Did you write up last night?"

"I'll do it now."

"Good. Meanwhile, I'll think."

At noon, Freedman was still thinking, and Ramos had finished his report, interviewed a hysterical woman who claimed her cat had been stolen, and restrained himself from killing a dealer who had sold crack to a ten-year-old black kid, who had gone into convulsions and died. "Put this scum into the number one cell, and take off his shoes and socks and belt and strip him to the waist, and write him down as suicidal," Ramos told the cops who had brought him in. The number one cell in the basement had not been used in years. It was icy cold, rat-infested, with at least an inch of filthy water on the sunken floor. Since it was never used, it had no cot.

Freedman, meanwhile, was thinking about how this country, his country, used to be. His father would tell him stories about New York in those days, in the 1920s, when the population of the United States was about seventy million, when a drug was medicine, and when kids could walk the streets at three o'clock in the morning without fear. New York, in his father's memories, was as close to paradise as a city could be. Freedman didn't trust memories. He had heard too many witnesses remember things that never were. Yet like his father, he remembered a New York of his childhood, when he was a kid in the 'fifties. Was it as bad as now? And what of the next ten years—the 'nineties?

Meanwhile, the simple lunatic day-to-day routine of a small, unimportant Lower West Side police precinct had been interrupted by the high forces of the nation. When a crime happened on the street, and the cops looked for witness, the almost universal response was "I don't want to get involved." Was that the way he felt? Freedman wondered. What do I love, aside from Sheila, who regards me as an unreconstructed pain in the ass. "I love my country" is what they all say. But define it: a cop treads a turf made of feces; that would have to be extracted from what you love. Consider the South Bronx or Bedford-Stuyvesant or Hell's Kitchen, where few enough sing "My country, 'tis of thee, sweet land of liberty," or consider Los Angeles, where there are at least five thousand doped-up gang members ready to do mayhem, or consider my own little island in the universe, where an old priest could be smothered to death, or a hooker stitched all over with an ice pick.

Yes, a tall, good-looking lady named Sylvia Mendoza, who made men happy for a few minutes or at least released them from the quiet misery of their daily lives.

Sylvia Mendoza. He was thinking about her, a slight smile on his lips, when Ramos looked into his office and suggested that since Jones and Leary were back at their desks, Freedman and Ramos could go to lunch.

"And no garbage. I am sick to death of the garbage we eat," Ramos said. "They brought in that bastard who sold the crack to the kid who died. I put him in number one."

"Number one?"

"Don't bleed for him," Ramos said. "You bleed to much for the garbage we collect."

"It's a hell of a world you paint. We eat garbage, we collect garbage, and the mayor sits and worries about how to get rid of the garbage of eight million people. It's the age of garbage. A ten-year-old kid buys crack and dies. When I was a cop in uniform, I was assigned to cover one of those diplomatic affairs that come out of the UN, and this Central American diplomat walks by, and believe me, I knew the face, and he's under suspicion of murder and drug trafficking and we can't touch him—"

"I think a cop goes crazy enough without trying to figure it out, so let's go to lunch, Lieutenant, and eat some decent Italian food at Marco's."

"Diplomatic immunity—what happened to the tape?" Freedman demanded as he put on his jacket. "Here's the biggest goddamn story of the year, and it disappears into thin air, and we got three murders right on the doorstep of our lousy little house, and nobody wants them solved and nobody gives a damn."

Ramos shrugged. "Nobody gives a damn about anything."

"Yeah. Let's eat."

At Marco's, on Fourteenth Street between Seventh and Eighth avenues, Marco himself took them to a quiet table in a corner of the room. He liked having the detectives eat at his place. He had come from Milan, and not only did he serve northern Italian food, but he was not connected in any way, and the presence of the cops eased his nerves.

They ate without saying much, except for Freedman ticking off the cases that might as well be closed, including Cullen, since Manhattan South would be following up on that, and then they discussed, somewhat hopelessly, the air conditioner that had been promised to them every fall during the past four years. "The trouble is," Ramos reminded Freedman, who was thinking of a petition from the entire force, "that every time they send an engineer around, he goes back with a recommendation that the whole building should be torn down and it's not worth air conditioning."

"Another year, another engineer," Freedman said. He was facing the front of the restaurant, and now he saw a man come into the place and speak to Marco, most likely asking a question. Marco's answer was to point to their table. The man was tall and good-looking, gray tweed coat with an English cut, no hat, but soft blond hair and a blond mustache, a little white in the hair, wide mouth, striped shirt, and dark tie. His eyes were a very pale and striking blue. He walked to their table, and said, "Forgive me for intruding. My name is Dumont Robertson, but I am better known to my friends as Monty. Perhaps Joe Cullen mentioned me to you."

· The two detectives stared at him in silence. Ramos left the initiative to Freedman, and Freedman took no initiative.

"May I sit down?"

Freedman glanced at the two empty chairs at the square table, but still said nothing. Monty moved around the table and seated himself.

Freedman turned to Ramos and said slowly, deliberately, "This sleazy son of a bitch had a tail on us." Then he turned to Monty and continued, "I'll push it a bit and charge you with loitering, being a public nuisance, and a general disturber of the peace. I think I can get you at least thirty days. Read him his rights, Sergeant."

"This shithead isn't worth the trouble," Ramos said. "Do you want any dessert, Lieutenant? They got the best zabaglione in the city right here."

"Why not? It rips the fat off you. Marco!" he called. The owner came to the table. "Two espresso, two zabaglione."

Marco looked questioningly at Monty.

334

"He's not eating!" Freedman said.

Marco turned away from the table, and Monty said, "We could talk more easily without the name calling."

Freedman said nothing. Ramos said nothing.

"I stopped in to tell you it's over," Monty said.

The two detectives said nothing.

"There was no tape," Monty said pleasantly. "Father O'Healey died in a plane crash in the mountains of Durango. The Mexican government was kind enough to conduct a wide search for the wreckage, but the body was not found until three weeks had passed. Understandably, the good father was buried in a sealed coffin. The burial took place only this morning. The bishop will be writing to you to tell you the details, and there will be at least a small acknowledgment of this in the back pages of the *New York Times*. A number of policemen in your precinct house may have heard Joe Cullen's confession, and I am sure that you will pass on to them the fact that the entire confession was a fabrication, a desire on the part of Mr. Cullen to get back at the small airline that had fired him. A little research on your part, no more than a few telephone calls, will convince you that West Texas Carriers had ample reason to fire him. As for the fecundity of Mr. Cullen's imagination, well, he was a cocaine user, and that should explain things. He did some small smuggling himself, but the amount was insignificant."

Monty rose from his seat at the table, looked from one man to the other, and nodded. "The main point is that it's over. What had to be done was done, and that's the end of it. Meanwhile, thank you for your courtesy in listening to me; I wish it would extend to our breaking bread together, but since that is impossible, I bid you goodbye." And with that, he walked out of the restaurant.

For a few seconds, Freedman and Ramos sat in silence, looking at each other. Then Freedman said, "That's not the end of it."

"No, I don't think it is."

"I'm going to get him," Freedman said. "I swear to God, I am going to get him."

The Harvard Club

I HAVE some plain pound cake. Is that all right, Lieutenant?"

He said it was all right. "Ginny, you don't have to feed me," he said.

"I don't have any liquor—except some brandy. But you don't want brandy. I don't drink." She did not add that men who wanted to drink did not come to her apartment, and that Cullen was the first man that she had asked to this apartment; but Freedman did not know that she had seen Cullen twice, nor would he ever know. That was her thing, and it would be kept as her thing.

Freedman tried to put her in a framework and then gave it up. Nothing fitted. He had watched her in court and had seen her tear a witness to shreds. She was an unremitting prosecutor, and yet this apartment, her refuge, her secret—he guessed that—was filled with light and color. But was there actually any separation? There was nothing feminine here, the lemon-yellow rug, the Chinese designs on the chintz-covered couches, the nonobjective paintings on the walls—well, perhaps feminine enough to someone else, but he made his comparisons with Sheila, the silks and the laces and the pastel colors that she loved so much. But Ginny was not Sheila, and Freedman really had little idea what she was or who she was, except that something connected her to Cullen.

She brought him tea. He had asked for tea. "The damn coffee's worse than smoking. It took me five years to kick cigarettes."

She sat facing him, intense. "You said a miracle would be needed to get them. What miracle? What changed?"

"Did you ever talk to Timberman about Tony Carlione?"

"Of course I did."

"About the possibility of prosecuting him?"

"Lieutenant, there's no evidence, not a shred of evidence that he killed Sylvia Mendoza. Twelve stab wounds—means nothing. If you had him cuffed over at your precinct house, I'd still say forget it."

"He killed her."

"Oh, come on."

"You ever feel something in your bones? I feel this in my bones. Tony Carlione killed her on a contract, and Dumont Robertson, our friend Monty, put out the contract. You want Cullen's killer—it's the same son of a bitch, Dumont Robertson, whether he pulled the trigger himself or whether he farmed it out."

"I'm listening," Ginny said.

"If you had a witness, say Carlione, to testify that Monty bought the contract, would you prosecute?"

"Oh, the whole thing's smoke. You know that, Lieutenant. Carlione was relocated. There's no way to find him, and if you found him, there's no way to get him to testify."

"You're wrong; he can be found and he can be made to testify."

"Yes, and pigs have wings. He's relocated. Don't you understand what that means? The Feds put their reputation on the line with their relocation program. That's how they get witnesses. There's no way into it."

"Who runs it? Not the Justice Department, but inside the department, who runs it?"

"They have a department for it."

"And who knows? You people used him. He was your witness, and you made the arrangements with the Feds. Someone in your outfit has to know where Carlione is."

She was silent now, thinking about it.

"Let me tell you something about Cullen," Freedman said. "He was a Catholic. I suppose you know that."

"I know."

"He wanted to confess to killing Father O'Healey."

"He didn't kill O'Healey."

"Maybe he did, maybe he didn't. We'll never know for sure, but I'm with you. I don't think he killed the priest, but neither do I believe his story is entirely true. What the hell, nobody tells the truth, if there is such a thing. You're a Catholic, aren't you?"

"That's right, Lieutenant," she answered stiffly. "And what has that got to do with it?"

"Everything or maybe nothing. In El Salvador, not too many years ago, there was a demented murderer of nuns and Catholic lay workers, women raped and murdered because they ministered to the poor. Then a bishop in San Salvador was murdered, because he took the side of the poor. A priest in El Salvador was shot to death because he was giving last rites to a woman a soldier had murdered, and in Nicaragua, the contras tortured a priest to death. I get all this out of reading the *New York Times,* so when Cullen told what had happened to Father O'Healey, I wasn't particularly surprised. Puzzled, yes, but not surprised. Me, I'm Jewish, and I learned street fighting from the Catholic kids who told me I had killed their God, which made no more sense than the stuff Hitler said, and then I grew up and did a turn in Vietnam and married a Catholic lady and became a cop, and found that practically everyone around me was Catholic if he wasn't Jewish or black, and then Father O'Healey entered my life and Cullen decided to confess to a priest in a church in my precinct."

"And what does all that add up to?" Ginny asked.

"I'm not sure it adds up to anything. Cops get sour, which is not unreasonable. You bring in a dope peddler and the next day he walks. I'm not blaming you or your crowd. I'm not blaming anyone, I'm just stating the fact. I'm forty-one years old and I don't see anything in my life that means a lot. Don't get impatient with me, Ginny. I'm trying to say something."

"I don't know what you're trying to say."

"Well," Freedman said, "I'll try. I want to bring Dumont Robertson in and I want to book him and I want you to prosecute him. This is something I have to do. Now, I started to tell you before that Cullen wanted to confess. He had to confess—I mean, that from what I've been able to put together, there was a force in him that drove him to confess. So he went up to this Church of Saint Peter the Rock, as I said in our precinct—"

"I know where the church is."

"Right. Now an old priest there, Father Immelman, hears his confession. Cullen wants absolution. The priest can only give him absolution if he states his belief in God, and Cullen, who is so desperate for this absolution, will not admit to a belief in God. That's one thing. On the other hand, Cullen has confessed to the priest, and in his covering of tracks, Monty has the priest murdered."

"What! Do you have proof?"

"No." Freedman held up his hand. "Hold on. Let me try to deal with this. I'm open with you, I want you to be honest with me. Cullen was here, wasn't he?"

"You know that's a lie, Lieutenant, and a rotten provocation!"

Freedman said harshly, "Cut out the crap, Ginny. When Timberman's right-hand lady, the smartest DA in the pack, and even money everywhere to run for Timberman's job when he retires, well, when she comes to a lousy little West Side precinct that doesn't rate high enough to investigate its own killings, and tells me to get Monty and his crew and make something out of Cullen's death, she is involved. You are involved, Miss Selby, damned involved. I don't know what puts you together with Cullen, but something does, and there's no other explanation for it except that Cullen, on the run after he killed Kovach, came here and you gave him shelter. You had to be face to face with Cullen; you had to see him in the flesh; otherwise, your involvement is senseless."

She shrugged. "So. What do you intend to do with it, Lieutenant?"

"The relationship puzzles me—to risk your whole career that way, to put yourself in an absolutely untenable position. Why?"

"I don't have to explain."

"All right. This dies with me. I give you my word of honor—no one will ever know. It's over, done with, finished."

"Thank you," she said softly.

"You see, something happened to me since Cullen made that tape in our squad room. I could use your words—I don't have to explain —but that's because I can't explain. Like Cullen, I don't believe very much in God, but I accept the fact that I don't know one damn thing about God, and the Pope in Rome and the Chief Rabbi of Jerusalem don't know one damn thing about God, except that their livelihood is bullshit and mine is being a cop. But I was brought up Jewish, and Jewish kids get stuff put on them, like any other kids, and some of the stuff that was put on me stayed with me. There's a Jewish legend about the La-med Vav—that means thirty-six. The legend says that always, in every generation, there exist in the world thirty-six righteous, good, and just men, and on their existence the existence of the world depends. They could be Jewish or Christian or Hindu or whatever, and no one of them ever knows in his lifetime that he is a Lamed Vav."

Ginny was crying. "What are you talking about?" she blurted through her tears. "He killed people, he was in Vietnam, he was—he was—"

"What was he, Ginny? Go on. You tell me. I think he was just a man, a poor bastard who swallowed the shit we all swallow—"

"No!" she said fiercely.

"Then what was he, Ginny?"

"God help me, I don't know." She wiped away her tears, rose, and went into her bed-room to fix her face. She came back into the living room and said, "Let's stop cutting away at each other and admit that we're in this to-gether."

"Good."

"Now tell me why you're here, Freedman, and cut the shit. We've talked enough non-sense."

"Yes. I'm here because I want to get Monty.

Men like Monty have been selling their line of goods for a long time. Nobody gets any of them. I want to change that." He said it lightly, almost with indifference.

"How?"

"I told you before. I want to find out where Tony Carlione has been relocated to. Then I will go there and convince him to testify against Monty, and bring him back here, and you will prosecute him."

"Just like that?"

"More or less."

"It's a dream, Freedman. You know that. You don't arrest people like Dumont Robertson. They go on doing what they're doing."

Freedman shook his head.

"And who knows where the relocation is?" she cried. "Who can find out? The damn Feds guard these places like the gold in Fort Knox."

"Timberman knows."

She hadn't expected that. She considered it for a few moments, and then she said, "Most likely. I imagine Timberman knows. Now how do I get him to tell me? Hit him over the head? Feed him a truth serum? Do you know what it would mean to get something like this out of Timberman?"

"I know," Freedman agreed. "I don't expect you to get it out of him. I'll take care of that. I just want you to set it up for me. I want you to persuade Timberman to see me. Alone and not in his office."

"And why not in his office?"

"Because his office is bugged."

"Oh, no." She shook her head. "No way." Her voice sharpened. "How the hell do you know it's bugged?"

"It would be a loose end. I've decided that Monty doesn't leave loose ends."

Hopelessly, she muttered, "Of all the damn things. I swear I don't know what to make of you, Freedman. Why don't you make this appointment with Timberman yourself?"

"Sure. I can see that. Freedman, who works in a third-rate West Side precinct, wants to meet the district attorney of New York County on a park bench in Battery Park. And why, Lieutenant? To get him to reveal the safe place where the Feds put Twelve-tone Carlione."

Ginny burst out laughing. It was the first time she had laughed that evening, or smiled, for that matter, and she was quite attractive when she laughed.

"But I convinced him," she said.

"He leans on you. Everyone knows that. You're the best he has; you're sensible and you're dependable. All you have to do is persuade him that a cop called Freedman—"

"Come on, Lieutenant, he knows who you are. Don't down-grade yourself."

"All right. Thank you. Don't tell him what I want. Tell him I'm paranoid and I think his office is bugged."

"What about a restaurant? I don't want to tell him you're paranoid, even if you are, and maybe you are, for all I know."

"A restaurant is fine, as long as we're not sitting cheek by jowl with strangers."

"You won't be," Ginny assured him. "It will probably be at the Harvard Club. All right—I think your whole shtick is hopeless, but I'll convince him to have lunch with you."

The next day, in the afternoon, Virginia Selby called Freedman and informed him that a lunch appointment for the following day had been arranged at the Harvard Club. When he told Ramos about it, the sergeant said, "There you are, Mel, lunch at the Harvard Club. Never happened to me, but it shows that cops are coming up in the world. I have something to look forward to."

Freedman had never lunched at the Harvard Club either, and when he told Sheila about it that evening, she informed him that she had dined there three times.

"That puts me in my place. How come?"

"Buyers who went to Harvard. It's a new world, Mel, and Seventh Avenue changes with the world. Come on, don't be angry."

He wasn't angry. The world changes, but

cops are not exactly in the world. They look at it sidewise. They're moralists without morality. "Have you ever thought of marrying me again?" he asked her.

"I've thought about it. What are you wearing tomorrow?"

"Gray flannels, blue blazer, and a white shirt."

"Nice. And a quiet striped tie."

"Fuck what I'm wearing tomorrow!"

"You're pissed off, sweetheart, because I go to lunch with buyers at the Harvard Club," Sheila said gently. "If we were still married, this would grow into a real brouhaha, and that always scared the shit out of me because I was living with a man who carried a gun. Now you're a pussycat. It's only a week since our first date after the divorce, and it's been wonderful. I love you. I love to sleep with you. We cry a little, we laugh a little. I think we ought to leave it this way."

"Honey, are you afraid of my gun? I been a cop twelve years and I never shot anyone. Have I ever raised a hand to you?"

"No. But when you used to be a few hours late, I died. Each time I died."

He had never given that much thought; there were many things he had never given much thought to. "I'll be away a couple of days," he said.

"I'll miss you, Mel."

When he left the following morning, he said to Sheila, "It's not an absolute professional affliction. I know cops married twenty, twenty-five years, and they manage. They even like each other."

"I'll keep that in mind," she said, smiling.

But even with his gray flannels and blue blazer and two-dollar shoeshine, the Harvard Club dining room intimidated him. It was filled with well-dressed people eating away under the great beamed ceiling, and Timberman welcomed him without pleasure and with only the minimum required politeness. Freedman wondered what possible ruses and devices Ginny had used to get him into this position. As if he read Freedman's mind, Timberman said, "I am here only because I have obligations to a wonderful woman who has worked with me for many years. I think the notion that my office is bugged is both presumptuous and outrageous, and I trust that if you have any evidence to back that up, you will present it."

"Have you had a debugger in recently, sir?" Freedman asked.

"I have not."

"There's a man on my squad, George Jones by name, who is as good as they come. May I send him around?" Freedman realized that

Timberman's act of opening his mouth and then closing it sharply meant that he was about to say, No, you may not. He didn't say it, gave the question a long moment, and then nodded.

"If you wish," Timberman said. "I would appreciate it."

"He'll come by this afternoon."

"Then let us get into it. You wanted to see me. Why?"

"About the tape that Joe Cullen made in my precinct—"

"I will not discuss that tape," the district attorney said flatly.

It set Freedman back. All morning he had rehearsed what he intended to be his arguments. He had conversations with himself and Timberman, internal conversations that concluded with Freedman making his point. Those internal conversations were simple and direct, convincing Timberman that we were a community of law, and that naturally the tape Cullen had made was central to the discussion. Now he saw himself as he imagined Timberman saw him, an odd Jewish cop, a person of no importance whatsoever, clownish, with outdated notions of law and order.

"If that is all you wish to discuss, then this luncheon was a mistake," Timberman said

352

with some irritation. "I allowed Miss Selby to persuade me, and that was also a mistake."

Freedman, trying to control the nugget of anger building up in his stomach, said coldly, "I will be happy not to talk about the tape. Evidently it's too damn hot and frightening even to discuss. That's all right with me. But you invited me to lunch, and I intend to say my piece. You can leave the table or you can have them throw me out. Or you can be a gentleman and listen for five minutes, after which I will be happy to go."

If Freedman's tone was cold, Timberman's face was frozen. "Go ahead, Lieutenant," he said in hardly more than a whisper. "I am listening."

"My father grew up during the Great Depression," Freedman said. "His father, my grandfather, worked in a garment factory—when he worked. When there was no work, my father did odd jobs and brought in a few dollars and the family survived on that. Nobody locked their doors, nobody was mugged, and nobody made ten million dollars out of peddling inside information. They were very hard times, but from the stories my father told me, they were also good times. There was something clean and decent about the country, and people had a passionate love for a thing called America—"

At this point, Timberman began to show signs of impatience and opened his mouth to interrupt. Freedman stopped him with "Please, sir, allow me to say my piece."

Timberman sighed and nodded.

"You see, sir, any sensible person wonders what is meant by loving your country—what do you love, mountains, rivers, a house? It's a crazy concept, because none of it means a damn thing, and the only thing to love in any country is the things people do and what they believe in, and through my father's eyes, I saw a country you could love. Destitute, desperate, tragic—all those things. But it was also something real. Well, my father enlisted. He was a rifleman, and he went through it all, from Normandy to Berlin, and I figured if he could do it, I could do it, and I went to Vietnam, but everything had turned to shit and I came back to a country where law was a farce, where greed had become a national religion, where the kids had sold their lives for crack, and where priests who were trying to believe in something were murdered in Central America, and where a man sits in my precinct house and tells me that people in our government, paid with taxpayers' money, are flooding this country with cocaine, and the operation is run by a son of a bitch named Dumont Robertson, a rich upstanding white Anglo-Saxon son of a bitch, and then this same malignant bastard comes into my precinct and murders a prostitute and an old priest and Joe Cullen, and you tell me I'm not to talk about the tape. Beautiful, sir—just beautiful, Mr. District Attorney. Thank you for listening!" With his last few words, Freedman's anger exploded and he pushed back his chair and stood up.

"Sit down, Lieutenant!" Timberman snapped.

"I'm leaving."

"You haven't had your lunch. You will god damn well sit down!"

The waiter, who had just approached the table with menus, now dropped the menus on the table and walked away. He had no desire to ask whether two men facing each other like angry wolves wanted to order drinks.

Freedman sat down.

"We'll both try to be civilized," Timberman said. "Do you want a drink?"

"I'm on duty," Freedman muttered.

"Yes, of course. Now suppose you tell me what you want of me, Lieutenant."

"I want to know where Tony Carlione has been relocated to."

Freedman was surprised that Timberman did not immediately reject the notion. Instead, he said, "You know what relocation means?"

"I think so."

Timberman signaled the waiter. "Bring me a Scotch, neat, and a glass of water." Then he turned to Freedman. "When the Feds take a witness and in return for his testimony offer him his life, there is a pretty important contract. You're asking me to break it. Suppose you tell me what you have in mind regarding Carlione?"

Suddenly, it was not the same man. Freedman, who had not rehearsed his speech and who now could hardly recall what he had said, was taken aback. He had not said what he had planned to say, and neither had he planned to say what he did. It had poured out, and trying to recapture his words was useless; but something he said had struck home and Timberman had dropped his cold and annoyed response.

"Carlione killed Sylvia Mendoza," Freedman said.

"Yes, that's what Ginny Selby thinks. Neither of you has any proof."

"I'm not talking about proof and evidence. I'm talking about a gang, men highly placed and connected in our government, who are bringing a river of cocaine into this country, who move their drugs without interference, and who at the same time are ripping us off for more millions, buying guns with taxpayer money, pocketing most of it, and exchanging the guns for cocaine in Honduras. We both know what I'm talking about. I'd love to bring in Carlione for killing Mendoza, but I'd get a lot more pleasure out of putting away the guy who's at the center of this, a certain Dumont Robertson, who they call Monty."

"Hold on," Timberman said. "I know Dumont Robertson. He wasn't mentioned by Cullen. My God, Freedman, he's a man with a reputation, known, trusted—you can't put him at the center of this. It's inconceivable."

"Is it any more inconceivable than Cullen's confession?"

"That was a confession by a disturbed man. There is not a shred of evidence to back it up. Do you think I would have backed away from it if you had given me one small piece of evidence?"

"I spoke to Monty, to your Mr. Dumont Robertson—"

"Not mine, Lieutenant. I resent that—and, damn it, what do you mean you spoke to him? When? How?"

Freedman spelled it out, word for word, adding, "And if you doubt me, I'll send Ramos down to your office."

"I don't doubt you," Timberman said softly.

The lunch they had ordered now came. It remained untasted, getting cold.

"Do you think he still has a tail on you?" Timberman asked.

"He had one on me. I shook him before I came here. You know, Mr. Timberman, with the kind of money they got, it's no big thing to put tails on a dozen people if they want to."

"That Robertson hired Carlione is only a guess. Robertson would have to have access to the relocation records."

"Yes."

"I hate conspiracy," Timberman muttered, finally putting a fork into his food and tasting it. "I hate to try a conspiracy case. I hate the people who want to turn every tragedy that hits our government into a conspiracy case. Furthermore, if Robertson—unthinkable as it sounds—did put out a contract with Carlione as his man, be sure that Carlione has an unbreakable alibi."

"That doesn't bother me, Mr. Timberman. I can handle Carlione. There's another one of the gang, a Colonel Yancy. I have a feeling he'll talk."

"Why?"

"Because from what I read, the general staff would be so enraged at a scandal like this, at a time when they're pushing Congress for every dollar, that they'd throw Yancy to the dogs. If we could offer him something—"

"Freedman," Timberman said, "suppose I

were to sit down with the police commissioner and the federal attorney and give them what we have and blow this thing wide open. That's what Miss Selby suggested, and I respect her judgment."

"And the day you do that, Carlione will turn up dead, and then you'll have nothing."

"Yes? And if Dumont Robertson is as thorough as you say, why isn't Carlione dead?"

"He will be. Evidently, Monty doesn't like to muddy too many waters, but the day you open this, Carlione is finished."

"And what do you do?" Timberman asked with annoyance. "If he killed Mendoza, that's murder one. Do you believe Carlione will walk into that?"

"Give him immunity."

"If he killed Mendoza?"

"We don't want him! He's not the dope smuggler. I want Monty."

"Are you sure you're not obsessing?"

"So I'm obsessing. It's worth giving Carlione immunity if it means getting Monty."

"If it means getting Monty. Lieutenant, there are so many ifs and maybes in your plan—damn it, I'd have to go to the Feds—"

"No!"

"There's no other way."

"You go to the Feds, and Carlione will be dead before I ever get to him."

"Do you know what you're asking me?" Timberman said unhappily.

"Yes, sir, I know."

"If the whole thing washes out—I hate to put it this way—but if the whole thing washes out, how did you find the place?"

"That dies with me," Freedman said flatly.

And after a moment or two, Timberman said, "I think I believe you. Let's order some hot food."

But before Timberman touched the hot food, he said to Freedman, "This is the first time . . ." He couldn't finish what he had begun to say. He was still Harold Timberman. He couldn't ask for sympathy from an ordinary precinct cop, who, even in his dark blue blazer and gray flannel trousers, looked so out of place in the Harvard Club. Perhaps it was the tangled mess of red hair, which Freedman had never found a way to control.

At the precinct house, the lieutenant's costume brought forth a few whistles but mostly admiring responses. In the squad room, with only Ramos and Jones present, it was solid admiration. "You're coming around, Lieutenant —you certainly are." Jones, who was black, was the only one on the squad who always came to work wearing a tie and a freshly ironed shirt. He was usually in a suit, and if he wore a sports jacket, it was either Armani or

Perry Ellis. Jones wasn't married and he could afford such clothes. Ramos followed Freedman into his little office and asked him how it came out.

"It's a class yuppie place, and the older men look like mob bosses who get sixty-dollar haircuts. That's just sour. It's full of high-class gentleman types, and if they ever make me chief of detectives, I'll join."

"You can't. You got to go to Harvard. They don't have exchange rates with City College. How did it go?"

"I don't know. At first he was as cold as a witch's tit. You know, class gentleman suffering a plain cop. I guess Ginny must have bullied him into it. But we talked and he softened up. He didn't say yes and he didn't say no."

"Do you know we were bugged?"

"No, you got to be kidding."

"I just had a crazy notion," Ramos said, "and I sent Jones down into the basement to check the wiring. They had turned the telephone into party lines. Jones took it apart."

"They're very thorough."

"Too damn thorough to suit me. What is it with you, Mel?" Ramos rarely called him by his first name. "We're not going to change anything. We're a couple of street cops who don't mean a damn thing in the scheme of things. My mother worked herself to death, hoping I'd go to Fordham. She had it all worked out for me to be a doctor or a lawyer, and I end up a street cop because you make your peace with the way it is."

"You're right."

"So what's eating you?"

"Monty. Yeah, until he walked into the restaurant, I was ready to let it go. One more pile of garbage on the mountain of crap that we spend our lives rooting in. But when he walked in and sat down, I said to myself that somehow, some way, I am going to get that bastard and put him in a cell."

Ramos smiled thinly.

"Pipe dream?"

"I don't know," Ramos said. "You ever think about Father O'Healey?"

"I think about him."

"Yeah, I think about him," Ramos said. "I'm the worst kind of lapsed Catholic there is. I hate the damn Irish priests that looked down their noses at me at school. I hate the damn chanting and candles and telling lies to little kids that they're going to burn in hell when they been living all their lives in hell, and nobody ever gave a damn about it, and some Pope talks to God the same as Jerry Falwell and those redneck nuts in the South—talks to God! Sweet Jesus, why doesn't he come to Brooklyn or the South Bronx and tell God about what he finds there—so that gives you a notion of what kind of a Catholic I am, and then this Francis O'Healey. I try to put it together. Here's a nice guy. Put him in our squad, and you'd say, O'Healey, a good cop, run of the mill. And then what does he do—he goes down there to Honduras, commits himself to those poor people, no pay, no pension, no side benefits, just these poor, driven people that he can help a little, and he gives up his life for them—and nobody gives a damn."

"That's right. Nobody gives a damn about much of anything."

"I think about him. I do a lot of thinking about O'Healey."

"I think more about Monty," Freedman said.

Ramos grinned. "Dumont Robertson. Man— that's beautiful. Dumont Robertson."

The rest of the day spun away. There was a bad three-car auto crash over by the river under the old abandoned West Side elevated highway—a police car in hot pursuit, the car they were after, and a civilian car that happened to get in the way. One of the cops was killed, the other severely injured, and in the car they were after, one man badly hurt and the other escaped. In the third car, two women, both of them badly injured. It was well past dark when Freedman finished his paperwork at the morgue and made his way back to the precinct house.

The night shift was on now. At some time during the day, Freedman had stuffed his tie into his pocket, and the blue blazer and gray flannels were now sufficiently rumpled to excite no comment among the men. He went into his office, looked through his telephone messages, and then tried not to think about the dead cop and the others in the accident. It happened. Normal course of events: robbery, mugging, murder, accidental killing. His telephone rang.

It was Virginia Selby. She said to him, "Will you be there for a while? I'm sending something."

"I'll wait for it," he said.

A half hour later, a pretty young woman was ushered into his office. "I'm an ADA," she explained. "I work for Ginny. She asked me to give you this." She handed him a sealed envelope.

After she had gone, Freedman wiped his glasses thoroughly, glanced around to see that the detectives were occupied, and then opened the envelope. On a slip of paper was written:

123 Custer St.
San Fernando, California

Carlione

SEATED in the tourist section of the big 747, bound for Los Angeles, Freedman turned down the offer of a headpiece for the film. He had too much film to run through his own head to be diverted by a movie. He had to plan his steps very carefully and slip up nowhere. After all, he had arrested Tony Carlione. If they were not old friends, they were certainly old acquaintances, and it was Freedman, noticing the twelve wounds in each of Carlione's victims, who had named him Twelve-tone Tony, giving it to the press. They made the most of it, and Freedman had had one of those brief exposures to fame that cops sometimes get. Carlione was a short, broad, fat man of great strength with an absurd angelic face,

round as a baby's, and with innocent blue
eyes. The fact that he was a vicious killer, a
man without a shred of decency or compas-
sion, was in no way evident in his appearance;
and it was his total lack of loyalty that enabled
Freedman to talk him into becoming an in-
former.

Now, Freedman decided, he would have to
do it once again—persuade Tony Carlione that
his best chance of surviving was to give evidence against Dumont Robertson. Of course,
Freedman was betting that Monty himself had
hired Carlione. He had a deep feeling that
Monty did not delegate such jobs. Anyway,
that was his bet.

Then there was Tony's wife. She was his
apostle of survival, a woman who resembled
him in form and appearance and apparently
loved him dearly. She too would have to be
convinced, but since she had always opted for
Tony's survival, the chances were good that
she would see the soundness of Freedman's
proposal and come in on his side.

Mrs. Carlione was also a good cook, and
Freedman recalled that in the rundown on
Tony's habits, there was mention of his
penchant for eating at home. Not for Tony the
dictum of eating breakfast like a king, lunch
like a prince, and dinner like a pauper. The
meals were solid, substantial preparations. If

his habits in exile had not changed, and Freedman saw no reason why they should have, he and his wife would be sitting down to lunch at twelve-thirty. Freedman's plane arrived at Los Angeles at twelve noon, and allowing two hours to rent a car and drive to San Fernando, he should reach 123 Custer Street just as the Carliones finished lunch. They would be relaxed, feeling good, each of them containing half a bottle of red wine.

On the other hand, that too was a presumption. What does a killer do on relocation? Obviously, he avoids anything that smacks of the mob, because even if the mob is another family in another city, they all share a dislike of informers. What then? Does he open a shop, or does he stay at home and grow flowers? But since less than a year had passed since Tony was relocated, he might well be resting and enjoying the very nice pension the government provided.

Freedman had never been to Los Angeles, his return from Vietnam having been by plane through Europe and to the East Coast, but he had supplied himself with maps of the Los Angeles area and the thruway system. San Fernando was not a very long or difficult drive. He had very specifically not gotten in touch with the local cops. He didn't want them interfering or cramping his approach, and he expected few difficulties with Carlione. He felt certain that he could convince Carlione that the only alternative to his coming east with him was an executioner's bullet in San Fernando.

But this line of thought led him to wonder what he would do if Carlione refused to come east with him. He could make threats, but that's all, and the most direct threat would be to let the mob know where Carlione had been relocated. On the other hand, Carlione could call the Feds and demand another protective location.

Freedman shrugged it off. There was really no use trying to plan a line of approach before the fact. Somehow or other, he would work it out and bring Carlione home with him.

He wondered whether he had made a mistake in going alone. He had vacation days coming to him, and there was no one on the squad except Ramos that he wanted or would have wanted to be with him. It was a strange friendship that had grown between himself and Hosea Ramos. Ramos was an interior person, walled in completely, leaving no opening for a joke or a barb. He had fought his way through life with grim determination. Freedman joked about being chief of detectives someday, just as most lieutenants did; Ramos never spoke about it, but Freedman knew that one day it would be Ramos, not himself, never himself.

Well, his own ambitions were more easily achieved. He wanted to bring back Carlione. He wanted to arrest Dumont Robertson. He wanted to sit in a witness box and give evidence against him, and above all, he wanted to marry his ex-wife.

Well, perhaps, he thought. That should not be too hard.

Time passed. Freedman looked down at the great bowl of houses and streets that made up Los Angeles, and then the plane was dropping across the freeways and down onto the landing strip.

At the car rental, a pretty girl gave him papers to sign and informed him that there would be a Ford Escort waiting for him at the rental station.

"Just cross the street to the island, and the company bus will be by."

But first he went to the baggage return to pick up his suitcase, which contained his gun and extra shells. He had always thought it stupid of the airlines not to screen the baggage as well as the travelers and the carry-on items, but now it worked to his advantage. He then left the baggage area and walked outside to the concrete island where the bus to the car-rental station would pick him up.

He stood in the blazing sunshine, trying to fit this warm, hazy climate into the end of November, into the thin, cold rain that had accompanied him to Kennedy Airport just a few hours ago, and then the bus came to take him to the rental station.

"No way you can go wrong," the car attendant assured him. "Turn right when you leave here, and then left on Century Boulevard. Left lane, and you'll see the sign for the San Diego Freeway north. Oh, I'd guess about twenty-five, twenty-six miles north, you come on the San Fernando Mission Boulevard sign, and you exit there, and a few miles up the boulevard, you're in San Fernando."

There were no problems as Freedman drove the twenty-five miles. He was intrigued by the signs he passed—Wilshire Boulevard, Sunset Boulevard, Sepulveda Canyon—names that would be very exciting to Sheila. It was not simply a case of proposing marriage, but of breaking out of a frozen life style. He'd bring her back here—maybe drive the whole length of California, or take a cruise ship to the Hawaiian Islands. Even the flat, dull streets of the San Fernando Valley impressed him, roses blooming in November, lawns covered with giant Moroccan ivy, palm trees—all the things that made the valley the butt of a thousand snide jokes were seen with a sort of lonely pleasure by this policeman who had come to manhood in the Bronx.

At the same time, his nervousness increased. The signs of tension were always the same, and he had experienced them enough times in the past to recognize them: a flushed face, a tightening sensation in his heart.

San Fernando Mission Boulevard. He turned east, and at the first available roadside space he pulled over and examined his street map, and switched his gun from bag to pocket. He was determined that no one should see him, that he would speak to no one, ask no questions, and find 123 Custer by himself. That was not difficult. He located it on the map and then placed himself in relation to it. No more than a mile and on the edge of the main center, a drab street with half a dozen old-fashioned California bungalows stretched on one side of the street and a single bungalow across the street facing them. The first bungalow, he noted driving through the street, was number 100. The single facing bungalow, across the street, was number 123.

It was now a quarter after two in the afternoon, hot, windless, a faint yellow smog beginning to tinge the air, making it even more unbreathable than the heavy heat. Nothing moved. No sign of life or of sound disturbed the totally surrealist street, and Freedman reflected that this was a place he would never bring Sheila to. He parked his car around the corner, and then he walked back to Custer Street and slowly and unhurriedly along the street to number 123.

The typical California bungalow of the period when these were built was a rectangle, a tile roof, stucco walls, and a small front porch, about three feet deep and stretching across the whole front of the building. Two wooden steps led up to the porch and the door. Freedman could see that the door was slightly open, no more than half an inch, but still open. Well, why not? Who would threaten the Carliones here? He could simply walk in. But did he want to? He did not want a confrontation with a gun in his hand; indeed, he believed profoundly that no one should ever have a gun in his hand unless he intended to use it. If he needed his gun, he could draw it and use it, but this was not a situation in which a gun would be helpful.

He did not draw his gun. He walked up the steps and pressed a white button that set off a musical clatter of chimes inside the house.

No one appeared. He sounded the chimes again. Still no one appeared at the door.

Freedman opened the door and entered. A shaded room, the blinds drawn, yet with the fierce sun giving it a sort of half light; and in

front of Freedman, on the floor, arms out-
stretched, Tony Carlione, blood still oozing out
of three bullet holes in his chest. And sprawled
on the couch, just glimpsed by Freedman's
side vision, eyes opened wide and a red hole in
the center of her forehead, Tony's wife, Maria.
All of it was peripheral; at the center of his
vision, facing him, standing just behind the
body of Tony Carlione, Freedman saw Dumont Robertson, gun in hand, silencer on gun,
smiling, blond hair in a graceful wave, blue
eyes encased in wrinkles of confident mirth.

"My dear Lieutenant Freedman," he said. He
was wearing knife-edge-creased, fawn-col-
ored twill trousers, two-hundred-dollar English shoes, a blue double-breasted blazer,
white shirt, and a striped tie that undoubtedly
contained the colors of his college.

"Please raise your hands—carefully," he
said.

Freedman raised his hands.

"You know," Monty went on, "I was thinking
of you as a stupid little Jew, but we think in
clichés. You're not small at all, but you are
very stupid. How could you imagine that I
would not think of Tony Carlione? Did I strike
you as either a stupid or an indifferent man?
Before I pull this trigger, I want you to know
that the things we do are not unlawful, but
rather the privilege of those who created this

country, who made it what it is today, and who intend to guide it in the future. It has always been that way, Lieutenant—"

It was at that moment that Tony Carlione convulsively grabbed Dumont Robertson's ankle, throwing him off balance, so that the two shots he managed to get off as he struggled to release his foot went wild, and as his third shot nicked the sleeve of Freedman's jacket, Freedman shot him in the head, just under his eye. He dropped to the floor and was trying to speak as Freedman approached him. He died as Freedman bent over him.

Tony Carlione was still alive, and he whispered a question to Freedman about his wife. But he died before Freedman could answer him. Freedman closed his eyes and his wife's eyes, but he could not bring himself to touch Monty's face. He found Monty's wallet in his jacket breast pocket, and he went through it for any mention of himself. There was no such mention, only seven credit cards, eleven hundred dollars in fifty-dollar bills, a driver's license, a pilot's license, and a gun license. There were no names, either there or in his other pockets, only keys, a clip of bullets in his jacket pocket, and eighteen dollars in small bills in his trouser pocket. He returned the money and cards to the wallet, and the wallet to Monty's pocket.

Freedman wiped clean everything of Robertson's that might register a print. He was still shaking, his heart racing, his hands trembling. The room looked like a charnel house, and it was entirely possible that someone had heard his shot and called the local police—possible but not too likely. He closed the door behind him, wiped the knob clean, and walked down the street and around the corner to where he had left his car. Still, there was no sign of human presence; the street lay quiet and silent under the yellow smog.

As he drove away, the problem of the gun remained. They would find the bullet, photograph it, enlarge the photograph, turn its shape and grooves into computer information, and begin a search. It would be a very thorough search, since Monty was apparently an important person.

Freedman's gun was not police issue, but the second gun that almost every policeman keeps —in Freedman's case, his third gun, since he had given his reserve gun to Sheila. He wiped it clean, removed the bullets and the firing pin. He had parked alongside a tangle of heavy brush, and now he flung the gun into it. If someone found it, they would have to find a firing pin to fit it, and in all probability it would be rusty and useless by then. They might, as a very long shot, connect it with Dumont Robertson's death. They could not conceivably connect it with him.

It wasn't until he was on the plane back to New York, on the redeye, having turned in the second ticket meant for Tony Carlione, that it came home to him that he had killed a man. In Vietnam, he had been a medic. He had never killed a man before.

You Pay Your
Money—

F REEDMAN managed a few hours of sleep on the redeye out of Los Angeles and back to New York. The plane landed at six-five A.M., and Freedman shelled out thirty dollars for a ride to his room in Manhattan. He took a shower, put on fresh clothes, buckled on his regulation revolver, and then walked over to the precinct house. The men on the squad were not sure whether he had called in sick or taken vacation leave the day before; anyway, he had been gone for only a day, and that attracted hardly any attention. Only Ramos raised a questioning brow.

"Let's you and me take a walk," Freedman said.

Out on the stoop of the old building, with

the uniformed patrolmen clustered up for the changing of the shift, Ramos asked, "Which way?"

"The river."

It was a lovely day, one of those rare, pure days that come close to Thanksgiving, and the two men were aware of the day and embraced it as they walked west from Tenth Avenue. Ramos took the opportunity to light a cigar, and he drew on it with pleasure as they walked.

"Your damn patience gets to me," Freedman said. "Ask me something."

"I can wait."

"I thought it through on the plane," Freedman said. "You and Sheila are the only ones I ever tell this story to."

"Are you certain you want to? Nobody's twisting your arm."

They reached an old pier before Freedman spoke. They sat in the sun and watched the golden glitter across the Hudson River, the slow-moving barges, and the circling gulls; and Ramos smoked his cigar and listened while Freedman told him what had happened in California.

"It's over," Ramos said. "No witness, no hit man, no case."

"Except that I killed Dumont Robertson."

"It was a just shooting," Ramos said.

"And how do I go about proving that it was a just shooting?"

"Who else knows?" Ramos asked.

"Only you."

"Then you put your life in my hands," Ramos said, in a manner that was almost courtly. "I would never betray you, Mel. We are friends. I am honored, and we are friends. But for God's sake, let it die with the two of us. Did anyone see you on that street?"

"No. But Ginny knows I was there and Timberman knows I was there."

"They've both forgotten by now, and they will continue to forget. What did you do with the gun?"

"Dumped it out there. No prints, and no way of ever tracing the gun to me. It was a reserve gun, no papers, not legal."

"You live dangerously, Lieutenant. The hell with it! Cullen and the murder of Father O'Healey are over. On the other hand, Tony Carlione saved your life."

"Light a candle for him," Freedman said.

That afternoon, Freedman went to the big newsstand on Forty-second Street and bought the *Los Angeles Times* and the *San Fernando News*. There was no word in either paper about the house on Custer Street. But when Freedman returned the following day, the story was there in the *Los Angeles Times*.

When Freedman checked the *New York Times,* he found the story in the back pages of the first section, and both stories were essentially the same. The headline read MOB KILL-ING IN SAN FERNANDO in the New York paper; Los Angeles wrote, MOB REVENGE IN SAN FER-NANDO. But while both stories made much of the fact that the highly touted federal reloca-tion plan had failed, they also accepted the suggestion that the three big Mafia families in New York had somehow discovered Carlione's safe house and ordered his execution. In both stories, there were detailed descriptions of the interior of the bungalow on Custer Street, but neither of them mentioned Dumont Robert-son.

"You're sure you hit him?" Ramos won-dered.

"Below his eye and out the back of his skull."

"That sounds final. They took him away."

"Someone knew where he was going," Freedman agreed. "They went to the house and hustled Monty off. It makes sense. They needed some explanation for a high-class gen-tleman like Robertson dead with a mob hit man and his wife, both done in by old Robert-son's gun."

"According to Cullen, he had friends. They won't sleep easy, Mel."

"No, I suppose not. But then, neither will I."

The following week, the *New York Times* ran an obituary for Dumont Robertson, who had taken off from Santa Barbara in a twenty-seven-foot power boat that he kept at the marina there. The Robertsons owned a winter home in Santa Barbara, where they had many friends, and Dumont Robertson frequently took his speedboat out alone. This time, he had mentioned Catalina Island as his destination. His speedboat was picked up by a coast guard cutter, about twelve miles southwest of Santa Barbara. Since a boarding ladder had been dropped over the side of the boat and since Robertson's clothes were in a heap in the boat, it was presumed that he had gone over the side for a swim. He was a strong swimmer, and since there was no evidence of a struggle or foul play, and since his wallet contained eleven hundred dollars in fifty-dollar bills, the only reasonable conclusion was that a shark had taken him. The obituary went on to say that Robertson left behind a wife and two children, both of them in college. His estate was valued at something over twenty million dollars, large for a man who had devoted so much of his life to public service.

Although Ginny put two and two together after reading the obituary, it did not come out precisely to four. She had cautiously refrained from getting in touch with Freedman, and indeed she was by no means sure that he had been to California. But now both the witness and the criminal were dead, and insofar as the New York City police and the Manhattan district attorney were concerned, the case was closed and would probably remain closed forever. There was much labor lost, for Ginny had put in many hours planning her likely prosecution of Monty. As she thought of her opening statement to the jury, it would have gone like this—of course with flourishes that she had entered in her thoughts but that would have had to be pared down or discarded:

"Ladies and gentlemen of the jury," she had planned to say, "this is no ordinary criminal case over which you will sit in judgment, any more than the cases tried in Nuremberg were ordinary criminal cases"—no, that would never be allowed, but nice to think about—"no, indeed. This is a case that cuts to the heart of whether a society, conceived as our nation is, can survive; for we have on trial here men highly placed in the administration of our government, men who set the law aside in the belief that they were above the law—not lawbreakers, as they saw themselves, not criminals, as they saw themselves, but men above and beyond law—men for whom words such as compassion, loyalty, and guilt were meaningless.

"In a society where greed has been turned into a virtue, these men betrayed their country and its laws again and again. As with the Mafia, they disposed of their opponents by murder, killing as casually as one would kill insects. They sold guns to wage a war that they had created and to arm a group of thugs who murdered women and small children with as little thought as the men who armed them, and in return for the guns, they received cocaine, which they brought into our country—"

Ah, well, it was an opening address that would never be spoken, and even if there had been a trial, she could hardly have approached it in those terms. Certainly, Harold Timberman would never have countenanced it.

Mr. Timberman, on the other hand, said to his wife, Sally, "I hate loose ends, but what can I do?"

"You could ask Freedman what happened."

"Oh, no—no. He would have to lie to me. I don't for a moment believe that Freedman killed the Carliones. I've looked into his record. He's not a gun-crazy cop. As far as I could determine, he's never fired his revolver. On the other hand, it is possible that he shot Robertson."

"Then you don't believe the story about the boat?" his wife said.

"Of course not. Men like Dumont Robertson don't fall off boats to be eaten by sharks or go swimming in midocean. No sensible man takes a power boat of that size out to sea and then swims off it without a line, and Dumont Robertson was not stupid. Other things, but not stupid."

It always amazed Sally Timberman that, as many years as she had been married to Harold Timberman, there were things about him that she did not know.

"You knew him?"

"Slightly. I met him a few times."

"What was he like?"

"Handsome, charming . . ."

"The same evil monster?"

"Many evil monsters are handsome and charming. We are a society that hates homeliness and is willing to forgive any horror so long as the perpetrator is beautiful."

"And since you are so wise and philosophic about things, tell me who really did kill Dumont Robertson."

"Freedman, I suppose."

"Freedman. The same Lieutenant Freedman you took to lunch at the Harvard Club? Oh, come on, Harold."

"He's much brighter than they give him credit for."

"Then why this whole silly charade about the boat?"

"I would guess," Timberman said thoughtfully, "that his body was in the wrong place and that it was full of bullet holes. It's very difficult, at times, to explain a thing to the press. They are nosy and difficult, and they always want to know why a body is where it is. A missing body makes a simpler story."

"Oh." She paused, and then she asked her husband whether he intended to take action against Freedman.

"No, no. Absolutely not. There's no corpus delicti, and Freedman is much too wise a cop to leave evidence around. And if I even started, the Feds would put their foot down. The last thing a great many powerful people want is for the case of Dumont Robertson to be aired in a courtroom." Then he added, "It's a pity, though. I suppose Freedman had to do it. I think he wanted the trial more than anything. For that matter, so did I."

Ramos, on the other hand, was convinced that Freedman had to do it. No doubts shook him. He had worked with Freedman for ten years; he had watched him on the firing range, and he had no doubt about Freedman getting off a shot at close range on target. Through the years, he had watched Freedman's cool, un-flappable style, and had tried to pattern his own after it. He felt that the only way to be an effective policeman and not go crazy or blow out your brains was to abjure the macho image and play your hand quietly yet firmly. He had great regard for Freedman, yet he never really understood him. Freedman was the only Jew Ramos had ever gotten close to, and during this case of the murder of Father O'Healey, Freedman had become even more complex and more difficult to understand.

Yet in response to Freedman's request, Ramos went to the old Church of Saint Peter the Rock and lit a candle for the soul of Tony Carlione, thinking to himself, "Provided he has one." The church was empty. Ramos looked around to make sure of that, and then he knelt and remained in that position for a few minutes. Father Paul White, standing in the shadows, saw him but did not disturb him or show himself.

At two o'clock in the morning, knowing from her breathing that Sheila was awake beside him, Freedman observed that it was all so damned pointless.

"Why don't you try to sleep?"

"Because every time I close my eyes, I'm standing in that miserable bungalow looking at Tony and his wife and into the silencer at the muzzle of Monty's gun. Monty wanted to live forever, just like Tony and his wife. I guess everyone wants to live forever so that they can go on eating and fucking forever, and then a time comes when you don't give a damn. It all adds up to shit."

"That's beautiful," Sheila said. "I don't want to hear any more. When you went to California, I knew you were going to get Monty, and I said to myself if anything happens to you, I'm through. I don't love anyone else, just you. That's real. That matters. The trouble with you is that when everything's said and done, you're one of those smartass Jews who have to know everything about everything, and they want everything to make sense. Well, it doesn't. It's just there."

"And that's the way you see it? That's all there is?"

Minutes went by before she answered, and then she said, "No. That's not all there is. There are people. There's Father O'Healey. There's you."

"And you think I'm like Father O'Healey?" Freedman said softly.

"More than you imagine," she said.